THE
SAINT JOSEPH
PLOT

JOHN M.
PERSINGER

Thank you for your support! I hope that you enjoy The Saint Joseph Plot!

Best wishes,

John M. Persinger

12/11/2013

This book is a work of fiction. Except for Regis Philbin,
the characters and events in this book are fictitious. Any
similarity to real persons, living or dead, is coincidental and
not intended by the author.

ISBN-10: 0-9891841-0-2
ISBN-13: 978-0-9891841-0-6

Printed and manufactured in the United States.

To my wife Sarah, my father Joseph, and my mother Julia

for everything.

INTRODUCTION

Saint Joseph, the husband of Mary and the father of Jesus, is the patron saint of fathers.

"He was chosen by the eternal Father as the trustworthy guardian and protector of his greatest treasures, namely, his divine Son and Mary, Joseph's wife. He carried out this vocation with complete fidelity until at last God called him, saying: 'Good and faithful servant, enter into the joy of your Lord.'"

-A sermon by St. Bernardine of Siena

SATURDAY

CHAPTER 1
SATURDAY
1:37 P.M.

The frail, young woman recoiled from the blinding glare bouncing off the Golden Dome. Stumbling out of Sorin Hall, the all-boys dormitory, she put her hand to her mouth and suppressed the urge to vomit. Her face was bruised and her bottom lip was split open. She wore the same pale blue jeans from the night before.

She hobbled across the dorm's landing to the top of the stairs. Five lacrosse players, with IRISH painted in green on their bare chests, pushed past her and barreled loudly down the steps. None of them seemed to notice the pale brunette slumped against the pillar or the look of shock on her battered face.

As she summoned the strength to move, she watched the young men melt into the crowd. The campus grounds were crawling with people. Thousands of fans had flocked to the University of Notre Dame to see the Fighting Irish – undefeated and ranked second in the country – play the number-one ranked Trojans from the University of Southern California. For the first time in decades a national championship was within Notre Dame's reach.

The unseasonably warm October weather and the game day anticipation made for an electric atmosphere on campus. Students laughed and played Frisbee in the sunshine. Drunken fans knocked down steak sandwiches from the Knights of Columbus. Hordes of faithful Catholics lined up for tours of the Basilica. Members of the 380-piece marching band lingered outside the Main Building, ready for the Victory March to the Stadium.

The young woman stared groggily at the scene. A blast of trumpets from underneath the Golden Dome jolted her senses. She turned toward the noise and was hit again by the glare off the Dome and its 4,000 pound statue of the Virgin Mary. She pulled her head away reflexively.

Shutting her eyes, the woman knew she had to get away from the noise and the light. She clutched the metal railing to steady herself as she started down the steps. Her thin legs trembled throughout the descent.

Once she hit the ground she headed southward, inching slowly across campus. She pulled her broken body through the flood of people, eventually reaching the South Quad. No one seemed to notice the disheveled young woman staggering through the lush, green grass. Nor did they notice the dark blood stain running down from her crotch.

As she cut across the Quad, she heard a volley of cheers and whistles in the distance.

"RALLY SONS OF NOTRE DAME! SING HER GLORY AND SOUND HER FAME!"

The band erupted into the Victory March, Notre Dame's fight song, as it began its march across the campus grounds.

The woman continued to move onward slowly, dragging her right foot behind her. She left a smattering of small blood drops in her wake.

As she reached the corner of the South Quad and the beige brick buildings of the Law School, the noise of the band suddenly grew louder. She looked nervously over her shoulder. In the distance, she could make out the front line of the band. Resplendent in gold and blue uniforms, it marched directly at her. Panicked, she tried to pick up her pace, the dragging of her leg becoming more pronounced.

Swarms of people started lining the path to watch the band. Fans clutching beers and young families with

3

strollers craned their necks down the pathway.

"RAH, RAH FOR NOTRE DAME! WE WILL FIGHT IN EV-RY GAME!"

The sound of the drumline hammered in the woman's ears.

Breathless, she forced herself forward as fast as she could. She shuffled along the path in between the Law School and Notre Dame Avenue, veering left when she saw an opening in the crowd. She felt a momentary reprieve in the shade of the Law School's archway. For a second, she thought she had escaped the noise.

Looking over her shoulder at the oncoming band, the woman didn't see the leg of the lawn chair until it was too late. She tripped, stumbling face down onto the cold pathway. She tried to lift herself up, but felt faint. She had neither the mental nor physical energy. She slumped back on her face.

"AND WE'LL CHEER HER EVER, LOYAL TO NOTRE DAME!"

An obese middle-aged man, with a brat in one hand and a lukewarm Coors Light beer in the other, shouted at her from the side of the path.

"Hey lady! Move!"

His face flushed red with anger at the thought that someone might disrupt game day tradition.

"HEY!"

He shouted louder this time, spilling his beer. His Milwaukee accent reverberated underneath the archway.

He stormed over to the woman, grabbed her legs, and dragged her off the band's path. He dropped her on the pavement in front of the Law School's St. Thomas More Chapel.

"CHEER CHEER FOR OLD NOTRE DAME! WAKE UP THE ECHOES CHEERING HER NAME!"

The band grew to a deafening pitch as it approached

the Law School. The clash of symbols reverberated under the archway. Horns pierced the air.

Yet no one in the crowd paid attention. The Irish fans were fixated on the woman.

Lying on the cold cement, the woman stared vacantly into the blue sky. Her bruised face and bloody groin were in clear view for everyone.

Standing over the woman, the obese man gasped and slowly stepped away from her collapsed body. A young couple shielded their toddler's eyes. A nun gripped her rosary beads.

The band remained oblivious to the young woman. The Victory March continued. Cheerleaders bounced along the path, smiling and waving at the shocked faces of the crowd.

"SEND A VOLLEY CHEER ON HIGH, SHAKE DOWN THE THUNDER FROM THE SKY!"

The young woman was conscious long enough to see a Notre Dame police officer peering over her with a radio in his hand.

"This is Officer McKinnon. We've got a drunken student passed out underneath the Law School archway. Please send EMTs over here ASAP."

"Roger that."

The policeman leaned in closer, scanning the young woman's body. He grabbed the radio again.

"Dispatch, you're gonna need to send those EMTs right away," he said with more urgency.

"Roger that. EMTs are on the way."

The policeman continued staring at the woman's face, trying to look past the bruises and bloodied lip.

"Dispatch," said the policeman, hesitating to finish his sentence.

"EMTs will be there very shortly."

". . . someone better call Congressman O'Riordan."

5

That was the last thing the woman heard as she slipped into unconsciousness.

"WHILE HER LOYAL SONS ARE MARCHING ONWARD TO VICTORY!"

*If I was a little more under self-control, I would
have put the barrel against his forehead and fired. . . .*

George DeMarco sat hunched over a mahogany
table in Notre Dame's Kresge Law Library, reading an
awkward quote from Bernard Goetz. He looked up at an
oversized clock on the wall as he raced to finish the judge's
opinion from People v. Goetz.

From his perch under a stained-glass window,
George could see and hear the game day festivities around
him. Every few minutes a group of visitors streamed into
the library or a wave of cheers erupted from the South
Quad, just outside the Law School. He tried his best to
ignore the distractions and focus on the Goetz case.

As a kid growing up in Brooklyn in the 1980s, he
remembered the news about Goetz gunning down four
black teenagers on the Number 2 train. He had ridden that
train through downtown Manhattan years later. With this
background, George didn't need to waste time relearning
the facts today. He jumped to the case's holding.

His first-year criminal law class was scheduled to
discuss legal justifications on Monday. The Goetz case explained when someone was permitted to use deadly force in
self-defense. Scanning the arcane legal language quickly,
George found what he was looking for and repeated it in his
mind.

*The use of deadly force is okay as long as someone
has a reasonable belief that it was a necessary defense
against imminent harm.*

Got it.

George slammed his criminal law textbook shut and powered-down his laptop. He threw his pen and highlighter into his backpack. And he took off.

George didn't have tickets for this afternoon, but he had promised himself that he would watch it on television. Today's game was too historic for even a casual football fan like George to miss. His plan had been to study all morning, leaving himself enough time to visit Macri's Italian Deli for a sandwich before heading home for kick-off.

He hustled out of the library with his backpack slung over one shoulder. George bounced down the steps leading to the Law School's first floor. He threw open the doors and emerged outside the St. Thomas More Chapel.

And then he stopped.

George walked into a hushed crowd, gathered underneath the archway. He felt a somber cloud hanging over the area. It was a stark contrast to what he had heard coming from the South Quad.

"Excuse me," said George to a six-foot Midwestern farmer blocking his path.

Without saying a word, the farmer leaned forward to let George pass. As he shifted, George caught of a glimpse of what everyone was staring at. He now knew why everyone was quiet.

A woman in her mid-twenties was sprawled out in front of the Chapel. Her face was battered and bruised. Her hair was matted with clumps of dirt and blood. Her jeans were stained with a thick red blotch.

George's stomach dropped. When he was boxing as a kid, he had taken some serious beatings. But his face had never looked this bad.

He felt instant compassion for the woman. He felt sadness for the family that had to deal with this incident. And he felt a surge of anger at whoever had committed this brutal act.

8

As he got over his initial shock, George felt something else. He stared more intently at the woman's face. He narrowed his eyes.

I've seen that face before.

He couldn't place where he had seen her, but he was positive that she was familiar. He rarely forgot someone, even after only meeting them once.

But where do I know her from?

Standing frozen in the crowd, he thought about various stages of his life. *Brooklyn. Regis High School. Harvard. Washington, D.C. Capitol Hill.* He tried to connect that face to one of these periods of his life.

He wracked his brain until a pair of EMT personnel broke his concentration. The medics pushed their way through the crowd, lifted the girl onto a stretcher, and wheeled her into the back of an ambulance. It drove off, sirens blaring. George stood with everyone else, motionless, as the flashing lights faded in the distance.

A group of students with cans of Milwaukee's Best in their hands cut through the crowd toward the Stadium. "GO IRISH!" bellowed one in green shorts and oversized clown glasses. People took it as a signal to start acting normal again. The crowd dissipated.

George headed in the opposite direction from the hoards heading to the Stadium. He'd been in a rush to get home before the game. But the sight of that beaten face had taken the wind out of his sails.

He walked slowly toward the South Quad as the image of the woman flashed in his mind. He kept wondering how he knew her. The more he thought about it, the more he was overcome by sorrow.

The savagely attacked woman evoked a dark memory from his past. He had been born to a single mother in Santiago, Chile. After his mother disappeared, George was rescued from the streets by Catholic Charities and placed

9

into the arms of an American couple. He was so young when it happened that he barely remembered his mother. It wasn't until he was a teenager that he finally learned the truth.

A reticent Catholic Charities employee showed him the pictures and explained what had happened. George's mother was one of thousands of activists that had protested against General Augusto Pinochet's regime. She was rounded up, along with other activists, and tortured by Chilean state security.

The faded pictures of his dead mother were gruesome. George never forgot the images. And he had never seen a face that pulverized until he saw the girl beneath the archway.

He paused at the corner of the Law School and the South Quad to reflect on all these thoughts. With his head down, he fought off a surge of emotions. Then he looked up.

It was a straight line across the South Quad to the parking lot. He could be at his car and off campus in just a few minutes. He checked his watch. He figured he had time for a quick detour.

George walked north. He passed Walsh Hall, then Sorin Hall, and turned left at the Basilica. He made his way down a short hill until he came to the Grotto.

Although kickoff wasn't far away, a crowd of Notre Dame and USC fans cluttered the stone shrine. They lit candles and kneeled to pray. George stood quietly in the back, bowed his head, and whispered to himself.

"Lord, have mercy on that young woman. Relieve her suffering and the suffering of her family. Protect us all from the violence of others. Keep us safe from the weapons of hate."

George raised his head, exhaled deeply, and turned toward Saint Mary's Lake. A path wrapped around the lake and led to the parking lot. Since it was at the opposite end of campus from the Stadium, the path was practically empty. He checked his watch, then he took off at a hurried pace.

George walked briskly for several hundred feet until he came to a solitary figure wearing an untucked black shirt and crinkled black pants. From the back, George could tell that it was a heavyset man. George watched as the man teetered back-and-forth, stumbling along the path.

"Excuse me," said George, as he tried to pass the rotund, disheveled figure.

George glanced backward as he stepped-off of the path and walked around the man.

"Father Finnegan?" asked George, instantly recognizing the priest's white hair and ruddy face.

George's inquiry startled the man, and at first he didn't respond. George stopped in his tracks and extended his hand.

"Hey Father, how ya doin'?" asked George in his thick New York accent.

It took the priest a few seconds to compose himself.

"Oh . . . uh . . . yes . . . uh . . . how are you, my son?"

It was an odd response. George had expected a more enthusiastic welcome. At least, George thought, the priest would have recognized him.

The two were more than familiar with each other. George was in Father Finnegan's criminal law class that met three times a week. More importantly, Father Finnegan had been best friends with George's adopted grandfather, Frank DeMarco. A third kid from the old neighborhood in Brooklyn, Father Sean McCarthy, rounded-out the trio.

Growing up, the three did everything together. They played stickball in the streets. They sold newspapers for pocket money. They even served in the Korean War

11

together.

And when they returned from the war, McCarthy and Finnegan joined the seminary. Frank almost joined them, but he met and fell in love with George's grandmother. The couple raised five children, including George's adopted father, and then raised George when his adopted parents unexpectedly died.

When Frank passed away, George relied on his grandfather's two best friends. Father McCarthy took George under his wing, getting him into the prestigious Regis High School in Manhattan and setting him on the path to Harvard. Father Finnegan did his part by getting George into Notre Dame Law School, after George's other admissions offers were unexpectedly rescinded. Because of this history, George expected a different reaction.

At first, George chalked up Father Finnegan's slow response to a hard night or maybe too much tailgating. The man stunk of stale beer. His priestly cleric was wrinkled and stained.

George knew that Father Finnegan had a reputation for hitting the booze. Nicknamed the "Pelican" by his students – for the large mouth with which he drank – Father Finnegan often showed up, already intoxicated, at the tailgates or Corby's Bar on a weeknight. Students in his dormitory, Sorin Hall, frequently heard the clinking of empty wine bottles behind Father Finnegan's closed door.

George pushed those thoughts away as the images of the battered woman came to him again.

"Father, you wouldn't believe what I just saw. I was coming out of the Law School, and a girl had collapsed underneath the archway. Her face looked like someone had pounded on it pretty bad."

"A girl . . . um . . . uh . . . what kind of girl?" asked Father Finnegan, with a hint of nervousness that George did not pick up on.

"Probably mid-twenties, a brunette, hair down to the middle of her back. She was really banged-up."

"Did anyone say who this girl was?"

"Not when I was there. She was definitely too old to be an undergrad. But she was still young. Couldn't have been older than twenty-five."

"What happened to her?"

"I don't know. No one said anything as the ambulance took her away. The cops just kept everyone back."

"Cops?"

"Yeah. Lots of ND PD."

George watched as Father Finnegan looked tensely in the direction of the Law School and then back at George. Finnegan placed his hand on George's shoulder, turned him to the direction of the parking lot, and started walking.

"Where are you headed?" asked Father Finnegan.

"I was . . . uh . . . headed to Macri's for a sandwich and then home to watch the game."

"Uh . . . well . . . how 'bout I buy you lunch?" said the priest, glancing back in the direction of the South Quad.

George hesitated. He had no desire for company on his one afternoon off. He did not want to think or talk about Law School. But George knew that he couldn't say no to his grandfather's best friend and the man that helped him get into Notre Dame.

"Uh . . . sure."

As soon as the words left his mouth, George sensed that he would come to regret them.

CHAPTER 3
SATURDAY
1:54 P.M.

"Can I help you?"

The woman posed an obvious question. Jimmy King stood in the "Self-Help" section at Notre Dame's Hammes Bookstore. Titles leapt off of the shelves shouting positive affirmations: "Costume Change: How to Start a New Act in Life"; "Embrace the New You;" and, "Positive People."

Jimmy appeared in need of help too. The boyish, twenty-five-year-old wore an oversized blazer and baggy dress slacks. He looked like he was wearing his father's hand-me-downs.

"No, thank you. I'm okay," he said curtly to the employee.

In reality, Jimmy did need the help. He was in a tough race for U.S. Congress. The most recent polls showed him to be only two points ahead of the incumbent, Congressman Michael O'Riordan. Jimmy knew this marginal lead would not hold going into the final weekend of the election.

He had made it this far on luck. He would need more than luck to survive on Tuesday. He expected the next four days to be a serious test of character.

At the start of this campaign, Jimmy never thought he would be ahead of Congressman O'Riordan at any point. He recognized his weaknesses, largely his lack of name recognition. He figured he could overcome this by running ads and meeting as many voters as possible. As people started to see his face, he would convince them that he was one of them.

Although he graduated number one in his class from St. Joseph High School and his parents taught at Notre Dame, Jimmy had spent the last seven years outside Indiana. He lived in Cambridge, Massachusetts for four years, studying government at Harvard. Then he moved to England to study Churchill's World War II writings as a Marshall Scholar at Cambridge University.

Over the previous year, he had worked as a foreign policy aide for one of Indiana's U.S. Senators. He returned home earlier in the year to throw his name in the primary ring. His plan was to lay the groundwork for a future statewide political campaign.

Until Jimmy jumped into the race, only one other candidate had stepped forward for the Republican primary: Michael Henry, a popular, tough on crime St. Joseph County judge who entered as the proverbial, primary day favorite. Henry had the name recognition and local ties that Jimmy lacked. Local party elders tried to convince Jimmy to get out of the race. They worried that he was jeopardizing the Republicans' best opportunity to recapture the district since O'Riordan was first elected in 1984.

Jimmy's refusal to drop out proved to be prescient. Two days before the primary, the *South Bend Tribune* broke a story about Judge Henry trading reduced prison sentences for sexual favors. The article quoted several local prostitutes extensively. The late-breaking news left no alternative candidates but Jimmy. At that point, the establishment rallied around him.

Though Jimmy was the Republican nominee, he had struggled to present himself as a serious candidate. His name recognition hovered at around fifteen percent. He raised a minimal amount of money. He couldn't afford staff, so he relied on a network of volunteers, mainly from the Notre Dame College Republicans.

Despite these shortcomings, Jimmy was still inching ahead of O'Riordan heading into the final days of the election. He had benefitted from factors largely outside of his control: Ten percent unemployment and a generally weak economy had created a "throw the bums out" mentality across the country. Special interest groups from Washington, D.C. had also put Congressman O'Riordan on the list of incumbents targeted for defeat.

Political action committees, representing various interest groups, swamped the congressional district with television commercials and mailers. Most targeted Congressman O'Riordan's votes against the recent free trade agreements with Colombia and Peru, branding him a "socialist." Unions thanked O'Riordan for "saving American jobs." The capitalists spent more money, driving up O'Riordan's unfavorable ratings.

Jimmy did not care where the money or ads came from. He simply cared about winning. When it looked like he might actually eke out a victory, Jimmy became even more competitive. The inner drive that propelled him to Harvard and a Marshall Scholarship drove him in these waning days of the campaign. The burning desire to win had brought him to the Hammes Bookstore.

"Well, if there's anything that I can help you with, you just let me know," said the bookstore staffer, a cheery, overweight woman in her 50s. "And just to let you know, Mr. Philbin's running a little late. He apologizes profusely. He knows that kickoff is soon, but he is still planning to sign a limited amount of books. He should be here in about five minutes. The line starts over there," she said, pointing to a line of people snaking out the door.

Jimmy gave her a tight smile.

"Um . . . okay. Thanks."

He had not come to get help from the legendary television star and Notre Dame alum Regis Philbin. He was there for Bob Jaworski's help. Based on their last three meetings, Jaworski would be arriving at any moment.

Sure enough, at 1:55 on the dot, the hefty union boss emerged from around the bookshelf. His weathered and weary face, with his graying mustache, showed no sign of emotion. He wore Levi's blue jeans, Timberland work books and a Notre Dame hooded sweatshirt. He blended into the game day crowd, just as he planned it.

Jimmy and Jaworski had met in the same location for every home game of the season. Jaworski wanted it that way. Dark alleys and vacant parking garages were too conspicuous. They needed a place where they could blend into a crowd. Jaworski did not want someone to publicly link the union boss and the young Republican.

"What do you recommend?" asked Jaworski, as the two men stared at the titles on the shelf and avoided making eye contact.

"Uh . . . Regis Philbin's 'How I Got This Way,'" responded Jimmy.

He pulled out a copy from a bookstore plastic bag he was carrying and placed it on the shelf. Jaworski grabbed the book, opened the first few pages and saw what he had come for. $10,000 in cash was stuffed inside the hollowed-out book.

"Is this the only copy?" asked Jaworski.

"Oh . . . uh . . . no. I've got another one right here," said Jimmy, as he fumbled to get the second book out.

Jaworski grunted in appreciation.

This is how the pair had done it for three previous home games, and it had worked seamlessly. The bookstore provided the perfect cover. A large crowd of out-of-towners swarmed inside, scooping up Notre Dame merchandise. No one ever noticed the young Republican and grizzled union boss swapping books by legendary Notre Dame alums.

If anyone had stopped him, Jaworski would not

have looked out of place carrying these books. At the opening game against Purdue University, he picked up *Tales from the Notre Dame Hardwood*, by former basketball coach Digger Phelps. Against the University of Michigan, the pair swapped former President Monk Malloy's *Monk's Tale: The Pilgrimage Begins*. For the Naval Academy game, Jaworski left with *Rudy's Insights for Winning in Life* by campus gadfly Rudy Ruettinger.

Each time two copies.

Each time $10,000 in a book.

Although Jimmy had spent the majority of his adult life in academic settings, he wasn't naïve about South Bend Democratic street politics. He knew that getting out the vote on Election Day required some "walking around" money. From a business perspective, he saw the $80,000 that he gave to Jaworski as a strategic investment in his campaign.

Jaworski exercised a lot of political clout in the northern part of the state. He served as President of the Teamsters Local 364 and, simultaneously, Chairman of the St. Joseph County Democratic Party. He had been in these roles for thirty-two years. His endorsement meant a lot in terms of getting voters out. His intimidating tactics, however, meant so much more.

The stories were a part of Indiana political legend, rivaling those from bigger city Chicago. Most infamous was the cautionary tale about the South Bend City Council member who initiated a primary challenge against Congressman O'Riordan. In the weeks after announcing his run, the Councilman experienced a series of unfortunate events. A car hit him on his early morning run, breaking his leg. South Bend Bank initiated foreclosure proceedings on his house. And perhaps most sinister of all, he came home one day to find his dog dead from rat poison.

Rumors circulated for months that Jaworski had set

up Judge Henry in compromising situations with local prostitutes. Whether or not he actually played any role in the
scandal was beside the point. His presence loomed over
every political maneuver in northern Indiana.

It was exactly why Jimmy wanted Jaworski working
for him. Jimmy figured that if it cost $80,000 to keep the
unions from deploying their foot soldiers and, more importantly, to keep his body intact, it would be worth it. He had
banked his campaign on a relationship with Jaworski, and
he hoped it would carry him through Election Day.

Jaworski had never accepted money from a candidate other than Congressman O'Riordan, mostly because
no opponent had ever had a legitimate shot at defeating
O'Riordan. People had approached Jaworski several times
with generous offers. He never bit because he didn't want
to be seen backing a loser. Jaworski knew that his reputation and, in turn, his wallet were at stake. If he lost one
election, the kickback checks would soon disappear.

With the polls leaning toward Jimmy, Jaworski
began to hedge his bets after Labor Day. He agreed to meet
with Jimmy for a price. When Jaworski helped Congressman O'Riordan plot his 1977 run, he received $10,000 for
his "advice and consultation." Thirty-two years ago that
was big money. In Jimmy's race, it paled in comparison to
the cash pulled in by various campaign consultants. Jaworski told Jimmy he would not work for anything less than
$80,000. Jimmy didn't flinch.

He agreed because he knew that he could trust
Jaworski. The two men had known each other for over
twenty years. Jimmy had been best friends with Jaworski's son, Tommy, from the day they met at preschool until
Tommy's death at the age of 10. Jimmy had slept over at
the Jaworski's house, eaten at their dinner table, and gone
with them on vacation to Lake Michigan every summer.

After Tommy's death, Jimmy stayed in close contact

with Jaworski. Tommy had been their only child, so Jimmy tried to fill the void. He rode his bike over to their house on the weekend. He worked for Jaworski on union organizing campaigns, during the summers in high school. Jimmy had raced to the Local 364 offices to open his Harvard acceptance letter. Jaworski gave him a big bear hug and Jimmy never felt prouder.

Jimmy knew the relationship meant a lot to Jaworski. But it meant even more to Jimmy. Jimmy's parents both taught at Notre Dame – his father in the biochemistry department and mother in engineering. Both were wrapped up in their own worlds and Jimmy had never developed much of a relationship with either. Jaworski, on the other hand, was always involved in his life. Whether it was football games or school debates, Jimmy could look into the crowd and see Jaworski's face.

The two drifted apart when Jimmy headed to Harvard. For one thing, Jimmy grew more conservative in his political outlook. He studied economics, penning his senior thesis on free trade agreements and the unions' efforts to undercut them. Jimmy's world had also expanded beyond South Bend. His internships and time abroad as a Marshall Scholar gave him experiences that Jaworski could not relate to.

Jimmy thought the campaign might pull them closer together. Despite their different political leanings, Jimmy never saw Jaworski as an ideologue. He considered Jaworski to be more of an old school political boss or local mafia don. He hoped that he could tap into the pair's relationship to neutralize the political opposition or, at the very least, avoid getting his legs broken.

"What are the talking heads telling you to say?" asked Jaworski.

"Basically, just to keep hammering his free trade votes and his votes to raise the debt ceiling," said Jimmy.

"That's insider baseball. No one gives a crap about that out here."

"So what I am supposed to talk about?"

"People know the Chicoms are taking their jobs. So they want to know what you are physically going to do about it. They want to hear you say, 'I will go to Beijing and bring back those jobs one-by-one myself.'"

Jimmy nodded his head as the pair continued to stare at the books, avoiding eye contact with each other.

"You're about to get hammered, so just brace yourself," said Jaworski.

"What do you mean?"

"No one's been paying attention to the race. You've been lucky that the Irish have been playing so well. People would rather talk national championship number twelve than about the economy being in the toilet. O'Riordan has saved his ammunition. Once this game is over, expect to be carpet-bombed by negative ads."

"I think I can handle it."

Jaworski snorted dismissively in response.

"This is gonna be stuff that would make your grandmother disown you. You got enough money to run counter attack ads?"

"We're okay on finances. About fifty thousand left."

"You're gonna need a lot more than that. You've shaken down all the rich alums?"

"Sort of. I'm headed to the press box now and can hopefully get a few more commitments."

"How'd you score that invite?" asked Jaworski skeptically.

"Father Price invited me."

Jaworski released a quiet, gravelly laugh.

"What's that supposed to mean?" asked Jimmy.

"Father Price is a snake."

21

"Why do you say that?"

"He slithers to power."

Jimmy thought that he would be hard-pressed to find another person describe the President of the University of Notre Dame that way.

"Where was he five months ago?" asked Jaworski.

"Where were *you* five months ago?" responded Jimmy.

With a scowl on his face, Jaworski turned away from the books and stared down Jimmy for several seconds.

"So is this all I get for $80,000?" asked Jimmy, pushing Jaworski further.

Jaworski started to get visibly angrier. He didn't appreciate the twenty-five-year-old kid trying to push him around.

"You don't worry about me. I'm working on something as we speak," responded Jaworski.

Jimmy wanted more assurance, but without knowing exactly what Jaworski was planning. If something went wrong, he could deny knowing what Jaworski had planned. Jimmy considered $80,000 money well spent for a political hatchet man. He stepped closer to Jaworski and grabbed the union boss's arm.

"You promised me," said Jimmy.

Jaworski looked down at the hand squeezing his bicep. He couldn't believe this kid. Jaworski remembered ten years earlier when Jimmy was a pimply faced teenager. He remembered just five years earlier when Jimmy was a pimply faced Harvard nerd. And Jaworski knew that even though Jimmy led the race at this point, Jimmy was still just a pimply faced twenty-five-year-old. The kid needed Jaworski more than the union boss needed him.

Jaworski got inches from Jimmy's face and issued an ultimatum.

"If you don't want my help, just say so."

The words lingered in the air for a few seconds before Jimmy released his grip from Jaworski's arm.

Jaworski reached down, grabbed the plastic bag, and started to walk away. He took three steps before stopping and turning around to face Jimmy.

"Don't you worry about a thing. You're gonna get your money's worth."

How the hell am I supposed to get out of here?

Bob Jaworski stood behind a tightly-packed crowd of people. The group blocked his path to the bookstore's entrance. People stood shoulder-to-shoulder, ten feet deep in a horseshoe formation. Everyone seemed to be staring anxiously at the main entrance.

Jaworski didn't have time to wait. In his rough manner, he started elbowing his way through the crowd. He didn't bother to excuse himself and people cursed as he shoved them out of his way. Jaworski stopped when he got to the front of the line. He watched as the doors flew open.

"GO IRISH!"

Regis Philbin stepped into the bookstore, waving to the crowd. Security personnel cleared space in the foyer for the television host. A table was set aside for Philbin to sit and sign autographs.

Philbin stood in the middle of the crowd, soaking up the adoration. He pointed to the men, blew kisses to the women, and gave high fives to little children. Trapped, Jaworski was forced to watch the scene unfold. He knew that Notre Dame had no greater celebrity fan than Regis Philbin.

"REGIS!"

Jaworski turned to see who had shouted Philbin's name. It was an obese, middle-aged woman with a mullet down to the shoulders of her vinyl Notre Dame jacket. She came charging directly at Jaworski.

He did not move fast enough to get out of the way. The woman crashed into him, pushing him to the ground.

She knocked the bookstore bag out of Jaworski's hands and sent it flying into the air.

Jaworski watched as the bag sailed through the air and one of the Regis Philbin books fell out. On its way to the ground, the pages flipped open. Several stacks of hundred dollar bills, wrapped in rubber bands, tumbled to the floor.

Jaworski moved faster than he had ever in his life. He scooped all the money back into the book. He grabbed the bag and quickly dumped the book inside. He leapt to his feet and pretended as if nothing had happened.

But then he realized something.

He looked in the bag and down at his feet.

There was no sight of the second book.

Jaworski scanned the crowd nervously. No one was paying any attention to him. Everyone was focused on the woman who now had Regis Philbin locked in a bear hug.

"I JUST LUUUV YOU REE-GIS!" shouted the obese woman.

Philbin appeared undaunted. From his years in show business, he was accustomed to women throwing themselves at him. It happened more often than not when he visited Notre Dame. While other celebrities would have been irritated by the woman, Philbin indulged every fan.

Philbin's security guards weren't as gracious. Two Notre Dame police officers sprung into action. One officer pried the woman's arms from Philbin's midsection. The other pulled the woman back by her waist. As they cleared a few feet from Philbin, the officers put the woman in a set of plastic flex cuffs. By this point, tears of joy were streaming down her face.

"Hey guys, please be gentle with the lady. She's only a fan," said Philbin, in his gentlemanly manner.

The call for mercy earned Philbin an ovation from the crowd.

25

Philbin heard the reaction and smiled. He pretended to dust himself off. He started at his shoulders and worked his way down to his knees. Rubbing his hands across his legs, he saw a copy of his book that had fallen at his feet. He scooped down to pick it up.

"Ma'am," called out Philbin to the obese woman. "You dropped your book!"

The woman did not hear Philbin.

"Ma'am!" Philbin called to her again.

"That's mine," grunted Jaworski.

He grabbed the book, wrapping his fat, swollen knuckles around the front cover.

"Oh, I'm sorry sir. Well, how about I autograph that for you?"

"That's alright," responded Jaworski sternly.

"But I insist," said Philbin. "Anything for a fan."

Philbin pried the book out of Jaworski's hands and sat down at the autograph table.

Jaworski knew that all the eyes in the bookstore were fixed on the front of the room and a book stuffed with $10,000 in cash. He initially thought about grabbing the book and running, but quickly dismissed that idea. He had just seen the ND cops manhandle a woman.

Running away from an autograph is not a crime. But Jaworski didn't need anyone asking questions about why he ran or what he was doing with a copy of Philbin's book filled with money. The fewer questions asked, the better his odds of slipping away undetected.

Philbin opened the hard cover of the book to the first page. Jaworski watched nervously, hoping that Philbin did not go any further.

"What would you like me to write?" asked Philbin, looking-up and smiling at Jaworski.

Jaworski stood there silent and stone faced. He didn't care what Philbin wrote. He just wanted to get out of there.

"Uh . . . sir . . . what's your name?"

"Bob is fine."

"Well, Bob, thanks for buying the book."

Philbin put his black Sharpie pen to the first page, but then stopped and looked up at Jaworski.

"You know Bob, it took me a lifetime to build up the stories in this book."

Jaworski, nervous that his cover might be blown, continued to stare blankly at Philbin. He didn't want to hear about what Philbin had done in his lifetime. He wanted to leave with his cash and not look back.

"But you know what, it only took me three months to write the thing!"

The crowd loved Philbin's cheesy joke. Regis smiled and laughed after they laughed. Then he put the pen to the first page again and began to write before he stopped, once again, to talk to Jaworski.

"My wife said to me, 'Why do you want to write a book? You never read books.'"

Philbin felt the crowd eating out of his hand and he played up to the moment.

Jaworski just stood there, paralyzed that this situation might never end.

"I said to her, 'Honey, you don't have to read them to sell them.'"

The crowd laughed even harder.

"Now, let me tell you about–" said Philbin, before an assistant reminded him that there was a line waiting.

"Oh yes. Well Bob, I hope you enjoy the book."

Philbin picked up the book with both hands and admired his picture on the cover. Jaworski felt as if he had been standing there for days. His heart beat rapidly as each second passed.

Finally, Jaworski just grabbed the book. Philbin

continued to hold on to it firmly. After a deep sigh, Philbin released it, smiled at Jaworski, and got back to signing autographs.

Jaworski looked around cautiously at the crowd. No one suspected a thing. He wanted to get out of there before anything else happened. He stuffed the book back into the bag and clutched it tightly to his chest. The crowd descended on the table where Philbin sat and Jaworski had to push his way through the people again.

Breaking free from the crowd at the side exit, Jaworski checked his watch. He was late. He was supposed to be at the Hesburgh Center for International Studies right now.

Jaworski still had more money to collect for this election.

CHAPTER 5
SATURDAY
2:04 P.M.

"Where the hell have you been?"

Mike O'Riordan snarled at Bob Jaworski. The tall and lanky fourteen-term incumbent Congressman hated to be kept waiting. He expected his staff to be prompt. And he definitely considered Jaworski to be staff.

"I . . . uh . . . had to pick up a few things."

O'Riordan looked at the bag Jaworski clutched in his arms. Then he looked back at Jaworski. He shook his head in disgust. The scowl remained on his face.

"We've got some kind hearted and faithful Catholics here that are interested in helping the impoverished children of South Bend. I suggested that the Teamsters might be able to get their generous contributions to those children in need."

"How much do they wanna give?"

"$10,000."

"That's it?" said Jaworski skeptically.

"That's it," replied O'Riordan firmly.

"What about the others?"

"What others?"

"Don't you normally have a number of fans at this type of event?"

"They all seem to be unable to contribute this year," said O'Riordan.

The amount explained why O'Riordan was in such a foul mood. The pre-game receptions at the Hesburgh Center for International Studies traditionally functioned as a campaign ATM for O'Riordan. The Center, home to both the Kellogg Institute for International Affairs and the Kroc

Center for Peace Studies, hosted wealthy alums and donors before every home game. Throughout the years, O'Riordan had courted many of these guests. In turn, many had supported O'Riordan in his political endeavors.

Since the Center was dedicated to studying global issues, a number of O'Riordan supporters held foreign passports. Political support from foreign citizens complicated things a bit for O'Riordan. Campaign finance laws strictly prohibited donations from non-U.S. citizens. Receiving foreign money was a potential political death trap. To avoid any problems, O'Riordan and Jaworski had developed a system.

Every dollar connected to a foreign citizen went straight into the Teamsters Scholarship Fund for Members' Children. The Fund raised an average of $250,000 a year from O'Riordan's political supporters. It awarded exactly one $500 academic scholarship. Jaworski took a ten percent cut for himself. He spent the rest advancing O'Riordan's political career.

Jaworski used the money for whatever was needed. He ran attack ads. He bought billboard space. He paid Union members and their extended families to get to the polls. And O'Riordan turned a blind eye to it all.

O'Riordan never asked Jaworski about finances. He never asked about how the money was being spent. As long as he kept getting re-elected, O'Riordan preferred to be kept in the dark. This would allow him to deny culpability if anyone ever uncovered the Fund's books. He finessed potential supporters and then left it up to Jaworski to collect.

In previous years, donations had flowed toward O'Riordan. The Kroc Institute's peaceniks loved O'Riordan's anti-war credentials. After graduating from Notre Dame in 1974, O'Riordan went to Ecuador as a Peace Corp Volunteer. In the early 1980's, he marched with other local activists against President Reagan's military buildup. Throughout his time in Congress, he had been a vocal critic of the military industrial complex. More recently, O'Riordan has used his spot on the House Permanent Select Committee on Intelligence to rail against the lawless War on Terror.

The pseudo-socialists associated with the Latin American-focused Kellogg Center were just as enamored with O'Riordan. They adored his stories about riding horseback through the Ecuadorean countryside. They listened attentively as he regaled them with his Ph.D. research on the Venezuelan military and political leader Simon Bolivar. And most of all, they loved that he always conversed in fluent Spanish.

The affection from both groups allowed O'Riordan to maintain a steady stream of campaign contributions.

Until now.

There were a number of reasons why his coffers were low. An older generation of revolutionaries was less anxious to talk about revolutions now that they owned nice homes and had healthy bank accounts. O'Riordan's foreign policy positions appeared out of touch given American counterterrorism support had helped Colombia free the Revolutionary Armed Forces of Colombia (known as "FARC") hostages. Most significantly, it looked like O'Riordan might lose to a twenty-five-year-old who had never held a serious job.

The slide in donations was not a result of O'Riordan's fundraising efforts. He had been at every home game reception this season, and worked the crowd hard. He cajoled them in a fiery Spanish tongue. He delivered emotional pleas for assistance. He even compared himself to Simon Bolivar, and spoke about liberating the impoverished. He pleaded with people not to quit on the revolution.

31

All of it fell on deaf ears. By the time the USC game rolled around, O'Riordan came across as pathetic. He used a professorial tone to lecture anyone within earshot. More and more people either tuned him out, or avoided him all together. Even the desperate graduate students stayed away from O'Riordan today.

Except for one.

"I'll join your revolution."

O'Riordan had cornered three master's degree candidates when he heard the soft voice behind him. He turned his attention away from the students, who instantly walked away.

As he looked into the eyes of the thin, thirty-five-year-old brunette, all his frustrations melted away. He inhaled a long breath through his nose and puffed out his chest.

"Do you believe in the cause?"

"I do."

"Are you committed to the cause?"

"I am," said the woman, her voice rising.

"Will you give everything you have to the cause?"

"I will," responded the woman, practically shouting at this point.

O'Riordan did not detect that she might be lying to him. He never suspected her ulterior motives. He believed in his heart that this graduate student nearly half his age had fallen in love with him.

"I am willing to do whatever you need."

"Thank you, Gabriella. You don't know how much that means to me."

O'Riordan honestly meant it. Her presence soothed him.

O'Riordan had never felt this way with the other graduate students. He had dated a number over the last fifteen years. What started as a cheap fling turned into a pattern of affairs with Latin American graduate students. When one graduated and returned home, O'Riordan moved on to another one. The pattern, however, ended with Gabriella Silva.

O'Riordan loved Gabriella. He hadn't loved any of the others. He only enjoyed the physical comfort and their naïve adoration. Gabriella gave him so much more.

O'Riordan planned to make Gabriella his wife as soon as the campaign finished. His 30-year-old marriage to Helen had only ever been one of convenience. He proposed to Helen without ever truly loving her. He figured he needed to be married before entering politics and he found himself a willing bride. But he wasn't about to divorce her before this election, given that he was on shaky ground.

O'Riordan had long used his family as a political weapon. He ran ads featuring pictures of his wife and daughter. The ads served as a vivid contrast to the young and unmarried Jimmy King. They also reinforced the message that Jimmy was a Harvard elitist and D.C. insider, with no ties to the community. The ads made no mention of O'Riordan's relationship with Gabriella.

Since asking him a question at one of his Kellogg Center lectures, the stunning Venezuelan had remained a constant presence in O'Riordan's life. She infused O'Riordan with a renewed joy and excitement, even though he faced such dim prospects on Election Day. After the election, O'Riordan planned to take her away for two weeks. One week in the countryside of his adopted home Ecuador. One week in the countryside of her native Venezuela. He bought an engagement ring to propose to her on the second week of the trip. He wanted to spend the rest of his life with her.

"How did you do today?" asked Gabriella.

"It's been a steeper climb than Chimborazo," said O'Riordan, referring to Ecuador's largest mountain.

33

"How much more do you need?"

"At least another $300,000. $500,000 would be even better. We have a number of ads to run over these next few days. And Bob here needs to mobilize his troops," pointing to Jaworski who had been standing silently next to O'Riordan this entire time.

"Well, I think that I can help you with that."

"Oh no, Gabriella. I couldn't take your money," responded O'Riordan, without seeing the irony of having just spent the last hour shaking down anyone with a checkbook.

"I insist. I believe in the cause! I am dedicated to the cause! I will give everything I have for the cause! Remember?"

O'Riordan loved this woman's confidence. The other graduate students had been too timid around him. Gabriella's maturity made her stand out from the normal grad students, who were straight out of college. O'Riordan liked the fact that she knew what she wanted and never backed down from a challenge. He sensed that she had won plenty of fights in the past. He loved her tough spirit.

"I can get the money from my uncle. He knows how much you mean to me. He would definitely see this as a worthwhile investment."

"Oh, Gabriella," started O'Riordan, until his cell phone started ringing. He pulled the phone out of his pocket. "Hello . . . yes, this is Congressman O'Riordan." Before continuing with the call, he held the phone away from his ear and whispered to Gabriella and Jaworski.

"Will you guys work out the arrangements while I take this call?"

O'Riordan smiled at both of them and then walked away. Gabriella smiled back at O'Riordan. Jaworski just stood there with a scowl on his face. It took several seconds before the union boss finally broke the ice.

"So . . . your . . . uh . . . uncle. He's gotta lotta concern for the people of northern Indiana?" asked Jaworski, skeptical about how a graduate student could come up with such a large sum of money.

"He believes in supporting a man of principle," responded Gabriella without skipping a beat.

"And he believes that a man who cheats on his wife with women half his age is a man of principle?"

"Oh, Bob," said Gabriella, laughing off Jaworski's snide comment. "You can't fault him for having such a big heart . . . Now, how would you like the money?"

"Cash would be great," insisted Jaworski, not thinking for one moment that Gabriella might come up with such a large amount on such short notice.

"Sure . . . I'll get you the money later today," she responded casually.

"You have five hundred grand in cash just lying around?"

"My uncle knows the high cost of an American education."

The quick response broke Jaworski's stern look. He smiled briefly. His stern demeanor returned just as quickly as it had disappeared.

"So what line of business is your uncle in?" asked a suspicious Jaworski.

"He does a lot of work in the oil industry."

Before Jaworski could probe Gabriella about the Venezuelan oil industry and why she had so much money from her uncle, O'Riordan returned. His arms hung at his side. He looked shaken by the phone conversation.

"Michael, what is it? What is wrong?" asked Gabriella.

"We've got to get over to Memorial Hospital right now."

"What is it? Are you okay?"

"I'm fine . . . But something's happened to Mary."

"We never expected a CIA officer to get involved here."

Neither did Lauren DeMarco. Never in her life did she think that she'd be mingling with aging peaceniks at the Kroc Institute for Peace Studies. Lauren didn't have anything against the idea of peace. She just had a different approach than these fading baby boomers. Rather than publish academic articles or sponsor lectures, Lauren had rolled up her sleeves and helped eliminate some of the most serious threats to peace on the planet.

She had joined the Agency straight out of Harvard. Her initial plan had been to work for her father at his boutique investment firm after graduation. But her life changed as she stood in front of her dorm room television on Tuesday, September 11, 2001. She was counting down the floors from the top of Tower Two to her father's office when the building began to crumble. She joined the Agency shortly after graduation wanting nothing more than revenge.

Her time in the Directorate of Operations took her all over the world. She tracked Hawala Islamic banking networks in Dubai. She broke up kidnapping rings in Iraq from May 2004 to early 2006. She uncovered a trade route in Beirut, where Venezuela funneled oil money to Iran and Iran sent weapons to Hezbollah.

She wanted to stay in Beirut longer, but events on the ground made it unsafe for Lauren. After she discovered the trade route, the intel agencies of Hezbollah, Iran and Venezuela put her on their hit lists. The CIA Director made the decision to recall her.

Upon her return to D.C., Lauren found herself a casualty of Beltway politics. Her identity was exposed in the *Washington Post* after she helped kill an African warlord that had been kidnapping children and turning them into child soldiers. He had drawn international ire for other atrocities like raping Peace Corps Volunteers.

Although the mission had been a success, the President's National Security Adviser had been advocating for a diplomatic solution. The President sided with CIA. The National Security Adviser, feeling that he had lost the President's confidence and wanting to be vindicated, hoped that Lauren's mission would fail.

When Lauren succeeded, the National Security Adviser made her the target of his envy. He knew that outing her as an operative would effectively end her career. After her name appeared in the *Post*, that is exactly what happened.

Her boyfriend, George, suggested that she come with him to South Bend to decompress and figure out her next move. Lauren, who had fallen in love with the man that reminded her so much of her father, leapt at the chance. In a self assertive and confident manner, Lauren told George that they had to get married if she was moving to South Bend with him. George's old family friend, Father Sean Finnegan, officiated their wedding in the St. Thomas More Chapel at the Law School and then helped Lauren get a job interview with Henry Sullivan, the Director of the Kroc Institute. Sullivan invited her to a football game reception.

"Well . . . I'm technically retired from the Agency," Lauren told Sullivan.

She laughed lightly as she made this comment. She suspected he would be suspicious about hiring a former covert operative. Going into the reception, she decided she would be as friendly as possible to put everyone at ease. Her calm demeanor and good looks had won over fanatical Islamists. She figured it would work on crotchety, self-important academics.

"Thank you so much for inviting me today," continued Lauren cheerfully. "I'm so excited to meet you."

"Well you come highly recommended from Father Finnegan."

"Oh, that's very kind of him."

"But Father Finnegan only told me a little bit about your background. You graduated from Harvard?"

"That's right. With a concentration in Economics."

"And then you went to work straight for the CIA after college?"

"Uh-huh. Obviously, I can't get into all the details. But I worked for the then-Directorate of Operations, which is now the National Clandestine Service."

"So you really are a spy?" asked Sullivan, in an astonished tone.

Lauren laughed at Sullivan's reaction.

"That's right. I worked clandestine operations during my time abroad and in D.C. But don't worry, it's not as exciting as it sounds," replied Lauren with a playful wink.

"When Father Finnegan said you worked for the CIA, I thought I was getting an academic desk analyst. Not some rough and tumble killing machine. But I have to say, the world is in trouble if all of our spies are this smart and beautiful."

Lauren forced a fake smile in response to Sullivan's creepy comment. She had dealt with plenty of lecherous old men in the Middle East. She didn't think she'd have to deal with them here at Notre Dame.

"Are you allowed to tell me where you lived?"

"That I can talk about. I was posted to Dubai, Baghdad, and Beirut, but I traveled all over the region."

"I thought Father Finnegan mentioned that you had lived in the Middle East. We actually have one of our scholars focusing specifically on the Middle East right now."

"Really? What's he working on?"

"I'll get him to explain that to you. His name's Ted Derring. Let me find him," said Sullivan.

Sullivan turned towards a long table of food. A shaggy-haired, fifty-year-old man stood with his back to Lauren and Sullivan. The man wore an academic's uniform: slacks, a faded tweed sports coat, and scuffed penny loafers. The man grabbed cookies one by one and stashed them into the pockets of his jacket.

"Ted!"

Lauren watched with amusement as the shout startled the disheveled academic.

"Ted," called Sullivan again. "I'd like to introduce you to Lauren Caputo. Lauren is eager to help us with some of our projects. She has extensive experience in the Middle East."

"Hi. I'm Lauren," said Lauren, extending her hand to Professor Derring.

"So where in the Middle East were you?" said Professor Derring, awkwardly ignoring a proper introduction.

"I lived in Dubai, Baghdad, and Beirut, but I traveled all over the region."

"Beirut, huh? I'm actually working on a project right now in Beirut."

"Really? What's the project?"

"I'm looking at the role that Lebanese women can play as peace builders in defusing conflict in Lebanon."

Lauren nodded politely. Having been a woman that tried to end Hezbollah's paramilitary operations, she wondered what contribution this man might make. It seemed awfully difficult to make an impact from South Bend,

Indiana.

"So does that mean you spend a lot of time in Beirut?"

"Oh no. None at all. I do most of my research from home. But we hosted a peace building conference here at Notre Dame. I invited a group of Lebanese women from a NGO in Beirut. My research assistant helped me interview them here on campus and we're in the middle of writing up a paper now."

Lauren nodded politely again. She wondered who would actually read it. How much insight could he possibly glean without visiting the region?

"I actually have a fantastic research assistant. She lived in Beirut for a while, so I leave most of the on the ground research to her. Plus, it's too dangerous over there right now."

"Where'd she live?" asked Lauren, ignoring the irony that a peacenik would refuse to travel to a conflict zone.

"I think she lived near the American University of Beirut."

"Really? That's the area that I lived in. Do you know when she lived there?"

"Oh . . . I . . . uh . . . I think from 2006 to 2008."

Lauren laughed at the coincidence.

"I lived there from 2006 to 2008. What's her name?"

"Gabriella Silva. Do you know her?"

"Hmmm... her name doesn't ring a bell. Do you know what she was doing over there?"

"I believe she worked for some NGOs. Actually, I saw her earlier. She may still be here."

Professor Derring scanned the crowd lingering in the Hesburgh Center."

"There she is. Gabriella! Gabriella!"

Lauren watched as Professor Derring waved at a tall, thin brunette standing across the room. As the brunette slowly turned around, Lauren's heart stopped.

It's her.

Lauren recognized the face immediately and instinctively reached into her bag. Her hand scurried around the bottom. It took her several seconds before realizing she no longer carried her reliable Sig – a Sig Sauer P239.

The lethal 9 millimeter had been a gift from the Navy SEALs that she had worked with in Iraq. When she lived in the Middle East, she always kept the gun within arm's reach. But when they moved to South Bend, she felt comfortable leaving home without it.

"That's her," said Professor Derring. "Gabriella, I'd like to introduce you to someone," shouted the professor, as he waved her over.

The brunette hesitated for a second. Then a smile slowly came across her face. She walked over to the group.

"Gabriella, I'd like to introduce you to . . . Sorry, you must remind me of your name again."

Lauren stood there in silence. During her time with the Agency, she had assumed numerous fake identities. At any given moment, she could regurgitate the most minute details of a fictional life. But now, when it came time to saying her own name, Lauren hesitated.

"Oh. Sorry. Hi. I'm Lauren DeMarco."

"Nice to meet you *Lauren DeMarco.*"

Gabriella repeated Lauren's name with extra emphasis. It was clearly intentional. Lauren figured it was the Venezuelan's way of saying, "I remember you from Beirut and Lauren DeMarco was not your name back then."

Lauren wasn't about to fall prey to the Venezuelan's head games. She had risked her life trying to bring this woman to justice, only to have her escape. She would not let her escape a second time.

"What's your name?" said Lauren.

"I'm Gabriella Silva."

Lauren didn't know if this was her real name and assumed it wasn't. She had only ever known her as "The Fox." That is how all of her contacts inside Hezbollah referred to the Venezuelan.

"Gabriella, Lauren was telling me that she lived in Beirut, in the same neighborhood, at the same time as you," said Professor Derring with a sense of amazement in his voice.

"Really? What were you doing over there?"

"I worked for the CIA," said Lauren, a cocky smile emerging on her face.

"Did you ever kill anyone?" the Venezuelan slyly asked.

"I sure tried my hardest," responded Lauren, keeping a playful tone but letting the Venezuelan know that she was still a force to be reckoned with.

"What were you doing over there?" asked Lauren, intrigued to see what excuse the Venezuelan would come up with.

"I was working for an NGO that provided humanitarian supplies to the war-torn areas after the 2006 Israel-Hezbollah War."

Lauren nodded politely, not buying one word of it. She really wanted to ask if cash and weapons from the Quds Force, Iran's paramilitary organization, constituted humanitarian supplies. She held off, and kept probing to get a better sense of why she was at Notre Dame.

"So why'd you leave Beirut?"

"Oh, you would know this better than me, Beirut takes its toll on you. What is your excuse?"

"I got a new job in D.C."

"So how did you end up here at Notre Dame?"

Lauren hesitated. She did not want the Fox to know

that she was married. She worried that George might become a target. But before she could say anything, the Kroc Center Director interjected.

"Lauren followed her husband here. He is a student over at the law school."

Lauren did not take her eyes off of the Fox. She watched as the Fox smiled slyly at this revelation.

"Your husband is a law student?" asked the Fox, rhetorically. "Interesting."

"How'd you end up at Notre Dame?" asked Lauren, trying to change the focus.

"After a year in Venezuela, my heart remained in humanitarian work. The Kroc Institute has one of the most well-respected peace studies programs in the world, so I applied for the master's program."

Lauren still wasn't buying it. She knew the Venezuelan had no interest in peace, especially not with the West. Lauren just could not figure out what operation required the Venezuelan to be in South Bend, Indiana.

"Wow. You two have quite the rapport," interjected Professor Derring. "I could use both of your experiences. How would you both like to work on this project with me?"

The two women, staring and smiling at each other, responded in unison.

"That sounds great."

"Not a bad view, huh?"

Jimmy initially didn't respond to University of
Notre Dame President Father Richard Price. He was too
busy looking up in amazement at all 136 sections of Notre
Dame Stadium. More than 80,000 seats were filled. Ush-
ers and local police stood in strategic positions. The entire
place was packed.

The Stadium itself wasn't unfamiliar to Jimmy. He
had worked in a concession stand here with Tommy Jaworski when they were ten. The two sold soda and popcorn
and listened to the Irish on the radio.

In all these years, however, Jimmy had never set
foot inside the Stadium. Not for a regular season game.
Not for a spring game. Not for an open practice. Not once.

From the ground, it looked just as it did on television, but even more majestic. On this glorious fall day,
with the sun draping down the east side of the stands, the
place felt magical. Touchdown Jesus, rearing his head
above the north end zone, looked more spectacular from
this viewpoint than in full view from outside.

"This is awesome," responded Jimmy giddily. "I've
never been down on the field before. I've never even been
inside the stands before."

"Well, we hope that this is not the last time that you
join us for a game."

"Any time you have an extra ticket, I'd love to join
you," said Jimmy, gushing.

Father Price, the forty-two-year-old priest with the
slicked-back, jet black hair, laughed lightly. The young and

charismatic priest had been chosen four years ago to lead Notre Dame in the 21st century. Standing in front of thousands of his flock, he slapped Jimmy on the back.

"I think we'll be able to find an extra ticket for you any time," said Father Price, smiling and winking at Jimmy.

Except for the oversized blazer, Jimmy looked right at home on the sidelines. His youthful appearance made him a dead ringer for one of the Irish student managers who carried water bottles and extra athletic tape. The student managers looked much more focused than Jimmy, though. Jimmy's wide eyes and big smile revealed how much he was enjoying the moment.

"What do you say we head to the press box? There are some people I'd like to introduce you to up there."

"That sounds great, Father."

Jimmy's smile grew wider as the two men strolled together along the sidelines. The crowd parted as Father Price and Jimmy headed off the field and into the bowels of the stadium. Jimmy soaked in every second, smiling extra wide as the television and still photographers captured him with Father Price.

Walking shoulder to shoulder with Father Price, all the resentment that Jimmy had harbored towards Notre Dame at the start of his campaign vanished. He had tried in vain to rally the university's hierarchy behind his campaign, but no one, especially not Father Price, took him seriously. When Jimmy came across the university provost on a Saturday of door knocking, the provost asked him, in a mocking tone, if Jimmy was even legally old enough to be elected. As an institution, Notre Dame had snubbed Jimmy.

But that attitude had changed this week.

With the polls tilting towards Jimmy and O'Riordan acting more erratic, the university's chattering class began talking up the young, ambitious Harvard grad. Father Price's appearance with Jimmy on the sidelines would give them even more to talk about.

Jimmy's walk with the President of Notre Dame sent an important political message, and Jimmy knew it. Father Price never endorsed any candidate for office. Yet he always managed to discreetly signal which candidates had his support, from the President of the United States down to the local St. Joseph County dogcatcher. The fact that Father Price was with Jimmy on the sidelines of the biggest game of the year – just days before the election – was a pretty obvious sign as to which candidate the Notre Dame establishment should back.

And with that backing came cash and lots of it. Notre Dame alums donated generously to all kinds of causes, including political campaigns. The university's top donors – men and women who wrote six figure checks without blinking – would be gathered at the reception. Jimmy hoped to meet and woo possible donors.

Even before Jaworski told him about O'Riordan's attack ads, Jimmy knew he needed more money. His campaign war chest had dwindled rapidly and he had no personal resources to speak of. He had spent the bulk of his cash on retaining Jaworski. He desperately needed money to run ads to boost his name recognition. He was banking on the reception to remedy his financial woes.

Before Father Price and Jimmy headed into the tunnel and off the field, the President stopped in front of the student section. He wrapped his right arm around Jimmy's shoulders and thrust his left arm into the air, pumping it up and down. The 10,000 plus mob of undergraduates and graduates responded with fervor.

"FA-THER PRI-ICE . . . CLAP-CLAP . . . CLAP-CLAP-CLAP!"

The students chanted and clapped over and over again.

Jimmy followed Father Price's lead. He wrapped

his left arm around the priest and waved to the crowd with his right arm.

"JIMMY KING!" shouted Father Price several times, as he pointed to Jimmy.

The students picked up on Father Price's motioning.

"JIM-MY KI-ING . . . CLAP-CLAP . . . CLAP-CLAP-CLAP!"

The pair's outward embrace and the students' response attracted even more cameras. Jimmy loved the attention. The smile stretched on his face. He did not stop waving to the crowd.

"Not a bad life, huh?" said Father Price.

"Not at all," responded Jimmy.

The pair reveled in the adoration from the students for a few more seconds and then walked off the field. As they made their way up to the press box, Father Price asked Jimmy about his plans once in office.

"Father, I think it's a bit too early to start thinking about that. I just want to focus on Tuesday. There is a lot of work to get done between now and then," said Jimmy diplomatically.

Despite all of the attention of the past fifteen minutes, Jimmy didn't want to appear too confident about the election. That's why he gave a non-answer. As he spoke, however, he couldn't stop thinking about winning and standing in front of that student section just one more time.

"You are smart not to get ahead of yourself. But you need to hit the ground running. You have to be ready to govern. Have you given any thought to committee assignments?"

Of course Jimmy had, but he tried to stay on message.

"I have, but I know that it's tough for a freshman to get the committees of his choice."

"You don't worry about that. You won't be the

47

average freshman Congressman," responded Father Price, playing up to Jimmy's ego. "You'll get your choices. Have you given any thought to the Foreign Affairs Committee? With your expertise, you'd be a great fit. Plus, you'd be a natural for Secretary of State one day."

Jimmy turned red and smiled at Father Price's suggestion. Ever since his time at Cambridge, studying Churchill's war-time writings, Jimmy had envisioned himself as a grand statesman. He believed he would make a great Secretary of State one day. He lapped up the compliments with glee, oblivious to the fact that Father Price was intentionally stroking his ego.

When the pair arrived at the press box's reception room, the entire room turned from watching the field toward Father Price and Jimmy walking in. As a thank you to its major financial supporters, the university hosted a private reception in the press box before every game. The guest list traditionally featured the wealthiest and most generous of donors. These were the families that had their names on buildings – the Ecks, the Comptons, the DeBartolos.

Despite the prominence of the guests, Father Price remained the star attraction. The crowd burst out into a spontaneous round of applause for the President. Jimmy stood next to the priest, smiling broadly and basking in Father Price's glory.

"C'mon Jimmy, let me introduce you to some folks that could make a difference in your campaign."

"Sounds great," said Jimmy, sticking by him.

Father Price, approached a middle-aged couple with outstretched arms. The pair wore matching blue Ralph Lauren blazers, with gold Notre Dame buttons specially designed for their garments. The man held a glass of scotch in his left hand and his wife cupped an apricot sour. A Notre Dame scarf covered her shoulders.

"Joe and Julia – so lovely to see you both. How are you?"

"Hi, Father. We're great. Kids are wonderful, perfect as always. Business is going great. Really no complaints. Just excited to be here for the big game."

"I'm so glad that you are both well and that you were able to join us today. You both mean so much to the university."

"Well, thank you for including us. You know how much we love Notre Dame and love Irish football. We wouldn't have missed this for the world."

"Now Joe and Julia, I'd like to introduce you to a good friend of mine. This is Jimmy King. Jimmy is the Republican candidate in our local congressional race. This guy has a great future ahead of him. Cabinet position one day, maybe even the White House itself."

Jimmy tried hard not to blush at this gushing description.

"Jimmy – the Lisas have been long-time supporters of the Republican Party. Joe and Julia funded several Super PACs that made the difference in a number of congressional seats during the last election cycle. I thought you like-minded folks would enjoy meeting each other. Now, if you'll excuse me, I have to say a few more hellos," said Father Price, shaking the husband's hand and then moving on to the rest of the crowd.

"Thanks, Father," said Jimmy, as he turned to the husband and wife duo. "It is a pleasure to meet you both. Where are you from?"

"We live in New Jersey."

"But you contribute all over the country?"

"Well, there are not too many strong conservative candidates in Jersey, so we are happy to lend our support to other areas of the country."

"You know, your support would go a long way here

49

in South Bend. I could really use any contribution that you would be willing to make."

"Consider it done. Any friend of Father Price is a friend of mine. I'll write a check as soon as I get back to the hotel tonight."

"That would be great. Thank you so much," said Jimmy, astonished at how easily it went. If Father Price's endorsement meant that much, Jimmy figured his campaign coffers would be replenished in no time. Winning on Tuesday seemed to be a more vivid possibility.

"Say, how do you think today's news will affect the race?" said Joseph Lisa.

Jimmy thought the man was referring to the polls that had been released this morning. They had showed Jimmy opening up a four-point lead over O'Riordan. He gave a canned response.

"I feel quite good. It's a reflection of all the hard work that we've put in over these last several months and it's a sign that our message is resonating with the people."

The husband and wife exchanged curious glances.

"Uh . . . no . . . I meant the news about the Congressman's daughter."

"What are you talking about?" asked Jimmy skeptically.

"Didn't you hear? Walking in, someone told us that the local Congressman's daughter had been attacked and that she's in the hospital."

"Are you serious?"

"Yes, that's all that people were talking about when we first arrived."

"Do you know what happened?"

"Apparently, the girl collapsed on campus. She was all bruised and battered and had some serious bleeding. Paramedics took her away in the ambulance."

"How do you know that she was related to Congressman O'Riordan?"

"That's what people were saying. They said that she was related to the local Congressman, and I know O'Riordan. I've spent a lot of money over the years trying to put him out of a job. He's a masquerading socialist who's ruining this great country."

Jimmy tuned out the man as his vitriolic attack began. He tried to process the information in his head.

Why hadn't I heard about this already? What happened? Should I suspend campaigning out of respect for O'Riordan? Will the polls swing toward O'Riordan out of sympathy? What's O'Riordan's next move?

The thoughts raced through his head and Jimmy felt suddenly deflated.

All his excitement from walking arm-in-arm with Father Price disappeared.

If O'Riordan gets a major sympathetic swing, then the election is over. No more standing on the sidelines for big games. No more VIP receptions with super donors. No more Secretary of State talk.

"Excuse me for a second," said Jimmy politely to the Lisas.

He stepped out of the reception room and pulled out his cell phone. If anyone knew what was going on, it would be Jaworski. Jimmy figured that his $80,000 might finally be worth something. He selected Jaworski's cell from his contacts list.

No answer.

Jimmy grew frantic as he tried again.

Where the hell is he and why isn't he taking my call?

"Hi . . . "

"Bob – it's me."

". . . leave a message."

Jimmy wondered why Jaworski had ignored his call

when he had been with him only thirty minutes ago. He hoped he was with O'Riordan, figuring out what had happened. Time was running out though and Jimmy needed more information to make the right response.

"Hi Bob – it's me. You have got to call me as soon as you get this."

Hanging up the phone, Jimmy couldn't stop his hands from shaking. He became more frantic as he thought more about the situation. He feared that his chances of victory on Tuesday were slipping away.

He tried to regain his composure by breathing deeply. He slowly inhaled through his nose and exhaled through his mouth. His mind and heart stopped racing.

But then he remembered.

I saw Mary O'Riordan last night.

"So this is us. The little white one up here on the right."

George pointed at a small Cape Cod-style house.

"Oh . . . uh . . . what a great little house," said Father Finnegan.

George looked at Father Finnegan, but the priest wasn't paying attention. He wasn't even looking at the house. His eyes darted around, scanning the street.

George couldn't figure why Father Finnegan was acting so strangely. The normally gregarious and engaging priest seemed nervous and withdrawn. His eyes shifted around. He insisted on waiting in the car while George went into Macri's to get the sandwiches.

What is up with him? What is he looking for?

George tried to put those thoughts out of his head. He was finally home, and even though Father Finnegan was with him, he'd still get to watch the game. For one afternoon, he didn't have to think about law school.

When they got to the front door, George pulled out a set of keys and let Father Finnegan into the house. The front door opened to the living room. An L-shaped couch sat against the far wall. A flat screen television hung above the fireplace.

"Father, why don't you make yourself at home and get the game on. I'll go get us some plates. What would you like to drink?"

"Glass of wine would be great if you have one."

"No problem. Red or white?"

"Red would be great."

George headed into the kitchen. He opened a bottom cupboard to a slim selection. The only alcohol George and Lauren had in the house was leftovers from a dinner party with classmates. The choices ranged from a cheap box of Franzia Fruity Red Sangria to a $4 bottle of Boone's Farm Snow Creek Berry.

"Father, I'm sorry about this, but we have a very limited selection. Is Snow Creek Berry okay with you?" he called out sheepishly, expecting the priest to decline.

"Of course, that's fine," said Father Finnegan.

George poured a glass and walked out to the living room.

"Here you are Father."

"Thank you so much."

Father Finnegan took the wine and drank the entire glass in one motion.

"That was good. Can I get another one?"

"Uh . . . sure," said George, mildly shocked.

George went and poured another glass. He gave it to Father Finnegan. The priest downed this one as well.

"Thanks. I needed that," said the ruddy faced priest.

Amazed at what he had just seen, George turned his attention to the television.

"Perfect timing. Looks like the game is about to begin. Do you mind turning it up a bit?" said George.

"Oh, let's keep the sound off. Those commentators never have much to add. Every other word out of their mouth is something bad about the Irish."

George found it odd that Father Finnegan wanted to watch the game in silence. But he wasn't about to get into an argument with a priest. He took a seat next to Father Finnegan on the couch and settled in to watch the game.

"By the way, my son, do you mind closing the blinds? I'm afraid it's too bright on my old eyes. I can't see the television."

George found this request odd as well, but once again, he didn't argue. He closed the blinds and returned to the couch. Before he sat down, Father Finnegan piped up one more time.

"Oh . . . and do you mind making sure the door is locked? A lot of break-ins happen during home games."

George could not understand what was going on with all of these requests. But he dutifully complied. He went over to the front door, made sure that it was locked, and returned to the couch. "

"Um . . . . George?"

Father Finnegan looked wistfully at George, as he raised his empty wine glass. George got the hint. He grabbed the glass, went to the kitchen, and poured the priest more wine.

"Anything else I can get you?" asked George, some-what annoyed because the game had already started.

"Oh . . . no . . . I think that's it," responded Father Finnegan, smiling slightly.

George did not know why Father Finnegan was acting so bizarrely. He had never seen him act like this. He thought it must be related to his drinking. But George didn't think about it for too long. The game was already in progress.

The pair sat quietly on the sofa for several minutes before a commercial for the nightly news came on. The ad ran images of a crowd of people gathered underneath the Law School's archway.

"Hey Father, do you mind turning up the volume," said George.

Father Finnegan fumbled nervously for the remote. He began pushing various buttons. None of them were the volume.

What is he doing?

"Um . . . Father, it's the up-and-down arrows on the right hand side."

By this point, he'd flipped through several stations. "Here, let me do it."

George grabbed the remote from Father Finnegan's hands. The priest reluctantly relinquished control. By the time George got back to the right channel, the commercials had ended and the game was back on.

"That was the scene from earlier today," said George to Father Finnegan. "I couldn't remember how I knew that girl. But then I realized, the first member of Congress that I worked for had an office across the hall from Mike O'Riordan. I must have seen her go in and out of that office dozens of times. She would chat me up in the hallways."

Father Finnegan sat there quietly, staring vacantly at the television.

"I personally don't like Congressman O'Riordan. He comes across like a real dirt bag. He always had girls half his age following him around . . . But man . . . I feel bad for him. That can't be easy for a parent. You know him at all?"

"Uh . . . no," said Father Finnegan, taking several seconds to respond and then downing his third glass of wine.

"Well, I hope Mary is okay. She took quite the beating. I don't know who attacked her. But whoever did gave it to her real bad."

"Say, would you get me another glass of wine," said Father Finnegan, interrupting George.

Father Finnegan's request did not immediately register with George. The images of Mary's face flashed through his head again. He couldn't understand why someone had attacked her so savagely.

"Uh . . . George?" said Father Finnegan, waving his

wine glass at George.

"Oh, yeah, sorry," said George, snapping out of his thoughts. He grabbed the wine glass and headed into the kitchen. He picked up the now half empty bottle of Boone's Farm and began to refill the glass.

"GEORGE!"

As he poured, a shout came from the other room. George slammed down the wine glass and raced out of the kitchen. Bursting into the living room, he looked at Father Finnegan to see what was wrong.

Father Finnegan stared back at him nervously.

"GEORGE!"

George looked over at the front door. His wife, Lauren, hurried into the house.

"George, you won't believe who I just ran into."

"Lauren, would you like to say hello to our guest?"

Lauren stopped in her tracks. She looked across the living room to see the disheveled priest sprawled out on the couch.

"Oh, I'm sorry. Father, I didn't know you were coming over."

As Father Finnegan stood up from the couch, he teetered back-and-forth. It took him a few seconds to steady himself and extend a hand.

"Hi Lauren . . ." said Father Finnegan, starting to slur his speech. "It's good to see you. Sorry for the lack of notice . . . *hiccup* . . . I saw George on campus and he was kind enough to invite me over for the game."

Lauren gave George a sideways glance.

"Lauren, I was just pouring Father Finnegan a drink. You want to come give me a hand. Excuse us for a second, Father."

"Uh . . . sure."

The husband and wife couple retreated to the kitchen. In his race to see the commotion in the living room,

George had placed the wine glass on the counter's edge. It fell off the side, shattering on the floor. George got on one knee to pick up the pieces.

"What's he doing here?" whispered Lauren.

"I ran into him on my way to the parking lot. We started chatting. He offered to buy me lunch. And before I could think about it, we were on our way to Macri's."

"Why's he sprawled out on the couch?"

"He's four drinks deep since we got here. And I think he may have had a few before I ran into him."

"How long is he staying for?"

"I don't know, but forget Father Finnegan. What were you screaming about?"

"Oh, yeah," said Lauren, shifting her attention back to the reason why she came flying into the house. "George, you won't believe it. Guess who I ran into today?"

"I have no idea. Who?"

He asked as he continued to pick up the broken pieces of glass.

"The Fox."

"In South Bend, Indiana?" responded George, skeptically and without bothering to look up.

"George, I'm not joking. She's here. I even spoke with her."

He stopped gathering the glass shards and looked up at Lauren.

"Seriously?"

"Seriously. She was at the reception at the Hesburgh Center. Some Kroc Institute professor introduced us."

George stood up.

"Did she recognize you?"

"Of course she did."

"What did you talk about?"

"Typical B.S. Enough conversation to pass the

time. Not enough to reveal any real details."

"What's her story?"

"She says that she's here getting a master's at the Kroc Institute and working with a professor about some research project in Beirut."

"Research project? You buy that?"

"I think the research project bit is legit. The professor she is working with was there as well. There is no way that guy is running covert ops. He was stuffing cookies into his pocket in full view of everyone."

"What about her? Why do you think she's really here?"

Lauren paused.

"I don't know her exact reason. But I think it has something to do with me."

George inched closer to Lauren and lowered his voice.

"You sure?"

"I don't know, George. But why else would she be here? Why else would a Venezuelan spy come to South Bend, Indiana?"

"C'mon, Lauren, you can't be serious. There's no way she could have applied for a graduate program, knowing that we were going to be at Notre Dame. We didn't even know that we would be here."

"George, I know it sounds crazy, but what other reason is there?"

"Maybe she is legitimately pursuing a master's."

"That's crap for two reasons. First, of all the places she could have studied at, why Notre Dame? And second, a master's in Peace Studies? Really?" asked Lauren, rhetorically. "I've dealt with spooks from all over the world. They are all the same. They are genetically wired to kill. They don't just become conscientious objectors over night."

George stood there quietly as his wife worked herself up.

"George, when we were in Beirut, I tracked her for months. I exposed her cover. I ruined her career. I'm not crazy. This woman tried to kill me once. She'd do it again in a heartbeat."

George saw the honesty in Lauren's eyes. He knew that she had a point.

"So what are you going to do about her?"

Lauren didn't respond. But she didn't need to.

George noticed Lauren furrow her brow and narrow her eyes. He had seen that distinct look once before and he would never forget it. It was right before she killed an African warlord. Based on that look, he knew what she planned to do to the Fox.

"No, Lauren . . . you can't."

Lauren still didn't respond.

"I'm telling you that you can't," pleaded George. "You're no longer with the Agency. You can't just take someone out and expect to get away with it . . . you could go to jail . . . for a very long time."

Despite George's pleas, Lauren remained silent.

"Lauren, I thought you left that life behind."

His words hung in the air for a few seconds.

"I did, George. But then that life found me here. The only way I'll ever be able to move on is if I finish this once and for all."

"Excuse me."

George and Lauren turned to see Father Finnegan standing at the kitchen door.

"Where is your bathroom?"

"I'll show you," said Lauren. "We're done in here."

CHAPTER 9
SATURDAY
2:48 P.M.

"How is she?"

"Why don't we sit down," urged the young, bookish doctor.

"It's my daughter, damn it. Just tell me what's wrong," snapped Michael O'Riordan.

"Well, she has some minor scrapes and bruises over her body," said the doctor, hesitantly.

"Minor scrapes and bruises?" asked O'Riordan in disbelief. "Then why the hell is she here in the hospital?"

The doctor took a deep breath. He was only a few years out of medical school. Nothing that he studied had prepared him for Mary O'Riordan. He exhaled and proceeded delicately.

"Both of your daughter's cheekbones are fractured. She has some internal bleeding. And she has what appears to be a stab wound in her abdomen. She lost a lot of blood from the wound."

"What happened?"

"That is something you'll have to discuss with the police."

"The police? What do the police have to do with all of this?"

"Based on the nature and severity of her injuries, we think that someone attacked her."

O'Riordan closed his eyes for several seconds, trying to wrap his head around what the doctor was saying.

"Is she going to make it?"

"We think so. But she is not in the clear yet. We are continuing to monitor her very closely. We are optimistic that she will make a full recovery, but we will have to proceed carefully.

"Can I see her?"

"She's in Room 103," nodded the doctor, gesturing down the hallway.

The doctor walked in silence with O'Riordan to the door. He thought he might want someone there with him. After a few steps, O'Riordan stopped the doctor.

"Do you mind if I spend some time alone with my daughter?"

"Of course. If you need anything, there is always someone at the nurses' desk at the end of the hallway."

O'Riordan grabbed the door handle. He hesitated before entering the room. He braced himself for the worst.

When he walked into the room he didn't see much at first. The nurses had turned off nearly all the lights to allow Mary to sleep. The only light came from the screens of medical equipment at the side of the bed, the muted images on a television in the corner of the room, and the dim light attached to the headboard of the hospital bed.

O'Riordan crept quietly to Mary's bedside.

Oh my God.

O'Riordan knew it was his daughter in the bed. But he had a hard time recognizing her. Her high cheekbones were swollen and purple. Her thick brown hair was matted with dirt and blood. Her fair Irish skin was covered in scratches and dried blood. Tubes and wires ran in all directions. O'Riordan's greatest nightmare was lying in front of him.

He was overcome by guilt. He had no idea what had happened, but somehow he felt responsible. He thought that he had failed in his duty as a father to keep Mary safe. He wished he had been there for her.

If she had been a younger kid, O'Riordan might have been there for her. The two had been inseparable for the first ten years of her life, especially come campaign season. O'Riordan brought Mary campaigning every chance that he got. And Mary proved to be a big hit.

Mary won over senior voters in retirement homes with her rendition of the Star Spangled Banner. At fundraisers, she pleaded with guests to, "Please help my Daddy." During parades, she shook the hand of each veteran, thanking them for defending her freedom.

Several local political commentators remarked that Mary O'Riordan, not her father, was the true politician in the family. Other commentators, mostly defeated Republican challengers, went further. They labeled it child exploitation.

The criticism had never fazed O'Riordan. He enjoyed bonding with Mary. And Mary seemed to enjoy bonding with him. O'Riordan had never worried about his daughter until about fifteen years ago.

When Mary's interest in campaigning waned, O'Riordan initially attributed it to a young girl growing up. He figured, like most teenagers, she would rather be caught dead than be seen in public with her parents. When Mary opted to stay home instead of visiting the elderly at Holy Cross Village, he thought nothing of it at first.

As she grew more withdrawn and rebellious, O'Riordan began to worry. Despite being only sixteen, Mary was seen drinking around town. The O'Riordans got a number of calls from Saint Joseph High School about Mary not showing up for class.

O'Riordan confronted Mary several times about skipping school and her drinking. Each time it turned into a full blown shouting match. He would accuse her of throwing her life away. She would scream back, saying that all he cared about was his political reputation.

Things were still tense when Mary moved out of the house for college. O'Riordan pulled some strings to get his daughter accepted at Notre Dame. He hoped the experience of living on her own, albeit under the supervision of a dorm rector, might help her mature. The experiment proved to be a complete disaster when Mary got kicked out after two months.

O'Riordan took out his frustrations on his wife. He blamed her for failing to control Mary. And he accused her of not doing enough to support his political career.

Frustrated by both his wife and daughter, O'Riordan turned toward the comfort of his graduate student mistresses. The first affair sprang from a sense of excitement and ego. The others were an escape from the deep pain he felt inside.

The students were interchangeable – young, naïve and optimistic. None of them expected a long-term commitment or that his devoutly Catholic wife would ever ask for a divorce.

Looking on at his daughter and reflecting on the years of family problems, he was consumed by guilt. The first affair had happened fifteen years ago. As time dragged on, he had spent more time pursuing affairs than with his family. When he wasn't in D.C. for votes or campaigning across the district, he was with a graduate student. He had failed to be there for Mary.

O'Riordan dropped his head. A single tear trickled down his right cheek.

When he looked up to take a deep breath, he noticed the television flickering in the corner.

It played images of an ad that he had seen several times before. It started with Jimmy King speaking earnestly into the camera. Then it cut to a shuttered Studebaker plant with a voiceover from Jimmy about his economic plan. It closed with a clip of King running along the Saint Joseph River, with a trail of school children following him. The image was a subtle dig at the incumbent and older

O'Riordan.

Standing at Mary's bedside, O'Riordan grew angry. He was angry about what had happened to his daughter. He was angry that someone had targeted her. And above all else, he was furious that he had not kept Mary safe.

Jimmy's ad stoked O'Riordan's rage. He stared at the television screen in the darkness, as Jimmy's pimply face smiled back at him. O'Riordan fumed about his campaign.

He could not believe that the election was even this close. He was not about to lose to a kid half his age. But as he stood there and thought more about the situation, he realized that Mary's attack gave him what he needed to finish this race.

O'Riordan stormed out of Mary's hospital room. He marched his way down to the waiting area. He found Bob Jaworski pacing with a cell phone to his ear.

"I'll call you back," said Jaworski, pulling the phone away from his ear. "How is she?"

"We need to find this person," said O'Riordan.

Jaworski had expected O'Riordan to be upset and looking for revenge.

"I'm working on it."

"We need to find this person . . . this is going to put us over the top."

Jaworski gave O'Riordan a puzzled look.

"This little freakin' kid has hung around for too long."

Jaworski did not know what O'Riordan was talking about, but he kept listening.

"There is no reason why the race should be this close. This kid hasn't even lived in the state for the last seven years. All of a sudden he shows up out of nowhere and expects to take my seat from me?"

O'Riordan's voice rose as he spoke about Jimmy

and the campaign. He leaned into the union boss and started poking his finger into Jaworski's chest.

"I'm the one who has lived here for the last forty years. I'm the one who raised his family here. And I'm the one who has risked his family for this job."

Jaworski stood in silence, taking the finger-jabs. He had encountered an enraged O'Riordan before. But he was taken aback by O'Riordan's comments about risking his family for the job. Jaworski couldn't believe how O'Riordan could focus on his campaign at this moment. He thought any father would only be concerned about the safety and well-being of his child.

"I want you to find out who was responsible for this attack," insisted O'Riordan.

"And then what?"

"We need to hold on to him until after the election."

"Why's that?" asked Jaworski, curiously.

"The longer we draw this thing out, the better it is for us."

O'Riordan's comments sickened Jaworski. He had been around a number of despicable politicians in his time. In fact, he thought most were low-lifes. But this was the lowest he had ever seen a politician stoop to save his career.

"We need to remind the voters about Mary every opportunity we get," continued O'Riordan, unprovoked. "This reinforces our narrative. My life, my career, and my family here in the district and the Harvard kid who was living in Europe only a few years ago. By Tuesday we need to make sure voters would never feel comfortable risking their families with someone who is unmarried and has no kids. Heck, someone who doesn't even look ready for high school graduation."

Despite his disgust with O'Riordan's moral compass, Jaworski knew that he had to play it cool. He couldn't reveal what he knew about the attack. Jaworski couldn't risk any suspicion right now.

"What if the cops get to this guy before us?" said Jaworski.

"You need to make sure that doesn't happen."

"And what do you want us to do when we find him?"

O'Riordan inched closer to Jaworski and lowered his voice.

"Hold him until I tell you to let him go."

That is exactly what Jaworski had already planned to do.

Now he just had to find the man that he was looking for.

"TOUCHDOWN NOTRE DAME!"

Gabriella Silva was oblivious to the roars echoing out of the stadium as she walked quickly from the Kroc Institute back to her campus apartment.

How did she find me?

Only a few moments ago, she had been playfully bantering with Lauren DeMarco. After the initial shock of seeing her face, Gabriella's training had kicked in. She acted as if the two had never met, let alone tried to kill each other.

But despite her dispassionate exterior, Gabriella was utterly bewildered.

How did she know I was here?

Gabriella had been painstakingly careful to conceal her identity after the Beirut incident forced her underground. She returned to Caracas and moved in with her widowed and disabled mother. The two rarely set foot outside the apartment. Beyond sharing mundane household chores, they hardly ever spoke.

Gabriella's intel bosses at Servicio Bolivariano de Inteligencia Nacional (SEBIN) kept a twenty-four hour watch on her. Banishing Gabriella to the four walls of her mother's tiny apartment was punishment for what went wrong in Beirut.

SEBIN had sent Gabriella to Beirut to funnel weapons and cash from Iran to Hezbollah. Venezuela, flush with profits from the spike in world oil prices, was eager to support its allies in the "war on imperialism." Gabriella assumed the role of an idealistic humanitarian, eager to save the world. She established a fake NGO, La Esperanza, under the guise of distributing medical supplies to areas in Southern Lebanon devastated in the 2006 Israel-Hezbollah War. The pipeline to Hezbollah worked flawlessly until Lauren DeMarco showed up and intercepted a medical supply bag carrying rocket propelled grenades.

News of the Venezuelan scandal provoked the usual international rebuke – a nonbinding resolution of disapproval from the United Nations Security Council. A harsher response came down from within the Venezuelan government. Party bureaucrats figured someone had to be punished. And all signs pointed to Gabriella.

The recall to Caracas was also a proactive measure. As with any intelligence agency, concerns about double and triple agents were rife. Rumors circulated within SEBIN about Gabriella's mistakes in Beirut. The whispering campaign was fierce. Some said Gabriella's affection for the West had blinded her from seeing how sloppy she had become. Others went so far as to claim that she was about to defect.

Recalling Gabriella meant that headquarters could keep a closer eye on her. With an informant on every city block, headquarters would be aware of every move she made and every person she met. The hierarchy could separate the truth from the rumors.

In reality, Gabriella had never once thought about defecting, especially not to the West. She would never dishonor her father's memory that way. She revered him for giving his life in the fight against the imperialist American invasion of Grenada.

She was only a young girl when her father shipped out. But she was old enough to know why he never came home. Gabriella's only motivation in life had been to kill the Americans that had killed him.

Stuck in Caracas, Gabriella was frustrated. She

wanted to be out in the field. She wanted to honor her father's memory rather than fold laundry with her mother. She begged headquarters to give her another assignment.

After a while, she was finally given that opportunity. One of her handlers unexpectedly arrived at her mother's apartment one night. Sitting at the Silva's small kitchen table, smoking a cigarette, he explained how the higher-ups had decided to give Gabriella a second chance. More importantly, headquarters wanted to send her to fight the imperialists on their own turf.

Through Venezuelan students studying at American universities, SEBIN operatives learned about an American Congressman with a passion for Latin American history and culture. The Congressman also had a passion for young Latin American graduate students. And, even better, the Congressman liked to share top secret intelligence during intimate moments.

Gabriella was pegged as a perfect fit for the Congressman's next girlfriend. She was young, smart, and knew enough about world affairs to pull-off the graduate student routine. She had the looks and confidence to make a man, especially one twice her age, fall in love with her. All that SEBIN expected from Gabriella was to keep the Congressman talking.

Headquarters also saw the operation as the perfect opportunity to test Gabriella's loyalty. SEBIN brass wanted to clear the rumors about her alleged affection for the West, once and for all. Without a shred of emotion, her handler laid down the guidelines.

If anyone discovered her true identity, Gabriella would be dead. If the Congressman had no interest in her, Gabriella would be dead. If the Congressman stopped providing her with information, Gabriella would be dead.

Gabriella nodded coldly and agreed to the operation. She saw it as the only opportunity to redeem her name and her father's honor. She knew she hated the West, and she had enough confidence in her abilities to pull off the operation seamlessly.

The only thing Gabriella had never considered is what would happen if the Congressman no longer had access to top secret information. Her briefing mentioned that O'Riordan had been in office for nearly thirty years. She assumed that American politicians served as long as they wanted, just like politicians in Venezuela.

With the polls showing Jimmy in the lead, O'Riordan's possible defeat was all that she could think about. Although Michael, as she called him, had reassured her that he would win on Tuesday, she knew she couldn't leave anything to chance. She devised several different strategies to guarantee O'Riordan's victory. She was not above simply killing Jimmy and making it look like an accident. But after Beirut, that seemed too risky.

That's why she didn't flinch when committing the $500,000. She knew the money would be well spent. SEBIN had no other agents with the access that she enjoyed with O'Riordan. If she explained the situation to headquarters, she was sure they'd approve the cash.

Gabriella had been on her way to call headquarters when she was sidetracked by Professor Derring. Her conversation with the American brought back a torrent of anger and resentment. Anger about being forced into house arrest in Caracas. Anger about not killing Lauren when she had the chance.

At first, Gabriella's reaction had been to finish the American on the spot. Just the sight of her across the room had filled her with rage. She snapped out of it quickly enough to realize the reception wasn't the place to take her out. If they had met in the women's restroom, it might have been a different story.

Faced with limited options, Gabriella figured her

best option was to pry as much information from her has possible. Gabriella hoped it might shed light on how the American had found her. Of course, the American refused to divulge much.

And Gabriella already knew her cover story from Lebanon. Her contacts in Hezbollah had warned her about a young American woman asking questions around the Dahiya, the Shiite ghetto and Hezbollah stronghold in Beirut's southern suburbs. They said that she claimed to be doing research for her master's at the American University of Beirut.

What Gabriella had never heard was the American's true explanation about why she came to Notre Dame. Was she really married, or was her husband an operative as well, and the marriage a cover? If the marriage was legitimate, then Gabrielle knew the American's husband represented a pressure point. But it seemed too much of a coincidence that he would choose Notre Dame out of all the law schools in the country.

Gabriella spent the entire walk back to the Fischer Graduate School dorms trying to figure out how Lauren had found her. Or, she thought, who might have told Lauren that she was here in South Bend.

Is my relationship with Michael attracting too much attention?

Did someone back at SEBIN tip off the Americans to set me up?

Did a local redneck report me to Homeland Security?

She churned over all the possibilities in her head. She couldn't figure out how, or even if, her cover had been blown. There was ultimately only one way to resolve the situation. But before that happened, Gabriella needed to get Jaworski the much-needed campaign cash.

When Gabriella entered her dorm room, she found

her roommate sitting on the futon with a textbook in her lap.

"So you decided not to go to the game either?" said her roommate, a twenty-two-year-old law student from Hillsdale College in Michigan.

"No. I forgot that I have a call with my Uncle," said Gabriella nonchalantly.

"You talk to your Uncle quite a bit. That's great that you have such a good relationship with him. I, like, don't even know my extended family."

"My family is very good to me," said Gabriella, entering her bedroom and closing the door behind her.

Gabriella had chosen to live in the dorms to be less conspicuous. She didn't want to give people any reason to think she was anything but a graduate student. As part of it, she had been forced to live with this immature blonde from the Midwest. Gabriella was kind enough to keep the girl from getting suspicious. She spoke to her in platitudes, so her roommate felt like she knew Gabriella, without learning a single thing about her background.

Inside her bedroom, Gabriella pulled out the chair from her desk. She placed it in the middle of the room. Standing on top of the chair, she removed one of the ceiling tiles.

Reaching into the ceiling, she brought down a stack of hundred dollar bills. She continued to bring down stacks until $500,000 in cash was spread across her bed. She put half of the money in an over-sized Adidas gym bag with the Notre Dame logo on it, and the other half in a North Face backpack.

She pulled a suitcase out from underneath her bed. She removed the suitcase's bottom to reveal an encrypted, satellite phone. She waited for the phone to power-on and then dialed a number.

"Uncle Luis, it's Gabriella, how are you?"

73

"Gabriella – what a wonderful surprise to hear from you. I was not expecting your call. How is school?"

The pair spoke in Spanish so Gabriella's roommate wouldn't understand. They also spoke in code to avoid any detection by the National Security Agency.

"It's good, except that I had some additional expenses this month, so I was hoping you would increase my allowance."

"I don't think that should be a problem. I know you are studying hard. I understand you have a big test coming up?"

"Uh . . . yes," said Gabriella, with mild hesitation in her voice.

"What's wrong? Are you prepared for the test? Do you think you are going to do well?" Gabriella's handler sensed something was not right.

Gabriella was unsure of whether to mention Lauren. She didn't want to alarm headquarters and have them think that she was in over her head. She also didn't know if someone inside headquarters had set her up.

But above all things, she realized that she needed approval before deviating from her assignment. She didn't want headquarters thinking that she was running rogue operations. Gabriella wanted assurance that she had the authority to handle the situation.

"I have been working very hard. I know I will do well. It's just that," Gabriella hesitated. " . . . I ran into an old friend today. It was a surprise to see her."

"Who is this friend?"

"An American girl I knew from Lebanon."

"Is she the one who had studied at the University?"

"Yes, my American friend from New York City."

Gabriella's handler knew exactly who she was referring to. He had studied Gabriella's file thoroughly. He knew what had happened in Beirut.

74

SEBIN's interest, however, was not in a former CIA agent. The Venezuelans had tapped into a rich well of information courtesy of Michael O'Riordan. The country had never had a source so high-up in the American government. No one in the bureaucracy wanted to see that dry up.

"Well your old friend should know that you are there to study and not to play. Your family has invested a lot of money in your education. We don't want it going to waste."

"Uncle – if you had a friend who was a distraction in your life, what would you do?"

"It would be time to get rid of that friend and make a new one."

That was all Gabriella needed to hear.

She had clearance to kill Lauren DeMarco.

"Lord, we give thanks for the food that we are about to eat . . . *hiccup* . . . We give thanks for the great blessings of friends and fellowship . . . *hiccup* . . . We ask that you shine your light upon us so that we can turn away from the darkness of sin and live in your image here on earth."

Father Finnegan struggled to the end of his pre-dinner blessing at the DeMarco's dining room table. George snuck a glance at Lauren when Father Finnegan mentioned renouncing sin. Sitting across from George, Lauren caught his eyes and shot him back an annoyed look.

Father Finnegan was oblivious. His head hung low over his plate for several seconds after the prayer. He wasn't thinking of them. He was praying for his own salvation.

He had a lot to ask God's forgiveness for. He specifically wanted help with his drinking.

Before dinner, he usually knocked off several beers. He preferred Kilkenny's Irish, but he'd drink whatever was in front of him. At dinner, he'd have several glasses of wine. To ease himself off to sleep, he'd often have a nightcap of Jameson's whiskey.

The ruddy faced priest was a gregarious drunk. The more he drank, the more he laughed and the longer his stories became. Sorin Hall residents knew to avoid Father Finnegan when he was tipsy, unless they felt like being cornered into a 90-minute lecture on the history of Notre Dame.

It hadn't always been this way. Father Finnegan had rarely touched the bottle fifteen years ago. He started drinking as a release from his guilt. Guilt that stemmed from his role in a life-altering confession.

Father Finnegan had heard thousands of confessions during his time as a pastor at South Bend's Little Flower Catholic Church. Most were from elderly Italian and Polish women seeking forgiveness for missing a daily mass or some other trivial indiscretion. Occasionally high school students – as part of mandatory confirmation preparation – would apologize for talking back to their parents. A downtown lawyer might seek absolution for abandoning his family for work. Father Finnegan listened dutifully and assured all that they wouldn't be locked outside the gates of heaven come Judgment Day.

Then, fifteen years ago, an individual stepped into his confessional booth with a much graver matter on his conscience. Father Finnegan sat quietly as the man revealed his story. He listened to every word without showing any emotion. Even when the man explained what he had done with the ten-year-old boy's body, Father Finnegan remained quiet.

Part of it was that he didn't know how to respond. Father Finnegan had never dealt with a mortal sin. So he urged the man to seek God's forgiveness. And he strongly suggested that the man turn himself in.

The man refused. He claimed it was an accident. Fighting back tears, he told Father Finnegan that he had too much at stake.

Father Finnegan accepted the man at his word. But he still urged him to come forward. Not to be punished, but simply to give the boy's family some closure.

The man then proposed a compromise. He would reveal the location of the boy's body to Father Finnegan. The priest could then tell the police where to find the boy without revealing his source.

The man knew that the confidentiality between

them was sacrosanct, protected not only under Church law, but civil law. Father Finnegan had no right to reveal his identity without his consent.

Under his deal, the police could locate the body and the family could at least bury their son. And he and Father Finnegan would ultimately avoid any legal repercussions.

It wasn't the resolution that Father Finnegan wanted, but he knew that he didn't have any other options. His hands were tied. Church law is clear and unbending about protecting the confidentiality of confessions.

So Father Finnegan went along with the compromise. He directed the police to a point on the Saint Joseph River, just west of the duck pond. The River Rescue Unit had to remove large rocks and branches to uncover the ten-year-old's submerged body. Standing on the river's edge with the South Bend police, Father Finnegan watched in horror as the boy's limp body was pulled from the cold water.

While the discovery brought some closure to the family, it didn't end things for Father Finnegan. The public cried out for justice. Even in this Catholic town, people wanted the truth. The press attacked him by name. The district attorney threatened legal action. Through it all, Father Finnegan never cracked. He kept his promise.

But doing so had taken its toll. The decision gnawed at Father Finnegan's conscience. His anguish grew as time went by.

Father Finnegan tried to numb his pain with alcohol. It started with a few beers at the football tailgates. The buzz from the alcohol and the game day excitement blotted out the memory of that child dying cold and alone, at least for a few hours.

When football season ended, he found other opportunities to self-medicate. In the winter, he became a fixture at basketball and hockey games, sneaking in a few pre-game beers at Legends, the campus pub. By spring-time, Father Finnegan's slurred speech and booming laugh could be heard at every home sporting event. It didn't matter if it was women's lacrosse or men's track and field. Father Finnegan would be in the stands, and he would be inebriated.

When the students left campus for summer, Father Finnegan sought refuge in the local bar scene. Since he didn't want people to know the full extent of his problem, he tried to frequent a different bar each night. Frank's Place on Saturday. Between the Buns on Sunday. Mulligan's on Monday. Corby's on Tuesday. CJ's on Wednesday. Madison Oyster Bar on Thursday. And the Linebacker on Friday.

Sitting at the DeMarco's dinner table, Father Finnegan vaguely remembered that he had been at the Linebacker the night before. He had gone there after the Pep Rally. He remembered elbowing his way through the crowd to the bar and ordering a few drinks. After that, things were hazy.

He didn't remember how long he had stayed at the bar, or how he had gotten home. He most certainly did not remember how the young brunette had ended up in his bed.

The first thing he saw when he rolled over in the morning was her bruised and bloodied face. He jumped out of bed and back pedaled out of the room in shock. Reeling in the hallway, he decided to get the hell out of there.

The crowds and sunshine had startled Father Finnegan as he had staggered out of Sorin Hall. He figured it would be quieter down by the lake. That was where George had found him, dazed and lost in his own thoughts.

At first, Father Finnegan didn't hear what George was saying. When he realized that George might provide a bridge away from the situation, Father Finnegan jumped at the opportunity.

From Notre Dame to Macri's to the DeMarco's house, Father Finnegan had kept a look out for anything or anyone that might help him remember the previous night, especially the young girl. He worried that someone might finger him before he had the chance to figure out what had happened.

Nothing triggered his memory until the girl's picture came up on the TV in George's living room. He realized at that moment that he knew her. Terrified that the TV story might implicate him, he pretended to fumble the remote when George asked him to turn up the volume. It worked, but barely.

Father Finnegan didn't know how long he could avoid arrest. He would have turned himself in, but he had counseled enough inmates to know that the cops rarely go easy on suspects claiming no memory of a crime. He needed time to recall what had happened. Imposing himself upon the DeMarcos bought him a little of that.

"Father, I was reading the *Goetz* case this morning," started George, passing him a bowl of mashed potatoes. "I know New Yorkers can be tough, but I was surprised at how violently Goetz reacted."

Father Finnegan grabbed the bowl and heaped a scoop next to the steak on his plate.

"We're going to talk about that case in class this week, Son. I don't want to ruin any of the surprise. How are your other classes going?"

Father Finnegan was in no mood to discuss violent assaults. Just referencing the *Goetz* name made the priest think about the girl's battered face. He felt sick to his stomach.

"My other classes are good . . . but . . . what was the deal with Goetz?"

"I'm sorry, I don't understand what you mean," said Father Finnegan, his face turning red.

"He unloads multiple rounds on these black kids. And then gets off?"

Father Finnegan sat quietly for several seconds before responding.

"Under the law at the time, Goetz had a defense for his actions. But like I said, we'll talk about that in class. I'm sure Lauren doesn't want to discuss boring old legal theories. How are you enjoying South Bend, Lauren?" said Father Finnegan, looking over at her and smiling politely.

George jumped in before Lauren could open her mouth.

"But even under the new law, a person can act that violent when they think someone's gonna kill them?"

Father Finnegan paused and drank what was left in his glass of wine.

"Could I trouble you for a refill?" asked the priest.

Lauren leapt to her feet.

"Of course not, let me get that for you . . . and Father, don't feel obligated to answer any of George's questions. He's just trying to suck up to the teacher before class."

Father Finnegan laughed awkwardly. Then he lowered his gaze. He stared at his plate, twirling his mashed potatoes, until Lauren returned from the kitchen. He did not see Lauren shoot George a stern look. He didn't look up until Lauren returned with a box of Franzia.

"I'm sorry, but this is all the wine that we have left," said Lauren sheepishly.

"Oh, lassy . . . *hiccup* . . . that will be just fine."

His thick, Irish, New York accent was stronger now that he was drunk.

Lauren put the box of wine on the table. With the spout hanging over the edge, she refilled his glass. Lauren and George looked on with astonishment as Father Finnegan picked up the glass and downed it again, placing

81

his empty cup under the spout for a refill.

"So Father," continued George. "Under the new law, a person cannot just attack another person, right? You can only attack someone if you are reasonably certain that they are going to attack you. Is that true?"

"That sounds about right," said Father Finnegan, wiping the sweat off his brow with a napkin.

"Reasonably certain means, like, someone is standing there with a gun about to shoot you. You couldn't just attack someone that you know. Not even if that person had tried to kill you in the past?"

"George, why don't you let Father Finnegan finish his dinner instead of bothering him with these questions," interjected Lauren. "Father, would you like more potatoes?"

Father Finnegan laughed nervously. He didn't notice Lauren giving George another annoyed glance. Or George staring back at her, stone-faced.

"No, Son . . . *hiccup* . . . you must be reasonably certain about an impending death or severe bodily injury . . . Now, I am reasonably certain I need to use the men's room. Excuse me one second."

"Reasonably certain," repeated George for effect, nodding his head and looking at Lauren.

"What the hell was that?"

George detected the anger in Lauren's voice, but he pretended not to notice.

"What?"

"Your little brown-nosing act."

"I just wanted to make sure I understood the holding of the case."

"And you couldn't wait until class on Monday?"

"You never know when someone in this family might need a claim of self-defense."

Before Lauren had a chance to respond, a loud crash came from the bathroom. The couple jumped from their seats and raced from the table.

Father Finnegan lay collapsed on the bathroom tiles.

George kneeled down next to him and shook the unresponsive priest.

"FATHER!"

Father Finnegan's head was slumped over. He snored and drool poured out of the corner of his mouth. He didn't appear to be harmed. He just looked like he had passed out.

"What do you think we should do with him?" said George.

"You think you can get him back to wherever he lives?"

"There's no way I can drag this guy across campus by myself."

"Well, then, just throw him in the guest bedroom and let him sleep it off. We'll deal with him in the morning," said Lauren, with anger still in her voice.

She felt George didn't fully comprehend the full gravity of the situation she was facing with the Fox. She was annoyed about his little act over dinner, and now they were stuck with a drunken priest passed out on their bathroom floor.

George wrapped his arms underneath the priest's armpits and dragged him into the guest bedroom. He rolled him on to a small, single bed in the corner of the room, lifted the priest's legs on to the bed, and removed his shoes. He threw two blankets over the priest.

When George returned to the kitchen, he found Lauren furiously scrubbing a pan.

"Sweetheart, listen, I wasn't trying to be a jackass out there. I just don't want to see anything happen to you."

Lauren continued scrubbing. Her jaw was clenched.

"You know how much I love you. I would kill this woman myself if it meant keeping you safe. And I know that you've been in these situations too many times to count. But this is a different game. You're no longer with the Agency. No one is gonna bail you out at the end of the day."

Lauren dropped the pan into the sink and turned to face George.

"George . . . do you love me?"

"Of course I do! That's why I don't want to see anything happen to you."

"Then you have to trust me on this one. This is my life. This is what I do."

"It *was* your life," stressed George. "You've got a new life now. And I'm part of that life in case you forgot."

"George, trust me. I know what I am doing."

George sensed it was a losing battle. It had been a long day already and he didn't have the energy to argue with Lauren. The day's events had taken a toll on everyone. He figured cooler heads would prevail in the morning. He left the kitchen and returned to the couch and TV in the living room.

With everything that had happened, George never got to relax and watch the game.

He knew Notre Dame pulled off a big win, sneaking by the Trojans 31 to 30. But he wanted to watch the highlights and see all the big plays again.

He flipped through the channels and came to the end of the highlights. Talking heads were on. One was shouting at the host, arguing whether it had been the greatest game of all time. George muted the sound and started to get up off the couch. He was startled to see Lauren standing behind him.

"Lauren, I'm sorry. You know how much I care for you. But let's just talk about this in the morning."

Lauren didn't respond. She stared right past George.

"Lauren? You hear me?"

"What's Father Finnegan doing on TV?" she said.

George turned around to face the television. He turned up the volume.

Father Sean Finnegan remains a person of interest in the violent attack on the daughter of Congressman Mike O'Riordan. The Notre Dame priest serves as a professor of criminal law and chaplain at the law school. This has not been confirmed by the South Bend Police, but our sources tell us that Mary O'Riordan had spent the night in Sorin Hall. This is the same residence hall where Father Finnegan serves as Rector. Father Finnegan was last seen walking around campus this morning.

We will continue to bring you more details as we learn them.

Back to you, Chip.

George muted the television again and turned to

85

Lauren. The tension between the couple dissipated. The pair now had a more pressing problem on their hands.

"You want to call the cops or you want me to do it?" asked Lauren.

"Not just yet," said George hesitantly.

"What do you mean? Why don't you just call the cops?"

"I can't do that."

"Oh yes you can. Here, you can use my cell."

"Lauren put it away. I'm serious."

"Why?"

"I don't know. I just don't think this guy did it."

"You don't think he did it?" said Lauren incredulously. "Aren't you the guy who says that if it walks like a duck and quacks like a duck, then it's probably some crackhead trying to steal your car radio?"

"Yeah, but this is different."

"Why? Because he's a priest? Everyone sins, George."

"I know he's been acting weird all day. And I know that he's a drunk. But I don't think he's the kind of guy to beat up women."

"You don't know that."

"Yeah, but I just don't think he did it."

"So why don't you let the cops sort this one out?"

"You and I both know enough cops to know that all they want is to get someone arrested and go home intact. There is no way Father Finnegan is gonna get a fair shake on this."

"So what . . . *you're* going to get to the bottom of this mess?"

The pair stood in silence for several seconds. George didn't know how to convey his feelings to his wife. He was normally not an emotional guy.

"You know how I told you about my biological

mom going missing in Chile under Pinochet?"

"Yes, what's this got to do with a drunk Irish priest?" said Lauren, rolling her eyes.

"Just listen for a second," snapped George. "I probably would have gone missing too if I had not been adopted. Catholic Charities found my butt, got me off the streets, and into the arms of the DeMarcos.

When they died, my grandfather took me in. My grandfather's best friends were Father McCarthy and Father Finnegan. He used to tell me stories about the three of them all the time. They were thick as thieves. I owe it to my grandfather to at least see if there is some way that I can help Father Finnegan."

Lauren admired George's passion and guts. Her father had embodied the same characteristics. She knew it would be hard to convince George to call the police.

"So what are you going to do?"

"I don't know. But trust me on this one. I'll figure it out."

Lauren did not like his vague response. But she knew that she had to trust George's instincts. They had served him well in the past.

"At least promise me that you won't spend more than a day working on this."

George stared intently at Lauren.

"Okay . . . no more than one day."

SUNDAY

What time is it?

Lauren rolled over and looked at the clock.

She had spent the night tossing and turning. Not a wink of sleep.

The last twenty-four hours had given her a lot to think about. She worried whether she had made the right decision to come to Notre Dame. She didn't regret marrying George for a second. She regretted walking away from the Agency when the Fox and others like her were still out there and intent on harming innocent Americans.

Then there was the issue with the priest. She decided that she couldn't worry about whether he had attacked that girl or not. George would have to deal with him.

Lauren's only priority now was staying alive.

She'd never worried about the consequences of her job before. From recruiting Hezbollah spies to hunting Libyan arms dealers in Beirut, Lauren had put her life at risk countless times before. What had made her an excellent operative was the fact that she didn't fear death.

She had no fear because she had nothing to lose. When her father died in the September 11th attacks, Lauren lost the only family that she had ever known. With no one to visit during the holidays, she could deploy to dangerous locations around the world for months on end.

Everything changed when George walked into her life. The woman who had shrouded herself in a head scarf in the Middle East started wearing make-up and high heels. The face that had stared down fanatical Islamists lightened-up, smiling and laughing with more regularity. Lauren experienced warmth in her heart that she hadn't felt since her father died.

Lying in bed, Lauren worried that the Fox had come to take it all away. In their five minute conversation, the Fox did not specifically say, "I want you dead." But she didn't have to.

Lauren couldn't figure out why the Fox would be here in South Bend, other than to kill her or, even worse, to kill George. Lauren was the one person who had exposed her cover and brought great disgrace on the Venezuelan government. She had expected the Fox to exact revenge. Lauren would have wanted the same thing.

Lauren considered all the ways the Fox might try to kill her.

It could be a single sniper's shot.

But that would mark the sign of a professional and expose the Fox's cover.

It could be a traditional car bomb.

But that would probably be the first car bomb in the entire Midwest and draw way too much attention.

She could strangle me in my sleep and make it look like a break-in gone bad.

Lauren was suddenly startled by a noise downstairs.

She stopped thinking about ways she might die and sat upright in bed. It sounded like a muffled voice.

"George . . . you hear that?" whispered Lauren.

No response from the other side of the bed.

"George . . . wake up. You hear that?" said Lauren again, still whispering but now shaking George.

"No . . . go back to sleep," said George groggily.

Lauren listened closely for any more sound.

She heard the faint noise once again. She was convinced that it came from directly beneath her. To Lauren, it sounded like someone was talking in a muffled voice.

Why would someone be talking in a muffled voice?

Did the Fox bring someone with her for back-up? Who else could be here?

The adrenaline started pumping throughout Lauren's body. Any restlessness disappeared. She was wide awake.

Lauren knew she had to react and do it quickly. The Fox wanted Lauren dead. Lauren had hoped to have more time to get to the Fox first.

She rolled over on-to her stomach and reached underneath the mattress.

She had strapped a Glock 17 to the bottom of the bed as a general security measure. George laughed when he saw Lauren with duct tape, sliding under there. They lived in a neighborhood of Notre Dame professors and families. In a heavily sarcastic tone, George had asked Lauren which one was the most dangerous – the linguistics or the accounting professor.

Lauren felt vindicated as she removed the gun from its holster. She eased herself out of bed and put her ear to the ground to get a sense of where the intruders were moving.

George and Lauren had converted the entire second floor into their main bedroom. It gave them plenty of room and tons of closet space. From her perspective, the only downside was that if someone did break in, they would be pinned upstairs.

The couple didn't have a fire escape, and it was about a twenty-foot jump out the window. She could land that jump. But she did not want to attempt it and have the Fox, or whoever was with the Fox, gun her down in the process.

Listening for movement, she considered her options. She could try to detect where the intruders were moving and then shoot through the floor boards. If she had a heavier weapon, a submachine gun like the Heckler and

Koch MP7, that might work.

With the Glock 17 in her hand, she neither had the strength nor the precision to pull it off. The handgun worked best in close situations. She would have to be face to face with whomever was downstairs.

A door closed off the stairs to the second floor from the dining room. She contemplated waiting behind the door. If one of the intruders opened the door, she could unload and then take her chances on the second one. Not ideal, but a better option.

She listened for more movement.

The muffled voice continued. She didn't hear anything else. No feet creeping through the house.

Where are they?

Lauren had never left anything in her life to fate and she wasn't about to start now. She resolved to take them head on. If she did not finish the Fox now – for good – there would be many more sleepless nights in the future.

She got back on her feet and crept slowly across the room. Dressed in pajama pants and a Notre Dame t-shirt, she slinked down the stairs, avoiding creaky spots in the floorboards.

She grabbed the door to the dining room with her left hand. In her right hand, her gun was drawn at her shoulder. With her pulse racing, she braced herself for a shootout.

She opened the door slowly.

Nothing.

No one in sight.

No attackers with knives or hatchets.

No guns jammed against her head.

The emptiness of the dining room provided only momentarily relief. She could still hear the muffled voice. It was coming from the other side of the house.

She moved quickly to the corner of the dining room.

And with her back against the wall, she listened. But she couldn't understand what the person was saying.

No going back now.

She knew she had to face what lay around the corner at some point.

She listened to the voice and steadied herself.

One.

Two.

Three.

"Don't shoot! Don't shoot!"

A frightened Father Finnegan, knelt next to his bedside, pleading for his life with his hands in the air.

"I didn't do anything. I swear," insisted the priest.

"Where is she?" said Lauren, with the Glock 17 aimed at the priest's forehead.

"I don't know. I don't know who she is. I promise. I swear. I just woke up and she was there in my bed. I don't know who she was or how she got there. I just left."

Lauren kept the gun aimed at the priest. She walked into the bedroom without taking her eyes off of him. Father Finnegan stayed on his knees.

"I'm so sorry. You've got to trust me. I didn't do anything wrong."

Lauren ignored the rambling priest. She scanned the room. Her eyes focused on the closet. She threw the door open with her left hand, again ready for a shootout.

Nothing.

Where is she?

She pulled back from the closet and checked on the opposite side of the bed.

Nothing.

She crouched down to look underneath the bed.

Nothing.

Still aiming the gun at Father Finnegan, she walked right up to the priest so the barrel was inches from his head.

"I don't remember anything. But I didn't hurt that poor young girl. God knows the truth."

"Who were you talking to?"

"I wasn't talking to anyone."

"I heard voices. You were talking to someone," insisted Lauren.

"I was praying."

"You woke up at 5:00 a.m. to pray?" said Lauren, not willing to accept that he was here by himself.

"I pray every morning. I've done it every day since entering the priesthood."

"Even after two bottles of wine?"

Father Finnegan's face turned red.

"I'm not proud of my drinking. But I've never slept through morning prayers. Even on my drunkest nights, I'm still up at five to thank the Lord for getting me through one more day."

"Every morning?"

"Every morning," said Father Finnegan.

"What are you praying for?"

"What all Catholics should being praying for . . . forgiveness for my sins and guidance to be a better person . . . But today . . . I also prayed for the victims of violence."

"That seems to be a prayer close to home."

Lauren watched Father Finnegan drop his head in embarrassment.

"Well, Father, if it helps, George believes you are innocent."

"He does?" said Father Finnegan, as he picked up his head with a hopeful look.

"Yeah . . . well . . . at least he feels like he owes it to his grandfather to help you out."

Father Finnegan broke into a wide smile. His eyes moistened.

Lauren didn't know what to make of the situation.

As she watched Father Finnegan getting drunk last night, she recognized a man with some deep problems. Whether he'd be driven to attack a young woman was another story. That would be for George to find out.

"Um . . . my dear, do you think you could point that somewhere else?" said Father Finnegan.

"Oh, sorry," said Lauren as she cautiously lowered the gun and stepped backward.

Father Finnegan brought his arms down. He put one hand on the bed to help himself up. As he steadied himself, he turned towards Lauren with an inquisitive look.

"What girl were you referring to?"

"Huh?"

"When you first came into the room, you asked 'where is she.' I assumed you were referring to a specific girl?"

"It's . . . uh . . . just someone that I have unresolved business with."

"And you needed a gun to finish that business?"

"I may need more than a gun, Father."

What am I looking for?

George stared back at his reflection in the rearview mirror. He was driving from his house to campus. He wondered what, if anything, he was going to find in Father Finnegan's dorm room.

After talking with the priest over breakfast, George figured they needed evidence to clear his name. If Father Finnegan didn't remember coming home with the girl, the two needed to prove it. He hoped that something in the dorm room might allow them to start building a case.

George still believed that Father Finnegan was innocent. He had probed him with questions all morning. George tried to catch the priest off guard. For the most part, Father Finnegan held up.

The only time Father Finnegan had acted strangely was when George asked him about Mary O'Riordan. Father Finnegan claimed to have not known the girl at first. But when George told him that she was the daughter of Congressman Michael O'Riordan, he saw his face grow pensive in recognition.

Father Finnegan had reacted to O'Riordan's name for a reason. George needed to find out why. Sorin Hall would be the starting point.

As George approached the dormitory, he spotted a cluster of journalists and television cameras behind a rope about fifty feet from the doors. Walking up the stairs to the main entrance, George put his head down and tried to walk casually past a Notre Dame police officer.

"Can I see your ID please?"

The officer moved in front of George, blocking the entrance.

"Oh . . . uh . . . yeah, sure. No problem."

George reached into his wallet, pulled out his Notre Dame student ID card, and handed it to the cop. The officer looked at the card and then at a piece of paper on a clipboard.

"Sorry, the dorm is closed to residents only. Your name is not on the list, so I can't let you in."

"I was just going to meet a friend of mine who lives in the dorm."

"You'll have to give him a call and tell him to meet you out here."

"But I don't have a phone on me, and my friend's waiting for me. Can't I just run inside real quick?"

"Sorry, but we are under strict orders only to let in residents. If your name is not on the list, then I can't let you in."

George took a step back to size up the police officer. The cop didn't budge. He stared back at George, clutching the clipboard with a sense of authority.

Alright, time for Plan B.

George could detect the journalists were watching, so he backed down. Retreating down the stairs, he figured that there had to be another way in. He decided to try the back entrance.

Rounding the corner, George saw his third-year mentor, Hank Cavanaugh, sticking a key into the backdoor of Sorin Hall.

"What's up, Hank?"

"Hey George. What are you doing here?"

"I was on my way to the library."

"This early? Damn, George. You've been working your butt off."

"Just trying to stay above water. What are you doin'

100

here? You live here?"

"Yeah, I'm one of the assistant rectors for the dorm."

"That sounds like a good gig. Don't they give you a pretty sweet room?"

"As far as dorm rooms go, it's not bad. Pretty much like a two bedroom apartment that has a small kitchen."

"What's the rest of the dorm like?"

"It's your standard dorm, except we have a chapel and we got a boxing practice room."

"A boxing room, really?"

"Yeah, it's a dusty old room with a couple of heavy bags, some speed bags, and some jump ropes."

"You know I was a Golden Gloves junior champ growing up in New York?"

"Seriously?"

"Yeah, I had some, uh, anger management issues so my grandfather sent me to the gym."

"You? George, you're like the most mild mannered person I've ever met."

George laughed.

"Back in the day, I was an angry little kid. I used to get into a lot of neighborhood fights."

"Haha . . . you?"

"Yeah," said George sheepishly. "So one day my grandfather says that you need to get your anger under control and that his buddy Mike is going to take me to the gym. The guys at the gym will work on you. So I get ready in a t-shirt and sweatpants and guess who shows up to take me to the gym?

"Who?"

" Mike Tyson."

"What? No way! That's awesome."

"Yeah, my grandfather used to race pigeons with Tyson back in Brooklyn. Tyson loved my grandfather so he took me under his wing. I trained with Tyson's crew for years."

"Wow. What a great story."

"Haha . . . thanks . . . that was years ago. I haven't boxed in a long time," said George. "It would be great to get into it again. You mind if I check out the room?"

"Um . . . well . . . it's not exactly the greatest time for the dorm. Did you hear what happened?"

"No, what?" said George with fake sincerity.

"You didn't hear what happened to Father Finnegan?"

"No, what happened?" said George trying to act surprised.

"Father Finnegan is the rector of our dorm. He's apparently suspected of attacking some woman that he brought back to his room. The dorm's been on lockdown. The guys are a bit shaken up. Me and the other assistant rectors have to meet with one of the university's psychologists to talk about how to handle the kids in the dorm."

"Oh man. I'm sorry to hear that."

"Yeah, it's pretty messed up. We're just all stunned right now."

"Hey listen, I don't want to disturb you guys. I'll just be in and out. You don't even have to stay with me if you have to go to your meeting," said George, fishing for an opening.

"Um . . . well . . . come on. We gotta be quick though."

Hank opened the back door to Sorin Hall and ushered George in. This entrance led into a stairwell on the basement floor. Hank walked down the basement hallway, past a vending machine, and George followed. Hank stopped at an old wooden door.

There was nothing on the door except for a painting of Sorin's mascot – an Otter – wearing boxing gloves.

Hank opened it to a dusty old room.

"Wow. This is great," said George as he scanned the room.

To George, it was the perfect training environment. The equipment was a bit worn down, making it tougher to handle. The temperature was hovering at around 80 degrees, hot enough to make you sweat. It reminded him of Gleason's Gym in New York where he learned the basics with Tyson and Tyson's crew.

"You do much boxing?" said George, as he stepped up to the speed bag and starting working the bag.

"I haven't. But I was thinking about doing Bengal Bouts this year."

"What's that?"

"No one's told you about Bengal Bouts? It's great. It's an on-campus boxing tournament for all the undergrads and grad students. You should sign up. They start training next month."

"Really? That sounds like a lot of fun."

George continued working on the speed bag to buy time. The only way he could get to Father Finnegan's room is if he ditched Hank. He needed to stall until Hank had to go to his meeting.

"Hey George, sorry to do this to you," said Hank, looking at his watch. "But I really gotta go."

"Oh yeah, no problem."

"I'll show you how to get out."

"Oh hey, did you say you had a chapel here?"

"Yeah, it's upstairs on the first floor."

Father Finnegan had said his room was on the same floor.

"Do you mind if I stop in? I didn't get to Mass this morning. I just want to say a few prayers. When you're in law school, every little bit helps, right?"

"Um . . ." Hank hesitated. He looked at his watch

103

again. "Well . . . uh . . . I guess so. I'll show you it real quick."

The pair headed back to the stairwell where they entered the dorm. George followed Hank up to the first floor. Coming out of the stairwell, the Saint Thomas Aquinas Chapel was on George's left.

"This is it. But do you mind making it quick? I've got to get to this meeting."

"Hey listen, you don't have to worry about me. I can show myself out. I just go down the stairs and out the back, right?"

"Um . . . well, I should really stay with you."

"Hey don't worry about it. I'll be in and out no problem. I don't want you to have to worry about waiting for me."

Hank checked his watch again.

"You sure you know how to get out of here?"

"Yeah, down the stairs and out the back. I'll be gone in a few seconds."

George stared at Hank's contemplative face. He waited patiently as Hank thought it over. Several seconds passed before Hank replied.

"Okay, just make sure you go out the back and close the door behind you."

George slipped into the chapel and sat in the first pew. Now that he was inside, he had to get to Father Finnegan's room without anyone noticing him. He prayed silently.

Dear Lord, please watch over me and guide me. Fill me with the courage to do your work.

Father Finnegan had told him that his room was the first room on the right as you entered the building's main entrance. It was the only dorm room with no posters on the door. The only identifying feature was a Crucifix attached to the top of the door frame. Based on that description, the room should be just around the corner.

George sat in the pew quietly, listening for any-one outside. Despite the media commotion in front of the building, the dorm was relatively quiet. It seemed safe to make a move.

George slipped out of the pew and crept down the hallway.

Silence.

He came to the corner. His heart rate picked up. He began to think about what he would do if he ran into some-one.

Ask for directions? Ignore them? Run the other way?

He turned the corner.

No one in sight.

His heart dropped back to a normal pace.

He saw Father Finnegan's room, with the small crucifix hanging on a tilt above the door.

George walked up and grabbed the handle. As he opened the door, he kept his eyes fixed on the hallway to make sure no one was coming. With his head turned, he didn't notice the man inside the room until it was too late.

As the door opened and George snuck into the room, he tripped over the foot of a stocky, mustachioed man. George stumbled to the floor.

"Sorry . . . I . . . uh . . . didn't see you there," said George looking up from the floor.

The man in the South Bend Teamsters jacket stared back at George.

"Um . . . is this Hank Cavanaugh's room?" asked George, thinking quickly.

"No. Who are you?"

"Sorry, I'm just a friend of his," said George as he picked himself up.

George took his time trying to get back on his feet.

He used it as cover to look around the room. He scanned it for any clues that might help Father Finnegan.

Nothing in the room was out of order. It was thoroughly clean. There were no signs that a struggle had taken place at all.

"You've got the wrong room."

"What floor is this?"

"First floor."

"Sorry . . . I was looking for the second floor," said George as he backtracked out the door.

The man kept staring at him.

George turned down the hallway and picked up his pace. He glanced over his shoulder to see the man now outside of the room, still staring at him. As he turned the corner, he heard the man on his cell phone.

"Hey, it's Jaworski . . . I need you to follow someone . . . It's for O'Riordan."

"As we head to the ballot booths on Tuesday, let us keep in our prayers our elected officials. Let us pray that the Lord will guide them with wisdom, prudence, and counsel. That they will govern with justice and mercy. That they recognize the awesome responsibility of serving in public office and that they never forget the Lord's compassion."

Jimmy King sat in the last row of Little Flower Catholic Church. He was filled with pride at the possibility that these people would be praying for him in just a few days. He thought about the prestige he would enjoy as a Congressman and the thousands of students that had chanted his name yesterday. He couldn't remember another time in his life when he had felt so fulfilled.

In the back of his mind, he had another thought.

No one prays for the losers.

He had heard several versions of this sermon already this morning. Not one priest had mentioned the candidates that would lose. Not one homily had discussed the names that would fade from memory. No one ever talked about what happened after the bumper stickers had been peeled off and the yard signs taken down.

Jimmy's concern about becoming a footnote in some other politician's career is what had driven him to church this morning. After hearing the news about O'Riordan's daughter, Jimmy knew that he couldn't host a campaign event. It would look too crass to be out campaigning while his opponent grieved.

At the same time, Jimmy was neck-and-neck with

O'Riordan and there were only a few days left. He knew that the news would be focused on O'Riordan. Even though it wasn't good news, O'Riordan would still be in the headlines.

Jimmy had to find a way to keep his name and face in the public eye.

He had called a meeting with his campaign team straight after the football game. His campaign manager and only paid staffer was a twenty-one-year-old Notre Dame political science senior named Ryan Humphrey. Ryan had volunteered on a couple of Saint Joseph County Council races before. But he had never worked in an official role on any campaign, let alone a federal congressional election run on millions of dollars. Ryan brought some volunteers to the meeting from Notre Dame's Republican Club – his girlfriend, a junior, and two freshman guys. "Miss Betty," a seventy-nine-year-old former neighbor of King, and a devoted member of the Saint Joseph County Right to Life Committee, rounded out the team.

No seasoned political operative would have called this a team. The Republican National Committee, the National Republican Congressional Committee, and the Indiana Republican Committee had all tried to send Jimmy reinforcements. He had refused their offers. He did so partially out of pride and partially because of Jaworski's advice.

Jaworski got it into Jimmy's head to keep the establishment at a distance. Jimmy didn't know if he had done this to help him or hurt him. But at this late stage, he figured he didn't need back up, given he had made it so far on his own.

I went to Harvard and Cambridge, for Pete's sake. I can figure this out.

The meeting was held at his campaign headquarters, a small former bakery on Main Street downtown. The site had been vacant for 17 months before Jimmy found the cash to start renting it six weeks ago. Gathered around an old wooden table, Jimmy spoke authoritatively to his team.

"We've got to get our name out there. We've got to connect with more voters. But we can't be seen as politicking. We can't make people think that we're out campaigning."

Jimmy paced the room. He weighed the pros and cons of various courses of action. He did this as a way of thinking out loud. He wasn't trying to solicit input from this rag tag group, until Miss Betty piped up.

"You ought to go to church and pray about it."

Jimmy stopped pacing. He looked right at Miss Betty.

"That is a great idea."

The Notre Dame kids were puzzled.

"We've got to get to church," said Jimmy. "Thousands of people go to church around the area on Sunday morning. We've got to be there as well."

"But how are you supposed to get to all of these churches?" asked Humphrey.

"I'm not. But we are going to get to as many as we can."

That is why Jimmy King had slipped into the last empty pew for Little Flower's 9:30 mass. Before that, he'd been at Queen of Peace at 7:30 a.m. and Christ the King at 8:45 a.m. He had two more masses on his list: Our Lady of Hungary's 11:00 a.m. service and St. Adalbert's at 1:00 p.m.

He had the same routine for each mass. He sat in the final pew or he stood in the back. He made sure that he was the last person in the entire church to receive Holy Communion. He wanted all the eyes in church to be on him. People had to know that he had been there.

The same was true at the end of mass. Jimmy refused to leave until everyone else had left. He made sure to make eye contact with as many people as possible. Some people recognized him. When they did, it thrilled Jimmy. He smiled back and counted himself one more vote closer to victory.

For those who didn't recognize him, Jimmy did his best to hide his disappointment. He tried to remind himself that there were still a number of people in the district that couldn't identify his face. That was the whole point of getting out to these masses and being the last person to leave.

"You're all set, Boss," said Ryan Humphrey.

Jimmy stood up from the pew and tightened his tie.

"How does my tie look?"

"Um, good."

"What about my hair?"

"Looks good Boss."

Jimmy wore an ill-fitting JoS. A. Banks suit, straight off of the rack, with a blue and gold Notre Dame tie that his father had received as a gift. The gap between his shoes and his pant legs revealed navy blue socks. He sported a fresh buzz cut, courtesy of the barbers at Rocco's. He looked more like a ninth grader at confirmation than a man on the verge of joining the United States Congress.

Jimmy stood up from the pew and put on a navy blue overcoat. The temperatures had dropped overnight, making the air much colder than yesterday's sun-filled morning. Jimmy buttoned up as Ryan Humphrey walked ahead to open the church's doors.

Jimmy exited the church and approached Little Flower's pastor, Father Stephen Flake, with an extended hand.

"Father, that was a great sermon this morning. I really enjoyed it."

"Well, thank you. That is very kind of you to say so. I don't often get compliments about my words from the pulpit."

As the two men spoke, Ryan Humphrey ushered over a press pool of two cameramen, one stills photographer, and two young reporters scribbling into their notepads.

"I'm sorry, but you don't look familiar. You're not one of our regular parishioners, are you?"

"Uh, no, Father. I'm actually a parishioner at Saint Joseph, so I usually go to mass over there. But this morning I thought that I would branch out."

"Well, it is great to have you with us. I do hope that you will join us more regularly."

Jimmy could hear the clicks of the stills photographer in the background, so he kept awkwardly smiling and shaking the priest's hand.

"You'll have to excuse our friends from the press. They've been here all morning. We've told them that they could be here as long as they kept a distance from the parishioners," said Father Flake.

"It's no problem. Actually, Father, I think they are here for me. I'm Jimmy King. I'm running in the election for the 2nd Congressional District."

"Oh yes, it's nice to meet you. I've read a little bit about you. I'm sorry that I didn't recognize your face."

"That's quite alright," said Jimmy as he gritted his teeth in annoyance.

As Jimmy made small talk with Father Flake, a thick, muscular man in a dark suit and a tall uniformed South Bend police officer approached the two.

"Excuse me, gentlemen," spoke the man in the suit. "Father, good morning. My name is Mike Walsh. I'm a detective with the South Bend Police Department. This is Officer Doyle."

"Good morning, gentlemen," responded Father Flake. "If this is about Father Finnegan, I already gave a statement to a couple of officers last night. I haven't seen him, and I really don't have anything else to offer."

"Actually, Father, we've come to talk to him," said Detective Walsh, as he pointed at Jimmy King.

The detective's claim took Jimmy by surprise.

What could they possibly want with me?

"Would you prefer if we went somewhere private to talk?" asked Detective Walsh.

Jimmy tried to play it cool.

"There's nothing that I could tell you gentlemen that I wouldn't say in front of Father Flake. How can I help you guys?" said Jimmy feigning enthusiasm.

"We're investigating the attack on Mary O'Riordan. You know that she is the daughter of your opponent, Mike O'Riordan, right?"

"Yes, I had read that in the papers."

"Didn't you two go to high school together?"

"Oh yeah, I guess we did. We went to Saint Joseph's together. Graduated in the same class, but I really didn't know Mary."

"Uh-huh," responded Detective Walsh, as he started to take notes. "Well, we've been trying to retrace all of her steps over the last forty-eight hours. You know, to get a sense of where she had been. Her friends told us that she was at the Linebacker on Friday night. You were also at the Linebacker on Friday night, right?"

"Uh . . . yes, I was. I went to see some old high school friends that were in town for the game," responded Jimmy cautiously. He was not sure where the detective was headed with this line of questioning.

"Some of Mary's friends said that you got into a shouting match with her?"

"Well, I wouldn't exactly call it a shouting match," said Jimmy, as he smiled at Father Flake.

"Her friends said that the two of you got into some

heated argument? That your voices were raised and there was even some swearing?"

Jimmy blushed in front of the priest.

"She was quite drunk. She bumped into me. I explained who I was. She got quite angry at that point. She started swearing at me. Yelling at me about being a politician. Saying all politicians are no good, except she used language that I won't repeat here."

"And you just stood there and took all of her abuse?"

"I may have said a few things to let her know that I didn't agree with her."

"Didn't you swear at her? Call her some vicious names?"

Jimmy's face, bright red at this point, appeared even more embarrassed. He gave Father Flake a look that asked for forgiveness. Trying to avoid the question, he looked over the detective's shoulder. He saw the journalists craning their necks to see what was happening and the cameras fixed on him.

Sweat poured from Jimmy's brow. This wasn't the type of media attention that he had hoped for this morning. He wanted voters to remember him on Tuesday because they saw him at church, not because they saw him being interrogated by the police on television.

"I may have said some things that I am not proud of. But I had nothing to do with what happened to her," Jimmy blurted out.

Detective Walsh, who had been scribbling away on his pad, stopped and looked up at Jimmy at this point.

"What did you do after you left the Linebacker?"

"Well, I stopped by my campaign headquarters and then I headed home to get some rest."

"Is there someone that could verify that you went to your headquarters and then home?"

113

"Um . . . well . . . it was late and all the volunteers had gone home at that point."

"So it was just you by yourself at your headquarters and then by yourself when you went home?" asked Detective Walsh in a skeptical tone.

"Um . . . that's right."

"Are you sure you need me to go? I really have some things that I need to take care of."

Gabriella Silva was fishing for an excuse. Any excuse. She didn't want to join O'Riordan at his press conference at Memorial Hospital.

Gabriella saw nothing wrong with the exploitative nature of the event. If O'Riordan hadn't decided to do it, she would have suggested it to him. It was a savvy political move, despite what people might think of him using his battered daughter as a political prop.

The polls this morning had shown O'Riordan coming back. He was now evenly tied with Jimmy. Gabriella thought that this was a trend in the right direction, but that they needed to do more to guarantee O'Riordan's victory. Exploiting Mary's situation would be the easiest way to finish Jimmy.

If it came to it, Gabriella had other ways to finish him off. Tactics that she had learned at SEBIN. But those options were risky and the consequences high. Plus, she already had to take care of Lauren DeMarco. Killing Jimmy King as well would seriously complicate things.

She was trying to keep her two problems – O'Riordan's election and Lauren DeMarco – separate. She did not want blowback from one bleeding into the other. Yesterday, once she turned over the $500,000 to Jaworski, she thought that she had a clear break to focus on Lauren.

The two had coordinated the drop exactly 17 minutes after the football game ended. Gabriella took her North Face backpack and Adidas gym bag to the port-opotties in the parking lot, south of the Stadium's Frank Leahy Gate. She went in to the first one on the right, dropped the bags, waited a few seconds, and then left. Jaworski was next in line to pick up the bags.

The plan worked seamlessly and Gabriella felt relieved. Surely, she thought, the $500,000 and the public support for Mary would be enough to propel O'Riordan to victory.

With one issue taken care of, Gabriella now had to figure out what to do with the American. She had to dispose of Lauren and do it without attracting any attention.

As she walked back to Fischer dorms, contemplating her next move, her cell phone rang. Having just dropped off the $500,000, she hesitated before answering. She looked around to see if anyone had seen what had just happened.

Even after O'Riordan identified himself on the phone, Gabriella responded cautiously. She expected him to be upset about Mary. It would be a natural reaction of any father who had just visited his brutalized daughter in hospital. Instead, he sounded relieved.

He was relieved about being able to cancel his campaign events. He was relieved that Mary's attack might turn the election in his favor. And he was relieved that he could spend more time with Gabriella.

Gabriella listened and feigned sympathy. She didn't want him coming over tonight. She had more pressing issues to tend to with Lauren. At the same time, she wanted to make sure O'Riordan was serious about exploiting Mary's condition to the hilt.

This was her opportunity to make sure that he wouldn't waiver. Gabriella told him to meet her at her dorm room. She put the issue of Lauren on hold, at least for the time being.

"Of course I need you there. It would mean so

much to me," called out O'Riordan from Gabriella's bed.

Gabriella stood in front of the bathroom mirror and rolled her eyes at his comment. She was brushing her teeth. She was scrubbing hard to get O'Riordan's taste out of her mouth. It was a foul mixture of cigarettes, coffee, and halitosis.

Gabriella and O'Riordan had spent the night in her dorm room, like they always did. With O'Riordan still living with his wife, Gabriella couldn't go to his house, even though his wife knew about his girlfriends. Gabriella did not want to create any additional drama by confronting Mrs. O'Riordan.

More importantly, Gabriella's dorm room offered more privacy. Except for her farm girl roommate, who spent all of her time at the library or at church, no one was around. It was within the four walls of this room that Gabriella extracted her best information from O'Riordan.

She never came out and asked direct questions about American intelligence. She'd lubricate him with a few glasses of wine first. She would then start flirting, playing the role of an awe-struck grad student. She would play to his ego by telling him that he was too smart for the House of Representatives. She would say that "Secretary O'Riordan" or "Secretary General O'Riordan" had a nice ring to it. She knew how to put him at ease.

Then she innocently prodded him for classified information. She knew his policy positions down cold, and she knew what issues provoked him the most. Asking why the U.S. did not just bomb Iran usually drew a ten-minute soliloquy about National Intelligence Estimates, the CIA's lack of sources on the ground in Tehran, and the military's long range missile capabilities.

Once she had him on topic, she could ask more pointed questions. That was when O'Riordan was most likely to reveal top secret information. This was the information that Caracas valued the most.

As a reward for his divulgences, Gabriella would end the night by sleeping with O'Riordan. She saw the powerful effect it had on his psyche. She knew that it would keep him talking.

Despite the act, Gabriella found nothing attractive about O'Riordan. The man made her skin crawl. He was neither the ugliest nor the oldest man that she had ever been with. Gabriella had been used as a honey trap in a number of SEBIN operations. What disgusted her most about O'Riordan was how pathetic he was.

In Caracas, a man of his stature would have gained more respect. He would have been much wealthier. He wouldn't have driven a run-down 1995 Saab 900. He wouldn't have had to grovel for campaign donations or prey on naïve graduate students to bolster his self esteem. She was amazed at how low O'Riordan had to stoop at times just to be noticed.

"Aren't you going home to get changed?" asked Gabriella.

She watched as O'Riordan pulled himself out of bed. The weight of the campaign, the late night with Gabriella, and the six glasses of wine had caused him to sleep in. He had started to put on the same suit and tie that he wore yesterday.

"There's no time. Press conference is scheduled for 11:30. Plus, I want the press to think that I spent the entire night by Mary's bedside. I'll make sure to add some comment about not even having time to go home and change."

As Gabriella applied her makeup, she smiled back at herself in the mirror. She liked where O'Riordan's head was at. She knew that he was going to make the most of Mary's misfortune.

"We should get going. I don't want to make you late," said Gabriella.

When they arrived at Memorial Hospital, O'Riordan's Press Secretary directed O'Riordan to a side entrance. Gabriella entered through the front doors.

Inside, Gabriella slipped into the hospital's nondescript conference room. Clutching a notebook, pen, and tape recorder, she pretended to be another member of the press. She maneuvered her way to the back of the room. There were seven television cameras set up along the back wall, the four local networks, plus CNN, MSNBC, and Fox News. Plastic folding chairs had been organized into five rows of ten. Fifty print, radio, television, and online journalists filled the chairs, with several on the sides and in the back.

Mary's attack had become a national story overnight. Rumors were swirling on left-wing blogs that Jimmy had orchestrated it. Right-wing commentators speculated that O'Riordan had set up his daughter to save his political career. The national media descended on South Bend to sort through the muck.

Cameras flashed as O'Riordan emerged from a side door and strode to a podium at the front of the room. He pulled a pair of glasses from his inner suit pocket and read from a prepared statement.

"Thank you all for coming this morning. And thank you for all the prayers and words of support for my daughter, Mary, and our family. Most of you know that Mary suffered a vicious attack on Friday night. As of right now, her condition is stable. The doctors are continuing to monitor her situation. I want to thank all of the doctors and medical staff here at Memorial for their work.

We are cooperating with the South Bend Police Department to find the perpetrator of this attack. We ask . . . we ask that . . ."

O'Riordan stopped reading. He appeared to be choked up. He lifted his head to reveal watery eyes. Then, just as quickly, he looked down at his statement.

Gabriella scanned the journalists. She wanted to see if they were buying his story. To her amazement, there didn't seem to be a skeptical face in the crowd. They were hanging on his words.

She sized up each journalist until her eyes stopped on a blond ponytail in the second row, three chairs in from the right.

Gabriella couldn't believe it.

What is she doing here?

Gabriella's two problems had just converged, and she didn't know why. She stared at the back of Lauren De-Marco's head weighing her next move. Gabriella did not even bother to look away when Lauren turned around and the two made eye contact.

She glared at her as Lauren gave her a tight smile. Gabriella didn't know what to make of it. But she knew that she also couldn't do much in a room packed with re-porters.

Gabriella kept staring until the journalists around her stood up and started shouting questions. She had been so focused on Lauren that she had missed the final words of O'Riordan's statement. She snapped back to her surround-ings to catch him fielding questions from the crowd.

As the press conference wound up, Gabriella fig-ured she should get out first. Slipping out the back door, she kept her eyes fixed on Lauren. Looking back over her shoulder, Lauren DeMarco did the same thing.

Outside, O'Riordan's Press Secretary ushered Ga-briella quickly past security and towards Mary's hospital room.

"Um . . . I can wait in another location," said Gabri-ella.

"Sorry, ma'am, this is where the Congressman asked for you to wait," replied the staffer.

He opened the door to the hospital room and Gabriella walked inside. She stood steps away from Mary's bed. The girl lay there, unconscious, with tubes running in and out of her.

"Was it your idea to host a press conference at his daughter's hospital?" said a voice from the corner.

Gabriella tried not to act startled, as she turned around to see Bob Jaworski sitting in a chair.

"It's important that the voters know that he is a loving father," said Gabriella, without a hint of irony.

"A loving father would never let his kid get into this situation," responded Jaworski.

By the disgusted look on his face, Gabriella could tell that she had hit a nerve. To her, it seemed like an attack on O'Riordan's character. Being a combative person by nature, she was not about to let his comment go.

Before Gabriella could reply, the hospital room door opened and O'Riordan walked in.

"Do you think they bought it?" asked O'Riordan.

"Oh, of course. You were great up there," said Gabriella, as she went up to hug him.

As she embraced O'Riordan, Gabriella looked over her shoulder at Jaworski. He remained seated in his chair, with the disgusted look still on his face.

"So, have we got any leads?" asked O'Riordan, turning to Jaworski.

"Yeah, right now, Father Sean Finnegan is still the main suspect. You know him?"

O'Riordan hesitated.

"Uh . . . um . . . yeah, I've seen his photo in the papers."

"Well, the cops don't know where he is. My guys are trying to track him down. We got one lead. We think some law school student, George DeMarco, has something to do with it."

"Law school student?"

"Yeah, we're not sure what the connection is, but we're working on it."

O'Riordan turned to Gabriella.

"You know any law students?"

"Uh . . . a few," responded Gabriella.

"You know this kid? What'd you say his name was again?" asked O'Riordan.

"George DeMarco," said Jaworski.

"No."

"Well, he just started law school. He's got a wife, Lauren DeMarco. You know her at all?" asked Jaworski.

"Uh . . . no," said Gabriella.

"Apparently, she's working up at the Kroc Institute. Don't you work with a lot of those people?" asked Jaworski.

"Yeah . . . a few."

"But you don't know Lauren DeMarco?" asked Jaworski again, with a look of skepticism on his face.

"Never heard of her," responded Gabriella without missing a beat.

"Who was it?"

"I have no clue. Never seen the guy before in my life."

"What'd he look like?"

"Late 40's, early 50's. Mustache. Stocky. Wearing a Teamsters jacket."

"What'd he say?"

"Asked me who I was and what I was doing."

"What'd you say?"

"Just made up some B.S. about being a student looking for a friend's room."

"He buy it?"

"I don't know."

"What was he doing in the priest's room?"

"I don't know that either."

"What'd you do?"

"I figured I'd blown my chance to inspect Father Finnegan's room, so I left."

"That's it?

"As I left, I heard him call someone and tell them to follow me."

"So where are you now?"

"I'm hiding out in the law library."

"How long are you planning on staying there?"

"Not much longer. I'm gonna head over to this bar to see if anyone knows anything about what happened Friday night."

"George . . ."

George listened patiently as his wife hesitated to

speak.

"What is it?"

"It's okay to go to the police on this."

"I can't, you know that."

"I know you feel a lot of loyalty toward Father Finnegan because he was your grandfather's best friend. That's one of the things that I love about you . . . that you are so loyal. But I don't think your grandfather would be upset if you went to the cops. Finnegan might have his name cleared in the end."

George wasn't upset by what she was saying. He could tell that she was speaking out of genuine concern and not because she thought that he was acting foolishly. He paused before responding.

"When your dad died, you felt that God made it your mission in life to hunt down those responsible and bring them to justice, right?"

Lauren's silence signaled reluctant agreement.

"Well, that's how I feel right now. I may not be able to explain it completely. But I feel as if God changed my path yesterday and brought me across Father Finnegan for a reason."

Lauren was silent for a few more seconds.

"You really think he's innocent?" she finally replied.

"I really do."

"Well, then you have to do what you have to do . . . At least be careful, will ya?" she said, sounding more light-hearted. "You're all I've got."

"Of course. You're all I've got too."

"I love you."

"I love you, too."

The couple let their sentiments linger before George spoke up.

"By the way, how's Father Finnegan holding up?"

"He seems fine. When I left, he was thumbing

through our bookshelf, looking for something to read."

"When you left? Where are you now?"

"Uh . . . at Memorial Hospital."

"So you just left Father Finnegan at home by himself?"

"Yeah, where else did he have to go?"

George knew she had a point.

"So what are you doing at Memorial?"

"I'll explain it all in a bit. I gotta go. She's on the move."

George heard the shuffle of feet and then Lauren hung up.

He didn't know why she had to run. He had more questions for her. He wanted advice on how to handle being followed. His wife was the spook in the family. George was just a street smart kid from Brooklyn. He could defend himself against a right hook and throw a counter-punch if necessary. But he'd never dealt with being followed.

Hiding out in the law library, he figured he couldn't worry about that now. If he wanted to save Father Finnegan, he had to deal with whatever was coming his way. He had to keep searching for clues.

George left the library and drove the short distance to the Linebacker Inn, on the southeast corner of campus. He parked next to a rusted 1997 Ford F-150 truck, with an American flag decal and a Teamsters Local 364 sticker on the back window.

This was George's first trip to the 'Backer. He knew it was popular with undergrads. From the outside he could understand why. It looked like a stereotypical college dive bar, a low-slung cinderblock building with no windows.

A neon martini glass and the slogan, "The Tradition Continues" flashed on a sign next to the building. It was as close to a 1950's Las Vegas marquee as South Bend got.

As he walked in, George was hit with the smell of stale beer. The wood paneled walls were covered with Notre Dame sporting memorabilia – the NFL jerseys of former Notre Dame players and photos of national championship teams.

George surveyed the dimly lit room. Five middle aged guys in Notre Dame gear sat hunched over beers in the corner. Two guys in their early twenties sat at the bar. One wore an Indianapolis Colts sweatshirt. The other wore a Colts Peyton Manning jersey.

George sized them up. The taller one with the goatee was about 6'4" and 180 pounds. The shorter one with the beard was about 5'7" and 250 pounds. They sat watching the TV with Bud Light bottles in hand, waiting for the start of the Colts and Tennessee Titans game. George pulled up a seat next to them.

"What can I get you?" asked the gruff barmaid, a woman in her late 60's.

She wore a "Notre Dame Football 1973 National Champion" sweatshirt. Her hair looked like she had just taken it out of curlers. A crucifix dangled from her neck. She gave George a once over as he scanned the menu.

"Uh . . . I'll just have a Coke, please."

The woman picked up a soda gun and sprayed it into a cup.

"You gonna order any food?"

George wasn't hungry, but he figured he should order something.

"Um . . . sure, I'll take a cheeseburger."

"How you want that cooked?"

"Medium is fine."

She wrote down the order on a pad of paper and walked back to the kitchen.

George turned to the two on his right.

"So . . . uh . . . who's favored?"

The pair stared silently at the TV, ignoring the question. George sat awkwardly waiting for a response. He also stared at the screen, until the woman emerged from the kitchen.

"You want anything else?" she asked.

"Uh . . . no. I'm good."

The lady turned her back on him to watch the game before he had a chance to finish his sentence.

This is going nowhere.

George sat in silence as they all watched the game. He decided on another route.

"So . . . uh . . . how's business?"

That caught the woman's attention.

"You some reporter?" asked the woman, with a snarl on her face.

"No, not at all," responded George. "Why do you ask?"

"We've had nosy reporters in and out of here all morning. Harassing the customers. Sticking their nose where it just don't belong."

"No . . . no, no. I'm not a journalist. I'm just a law student."

"Well why you so concerned about our business?"

"I was just trying to make conversation."

George sat there with an apologetic face as the woman shot him a dark look. She turned back to the television. George sat there quietly for another minute to let the tension dissipate.

"So why have all the media been coming in?"

The woman kept her back to him. George figured that the only thing he was going to get out of this visit was a stomachache from a bad cheeseburger.

"They're just trying to dig some dirt on what happened here on Friday night," offered the woman.

George perked up.

Okay, here's an opening.

"What happened on Friday night?" asked George, acting dumb.

With her back still turned towards George, the woman continued watching the TV. Again, it was a few painful seconds before she responded.

"Nothing. But the media are saying that he attacked that girl."

"Who are you talking about?"

"Father Finnegan."

"But you don't believe the media?"

"I don't believe much of what the media tells you. Most of it's just lies."

"Why don't you think he did it?"

This touched a nerve. The woman turned around to face George. The guys sitting at the bar also looked over.

"You swear you're not some kind of reporter?"

"Absolutely, I swear. I'm in my first year up at the law school."

The woman hesitated for a moment.

"Well, you're up at the law school. You know Father Finnegan. He is a good guy. He was awfully good to me and my family when my sister Maria passed away."

"So why do you think the media are saying that he did it?"

"The media is out to get Catholics any chance they can get. Those east coast elites don't like the Catholic Church. And they'll do anything to bring it down. That's why they're after Father Finnegan."

She finished her statement and placed her hands on the bar. She was inches from George's face and visibly angry. He could smell the cigarettes on her.

"Were Father Finnegan and that girl here on Friday night? Were they seen together?"

The woman pulled away from the bar.

"I didn't see nothing."

"Did they leave together?"

The woman remained quiet.

"Did they say anything to each other?"

George stopped. He waited for a response, any response.

"I think it's time for you to go," said the woman.

George lowered his voice.

"I'm sorry. Look, I'm a friend of Father Finnegan's. I'm just trying to help him out."

"Well why don't you go somewhere else to help him out."

George didn't move. He was trying to gauge if the woman was serious.

"You heard the lady, it's time to go," said the shorter, fatter Colts fan.

"What about my cheeseburger?" said George, with a smile on his face.

He was doing his best to lighten the mood. He knew he could take both of these guys if he had to.

"Find somewhere else to have a cheeseburger," responded the woman.

The intensity of her glare told George that she meant business. As she replied, the two Colts fans stood up from their stools. George stared them both down. He knew he could drop the two of them easily. However, he was quick to realize that leveling these two would not help him clear Father Finnegan's name. He slowly backed down.

"Okay, okay. I didn't mean any harm. I'm leaving."

George put on his jacket quickly. Without turning around to see if the woman and the Colts' fans were still watching him, he walked out into the parking lot. He pulled his car out and headed home on Edison Road, his head spinning. The more he thought about everything, the more he was frustrated by the entire situation.

Father Finnegan's gotta remember something else. Why can't he remember anything? Maybe he is guilty?

What then? Either I turn him in or he turns himself in. If he turns himself in, what happens to us? How do we explain it all?

George could see nothing good in the situation. All the scenarios ended in Father Finnegan going to jail and, possibly, himself and Lauren joining him there.

George came to a red light at the intersection of Eddy Street and Angela Boulevard. His eyes drifted to the rearview mirror. He almost missed it at first.

Then he turned around to look out of the back of his Jeep. The rusted F-150 truck, parked next to him at the 'Backer, was now two cars behind him. Two men sat in the front seats. George was certain they were the two Colts fans from the bar.

The light turned green. George continued driving west on Angela. His eyes darted between the rearview mirror and the road ahead. The F-150 truck followed.

Any thoughts about Father Finnegan or what he would look like in an orange prison jumpsuit left his mind. He tightened his grip on the steering wheel.

As he came to the intersection of North Michigan Street and Angela, the road split into three lanes. The right lane went to the highway. The center lane ran to the west side of town. The left lane took you downtown.

George got in the left lane.

The F-150 truck did the same.

He turned left on to North Michigan. The truck – still two cars behind – followed.

Up ahead was his street, Wakewa Avenue. Few cars turned right on to Wakewa, unless they lived on the street or were visiting someone in the North Shore Triangle.

George turned right. The green Nissan Maxima between George and the truck continued on North Michigan. The truck followed George on to Wakewa.

There were no cars between them now. George had one block to figure out what to do. He lived on the second block of Wakewa. He came to a stop at the intersection of Wakewa and Lafayette Boulevard. The truck crept behind him. In his rearview mirror, he could clearly make out the faces of the men from the 'Backer.

After pausing to see if there was any traffic, George continued through the stop sign. He drove at the normal speed limit – 30 mph – down his block until he came to his home. He slowed his car down to 10 mph. As he rolled up to the white house, he looked out the window and contemplated his next move. The truck, about twenty-feet behind his Jeep Cherokee, slowed down as well.

Without showing any sign of stopping, George held the Jeep's speed at 10 mph as he slowly drove past his house. He continued down the street. He did not stop until he came to the intersection of Iroquis and Wakewa.

George waited at the stop sign. His mind raced, trying to figure out how to shake these Colts fans from his tail. After sitting for about twenty-seconds, George finally saw an opening.

A white Buick LeSabre turned on to Iroquis from North Shore drive, approaching George from his left side. George recognized the car. It belonged to his neighbor Albert Canton, an eighty-five-year-old retired Notre Dame professor.

George flicked on his left blinker to throw off the two men following him. He watched as the truck put on its left blinker as well. The Colts fans stared and waited for George to make his move. As the LeSabre came to the intersection, George slammed on the gas, cutting out in front of the white sedan and turning to the right.

The LeSabre came to a screeching halt. The elderly Mr. Canton blasted the horn. The old man's car blocked the intersection of Wakewa and Iroquis.

The Colts fans had been watching George. Both of their heads were turned as the driver slammed on the gas pedal. Neither of the men saw the Buick LeSabre until it was too late.

The truck plowed right into the side of the white sedan.

George grimaced as he watched all of this unfold in his rearview mirror. He hadn't intended for Mr. Canton to be hit. He simply wanted some interference in order to get away from the truck.

He took a quick right turn on to Tonti, the street that ran behind his house. He went a third of the way down the block and then turned down an alleyway between two houses. He hit the garage door remote control that was attached to his visor.

He went careening down this small alleyway into his garage. He slammed on the brakes to make sure that he did not plow through the back wall. He pressed the remote control again. He sat in the Jeep looking into the rearview mirror. He watched as the garage door closed behind him.

No sign of any trucks.

No sign of any Colts fans.

His pulse was racing. He was sweating.

He sat in the darkness of his garage and took a deep breath.

He knew that this meant the start of his problems – not the end.

"What are we looking at?"

George recoiled as Father Finnegan opened his mouth. The priest's breath stunk of steak, wine, and beer. He hadn't brushed his teeth in over two days.

"Get down," said George, suppressing a reactive cough.

The two were kneeling below a window on the second floor of the DeMarco's house. George didn't think he could bear anything worse than the priest's breath. But then he got a whiff of his body odor. His stomach lurched. It took all of his self control not to vomit from the smell.

Kneeling inches from a filthy, alcoholic priest is not how George had envisioned his Sunday. He normally spent the day going to mass, working out, catching up on household chores, and reading for the week ahead. He didn't want to be in this situation, but he had no other choice.

George had bolted inside the house after making it to the garage. Swinging open the door, he had flown past Father Finnegan and raced up the stairs. From the window on the second floor, he could just make out the scene at the intersection.

The fat Colts fan was on the street, talking animatedly into his cell phone. The taller and skinnier Colts fan stood next to Mr. Canton's door, peering in on the old man. Mr. Canton's head was slumped over the steering wheel. Glass from the shattered LeSabre's windows littered the pavement.

Father Finnegan had followed George upstairs. Kneeling together on the floor, George explained what had happened.

"Those were the guys that were following me."

"Which guys?"

"The guys in the Colts jerseys. They were at the 'Backer, when I was asked to leave. And then they followed me here."

"You were asked to leave?"

"Yeah, the lady behind the bar asked me to leave."

"Jeanette?"

"I didn't get her name," responded George, somewhat annoyed that the priest was more concerned about her than what had just happened.

THUD-THUD-THUD.

The two were startled by a knock on the door downstairs.

"You hear that?"

"Shhhhh," said George.

The pair waited and listened.

They heard it again.

"Who is it?"

"Shhh. I don't know," said George tersely.

George's pulse began to race again. Father Finnegan stared at him, waiting for George to take the lead. They heard the knock a third time.

George rose up slowly and peered out of the window. The Buick LeSabre, with Mr. Canton still slumped over the steering wheel, remained in the middle of the intersection. The rusted F-150 truck was gone. George saw no sign of the Colts fans.

"Maybe they left," said Father Finnegan.

George looked at him skeptically.

"Otherwise, they'll probably be here any minute," said Father Finnegan. "And I'm no good in a fight, Son."

George stared at the disheveled priest. The comment didn't make him feel any better. He headed downstairs to find a knife, scissors, or anything sharp to use as a weapon.

As he hit the bottom of the stairs, George heard the knock again. Instinctively, he turned toward the door. He saw a face that he recognized through the glass window.

All of his anger evaporated. Curiosity took its place.

George walked to the door and opened it.

"Hi, George. Can I come in?"

"Uh . . . yeah, sure."

The appearance of Jimmy King on his doorstep took George by surprise. Over the last few months, George had seen his face scores of times in the papers and on mailers, billboards, and TV. But he hadn't seen him in person for years.

"Uh . . . hey . . . what's up Jimmy? How you doin'?" said George hesitantly.

He had no idea why Jimmy was here.

"Sorry to disturb you, but I needed your help with something."

"Uh . . . it's a little late in the campaign to be looking for volunteers . . . I might be able to help. But school is really busy so I don't have much time these days."

"This is . . . uh . . . not something for volunteers. I need you full time."

George couldn't tell why Jimmy was acting so cagey. He wasn't sure if Jimmy was nervous or just generally awkward.

"I'd love to help, but like I said, school's really busy and there are some things I gotta take care of," said George. He was trying to find any excuse to get Jimmy out of the house without seeing Father Finnegan. "I can ask around the law school?"

"No, this is only something that you can handle."

George looked at Jimmy skeptically. He didn't

know where Jimmy was headed with this.

"There's lots of conservatives up at school. I'm sure one of them would want to help out during the next two days."

"No, George, you're really the only person with the skills that I need. And I don't know if I can trust anyone else to do this job."

George took another look at Jimmy, and then it dawned on him. The reason why Jimmy wanted his help had nothing to do with politics or even the law. Jimmy needed some muscle.

Despite being at Harvard at the same time, George didn't meet Jimmy until the summer he moved to D.C. George had initially planned to go into the military after college. Like many of his fellow New Yorkers, the September 11th attacks had changed his life. He decided to postpone law school in favor of combat.

George was also inspired by his grandfather's service. The Italian kid from Brooklyn had enlisted in the Army to serve in the Korean War. George remembered hearing his grandfather speak with pride about repelling the Communist tide into Korea. Through many lessons, the old Army vet instilled in his grandson the value of serving a cause greater than oneself.

George wanted to join the Army, but pickup basketball games ruined his chance. George had torn the ACLs in both legs on New York City blacktops. He still felt physically capable. But the Army thought otherwise.

George pleaded his case, but it got him nowhere. The recruiting staff said he could take a desk job. George's idea of fighting terrorists didn't involve working inside a nondescript, government building.

Still determined to join the fight, George moved to D.C. with the hope of joining the F.B.I. The hiring process took longer than expected and his funds quickly dried up.

He tried getting a day job. No one wanted to take him on, knowing that he'd quit if he got a call from the Bureau. Through a Harvard connection, he ended up working as a bouncer at the trendy, Georgetown bar, Smith Point.

George was working one Friday night in mid-July when Congressman Robert Smith, a thirty-four-year-old Republican from the affluent suburbs of Indianapolis, brought his staff and interns to the bar. At the end of a long night, the group stumbled into the street. The young women in the group were drunk and trying to hail a cab.

George watched as two crack-heads accosted the group and tried to shake them down.

The Congressman and his male aides were paralyzed. George hustled over and dropped one of the crack-heads with a solid punch to his temple. The other guy fled.

Congressman Smith and his aides stood there in amazement. They had never seen someone react so swiftly and viciously. The Congressman offered George a job on the spot. George accepted, starting his career as a Capitol Hill staffer.

Standing in the group that night was a summer intern from Harvard. Jimmy King watched in awe, along with his colleagues, as George had single-handedly taken on the two drug addicts. He had never seen another Harvard student act so tough and in control. George earned demigod status in Jimmy's eyes.

Jimmy had come to the DeMarco's house with the hope that George might bring some toughness and control to his campaign. After learning about Mary and being interrogated by the police, Jimmy was worried about his own safety.

"Sorry," said George, as he walked to the door. "I think you need to find someone else."

As George walked by, Jimmy reached out and grabbed him by the arm.

"I think I'm being set up."

George saw the pathetic look on Jimmy's face. He felt sorry for the kid. The campaign and stress had taken its toll on him.

Jimmy repeated his plea with more desperation in his voice.

"George, I really need your help. I think someone has set me up."

"What do you mean?"

"Someone attacked my opponent's daughter and they are trying to pin the blame on me."

"How do you know they are blaming you?"

"Well the cops showed up at church this morning to harass me."

"What'd they say?"

"They started asking questions about Friday night and they insinuated that I stood to benefit from the whole situation."

"Wait, what about Friday night?" asked George, realizing that his upstairs and downstairs problems were coming together.

"Uh . . . well, I . . . uh . . ." stammered Jimmy, as he looked down at the floor. "I ran into Mary O'Riordan at the Linebacker on Friday night. She yelled at me. I lost my cool and yelled some things back."

"Then what happened?"

"That was it. Her friends pulled her away. I left and headed to my campaign headquarters to write thank you notes to donors."

"Did you see anyone else at the 'Backer?"

"Sure, there were lots of people."

"No one that stood out?"

Jimmy's confused look showed that he didn't know what George was talking about.

"Well . . . " started Jimmy.

The sound of books tumbling from a shelf thundered from upstairs.

"Who's that?" asked Jimmy.

"Oh that . . . uh, that's just my wife Lauren. She's . . . she's just doing some work upstairs."

George watched Jimmy as the kid's head turned toward the stairs. He was hoping that Father Finnegan had found a good hiding spot in case Jimmy wanted to inspect things for himself.

"Your house smells really bad," said Jimmy. "Are you sure everything's alright here?"

"Oh yeah. We had . . . uh . . . a friend over last night for the game and he just drank a lot and got sick."

Jimmy looked skeptically at George.

"So no one seemed to stand out on Friday night?" asked George, trying to deflect Jimmy's question.

After a few seconds of silence, Jimmy focused on George again.

"Just the usual crowd of people for a football game weekend. But I did hear that the priest was at the 'Backer on Friday as well. Do you know this priest?"

"Uh . . . no. What priest?" asked George feigning ignorance.

"Name's Father Sean Finnegan. Right now, he's the lead suspect. Press says he's a professor at the law school. You don't know him?"

"Oh him? Yeah, I know who Finnegan is. But I don't have any classes with him, so I've never met him."

George watched to see if Jimmy believed him. He prayed that Father Finnegan wouldn't come tumbling down the stairs.

"Well, he's apparently missing. I need your help finding him."

"Why do you need my help? Why don't you just go to the cops?"

"George, the police here are crooked and lazy and I'm not sure which is worse. They are all in the pocket of the Democratic Party. I can't trust any one of them to keep me safe. And if we don't find Father Finnegan, they're likely to pin Mary's attack on me."

"But why do you want me to help you?"

"Because you're an outsider – people in South Bend don't know you. You can ask questions and not draw any attention."

"There are plenty of other law students who aren't recognized around here either."

"But no one else has the street toughness that I need. What you did outside Smith Point was incredible," said Jimmy, still amazed thinking about that summer night.

Again, George demurred.

"I really think you should go to the cops," responded George, aware that he had disregarded the same suggestion earlier from his wife.

Jimmy didn't respond. He looked crestfallen. His eyes began to water.

George felt bad. The kid was clearly desperate. He didn't want to blow him off. But he didn't think that offering to find Father Finnegan would work out well for Jimmy, Father Finnegan, or himself.

"I can't go to the cops. They are already working against me," pleaded Jimmy, softly. "Please . . . you are the only one I can trust."

George looked at the kid. At this moment he wasn't a congressional candidate or an arrogant Harvard grad. He was a scared and vulnerable boy. George saw the same weakness in Father Finnegan. And as with Father Finnegan, he felt compelled to protect him.

"Okay . . . what do you need me to do?"

Jimmy perked up.

"Help me find Father Finnegan and clear my name."

George took a deep breath, knowing that what he was about to say might not be true, but he had nothing else to offer.

"I'll do my best."

"I didn't know you were a women's basketball fan."

"I'm not," replied Bob Jaworski gruffly. "I'm here to make sure chumps like you are doing your job. Now let me in."

Jaworski's comment triggered a laugh from the Teamster working a side job with Notre Dame security. The two men were on the south-east side of the Joyce Center where the basketball teams played their home games. The Teamster opened the door and ushered Jaworski into the bowels of the 11,418-seat arena.

It was the opening game of the women's basketball season. Fans had been streaming into the Joyce Center's Purcell Pavilion for over an hour.

Jaworski wasn't there to watch the Lady Irish. He came at the request of Jimmy King. Jimmy had called him in a hysterical state after his run-in with the cops that morning.

Jaworski did his best to calm him down over the phone. Jimmy insisted on a face-to-face meeting. Initially, Jaworski declined. But Jimmy insisted, sounding even more upset. With O'Riordan's schedule now free and Jimmy on the verge of a complete meltdown, he finally relented.

Jaworski wanted to meet somewhere other than the Joyce Center. Too many of Jaworski's Teamsters worked full or part-time jobs there, in security, lighting, and the concession stands. The women's basketball team also drew a number of fans from the South Bend community. Jaworski was worried that a neighbor might identify him and start asking questions.

Jimmy pushed hard for the Joyce Center since no one would be at the Hammes Bookstore on a Sunday. He thought the two could blend into the nearly 12,000 people expected to be there for the game. Not only did the crowd provide cover, but Jimmy reasoned that the arena had places where they could blend in, like the gift shop at Purcell Pavilion or the exhibit of sporting memorabilia outside the Monogram Club.

When Jaworski pushed back on the Joyce Center, Jimmy accused Jaworski of setting him up. Jaworski could not believe his ears, but he was in no fighting mood. He needed Jimmy to maintain his sanity, at least until Tuesday. Jaworski agreed to meet Jimmy outside the Monogram Club.

Jaworski was there on time. Normally Jimmy was the early one. The fact that he was late angered Jaworski.

Jaworski passed the time by perusing the Irish's various national championship trophies, pretending to be another obsessed fan. He looked the role too. He was wearing Timberland work boots, blue jeans, and a Notre Dame hooded sweatshirt that covered his middle-aged gut. It was the same outfit that he had worn yesterday.

While pretending to inspect the 1924 National Championship Trophy, Jaworski's eyes darted around the room. He scanned every face that walked in, every head that turned in his direction. He wanted to spot Jimmy, or anyone else who might recognize him, before they spotted him.

"What are you doing here?"

The voice came from behind him.

He didn't recognize it immediately. He tried to think of a quick story about checking up on Teamsters or coming to support the team.

"What are you doing here?" asked the voice again,

this time with more desperation.

Jaworski recognized it this time. Any hesitation that he had gave way to anger.

"What are you talking about?" said Jaworski.

"We were supposed to meet at the gift shop downstairs," replied Jimmy King.

"We said outside the Monogram Club, next to all the memorabilia."

"No, we said the gift shop," insisted Jimmy, his voice growing shrill.

Jaworski inched in, close to Jimmy's face.

"Lower your voice and get a hold of yourself. You look like a mess."

Jimmy stood there in the same Jos. A. Banks suit that he had worn to church. Except now, he looked completely stressed out. His suit was rumpled. His tie was pulled down. His shirt was untucked at the back.

He was clearly mentally fatigued from the long months of campaigning. The situation with Mary O'Riordan had only compounded his stress.

"What am I supposed to do?"

"For one thing, stop acting like a child."

"It's over though. My poll numbers are dwindling. O'Riordan's surging ahead. There's only two days left."

"Two days is an eternity in politics. There's plenty of time left."

"Yeah but O'Riordan's stopped campaigning. What am I supposed to do?"

"You need to go home and get some rest. You gotta be ready for the debate tonight."

"Why is he even going forward with the debate? How can he cancel all of his campaign events and not the debate?"

"Because he's in the position to call all the shots."

"So why'd he cancel his other campaign events?"

"He did it because he hates campaigning. The guy hates talking to people about their problems. All he ever wants to do is lecture people about Latin America. When the whole Mary situation happened, he saw it as an opportunity to put his feet up."

"But why keep the debate then?"

"Because he knows he is still behind and he realizes that he needs a final knockout punch to put you away."

"And he thinks he can out-debate me?"

"Looking at the shape you are in, he can definitely out-debate you," said Jaworski.

Jimmy looked down at his disheveled clothes to see what Jaworski meant.

"But he's not planning on out-debating you," continued Jaworski.

"What do you mean?"

"Like I said, he thinks he needs a final knockout punch. At some point in the debate, he plans to answer a question by making a reference to his daughter, Mary. When he invokes her name, he is going to act like he is fighting off tears. He thinks that this *spontaneous* moment will leave voters with the lasting image of a loving, caring father. And who could vote against someone like that?"

"You're kidding."

Jaworski shook his head in silence.

"Would he really stoop that low?"

"You better believe it. He's a major league scumbag willing to do anything to save his own ass."

"Did you tell him that he's crossed the line?" pleaded Jimmy.

"I told him that I thought he was despicable and that what he planned to do was despicable."

"But he still plans on doing it?"

"Like I said, he's a major league scumbag."

"So what question is he going to respond to?"

"Any question he can. Doesn't really matter. As long as he can connect it somehow to Mary."

"When should I expect it?"

"Who knows. Could come five minutes into the debate. Could come fifty-five minutes in."

"You think it will work?"

"What mother, father, or grandparent would not sympathize with a grieving father?"

"But the girl's twenty-five-years-old."

"Doesn't matter. She'll always be daddy's little girl."

"But doesn't she hate her dad? She was yelling at me on Friday about how all politicians are terrible human beings."

"She's no angel but what are you gonna do? Run an ad calling her an alcoholic, druggie slut? Yeah, you see how well that goes over. O'Riordan will just open up the doors to her hospital room so everyone can see her banged up mug."

"There's got to be some way to let people know the truth. What about O'Riordan's wife?"

"Listen, she's not fond of the man. But she's a good Catholic, a former nun, until O'Riordan swept her away. She won't divorce him, so she just acts like nothing bad is ever going on. There's no way you'll get her to say anything about her husband or daughter."

"So what do you expect me to do?"

"Go home, get some rest, get ready for this debate, and brace yourself for the fallout from his little stunt."

"And what do I do tomorrow?"

"Act natural, most importantly. Get out around the district. Make sure people see your face and hear your name. But make it look natural. Don't look like you're campaigning."

"That's what I was doing until your friends in the

police department came to harass me," said Jimmy, sounding less hysterical and more annoyed.

"They are just doing their job. Don't let them get to you. Do you have anything to hide?" asked Jaworski.

Jimmy shook his head "no" in response.

"Then don't give them any reason to get suspicious."

"I thought you had everyone in your pocket?" asked Jimmy.

"You don't worry about that."

"How come you can't get the police to release a statement or make an announcement clearing my name?"

"Not on this one. This one is too serious. Just let them do their job and don't worry about it. You take care of getting ready for this debate."

"And what are you going to take care of?" asked Jimmy, sounding even more annoyed.

Jaworski stared at Jimmy.

"I've got things under control from my end."

"Really? You keep saying that, but I don't see you having anything under control. I'm about to lose the election. I'm out $80,000. My name's being dragged through the mud. What are you doing to keep things under control?" asked Jimmy in his most demanding voice yet.

Jaworski did not appreciate Jimmy talking to him like this. He closed in on Jimmy's face again.

"I'm working on it," said Jaworski, as he gritted his teeth.

"That's all I've heard this entire campaign. 'I'm working on it.' Or 'It's under control.' Not once have I heard you say that you've actually done something. This has all been a complete waste of money."

Jimmy left it at that statement and began walking away from Jaworski, bumping his shoulder in the process.

Jaworski grabbed Jimmy's arm hard and kept him

from walking away.

Jaworski was pissed. No one ever spoke or treated him like that, especially not some hysterical, desperate kid. He started with a hushed, but stern tone. He wanted to remind Jimmy that he was in charge.

"Listen, my guys are close to finding the priest. When we find him, then your name is clear."

"How are you going to find him?"

"We've got some leads."

"Oh yeah, what leads?" asked Jimmy, skeptically.

Jaworski did not want to get into it, but he figured he had to appease the kid.

"We think he is hiding out with a law student. Once we find that law student, we've found the priest."

"What law student?"

"Kid by the name of George DeMarco."

Jaworski could tell by Jimmy's startled reaction that Jimmy knew the kid.

"You know where to find him?" asked Jaworski.

"Yeah, I was just at his house," stammered Jimmy.

He was shocked by what Jaworski had just told him.

"What?" asked Jaworski, trying to hide his surprise.

"Yeah, he lives over in the North Shore Triangle. Little white house at the head of Nokomis Park."

"What were you doing over there?"

"I . . . uh . . . went to go see him about some re-search for the campaign," said Jimmy, hesitantly.

Jaworski squinted his eyes at Jimmy. He didn't believe him. But it wasn't the time to press him on the matter.

"You see the priest over there?"

"No, but I did hear someone upstairs. George said it was his wife."

"How long ago was this?"

"Just right before I came over here," said Jimmy, as he turned from being angry to being hysterical again. "I've got to go. I've got to get back over to George's."

Jimmy started to walk away. Jaworski grabbed him on the arm once again.

"You let me take care of this," insisted Jaworski.

"I've got to get over there. I've got to talk to George about this."

"Don't worry about it. You've got a debate to get ready for. The election hinges on this debate. Go get some rest," said Jaworski faking a soothing voice. Jaworski did not want Jimmy to do anything to alert this DeMarco kid that Jaworski was looking for him.

The uncertain look on Jimmy's face told Jaworski that this kid really was conflicted.

Jaworski looked Jimmy in the eyes and reassured him.

"I'll take care of it. Trust me."

"Yalla habibis."

Lauren whispered "hurry-up darlings" to herself in Arabic as Congressman O'Riordan and Gabriella Silva finally emerged from building number four at the Fischer grad dorms. She had followed the couple there when the press conference ended. That was around 12:30 p.m.

Six hours later, Lauren was still sitting in her 1990 BMW 325i convertible. She had purchased the car as a gift for herself when she moved to Washington. It was a small indulgence after trekking around the Middle East in the back of bootleg taxis for so many years.

The BMW was great for cruising short distances, but Lauren was clearly uncomfortable now. Sitting still in a car or in an empty safe house for hours on end didn't suit the former Division I lacrosse player. Despite this, she still had the patience to wait out The Fox. She knew timing was everything, and tonight her window of opportunity was small.

O'Riordan and Gabriella were due at the congressional debate, which was scheduled to last an hour. While they were there, Lauren planned to move in and out of Gabriella's apartment as quickly as possible. She didn't want to risk confronting Gabriella with a shoot out in her own bedroom. She'd have a tough time explaining why she'd brought a gun into the graduate dorms.

Lauren perked up when the couple finally came down the steps at Fischer. Parked in the visitor's lot across Wilson Drive, opposite Gabriella's building, she saw O'Riordan give Gabriella a playful tap on the butt as they walked to his car. Gabriella giggled in response. Lauren shook her head in disgust. She couldn't believe that a United States Congressman – especially one on the Intelligence Committee – had fallen for this trap.

When Gabriella drove O'Riordan's Saab past the BMW, Lauren slunk down in her seat. She was certain the two were headed to the DeBartolo Performing Arts Center – the site of tonight's debate – on the south side of campus. Yet she waited another ten minutes just in case they returned.

With the Saab nowhere in sight, Lauren headed to the dorm. She had searched Notre Dame's directory so she knew where Gabriella lived and that she had a roommate. Lauren didn't think the twenty-two-year-old would give her any problems, but she was prepared just in case. She kept her Sig Sauer P239 loaded in her Kate Spade hand bag.

Gabriella and her roommate lived on the second floor – apartment 4A. Lauren walked up the one flight of stairs, found the door on her left, and knocked. She pressed her ear to the door to listen for any movement inside.

As soon as her ear touched the door, Lauren pulled back.

Someone was coming. She turned around, trying to act casually.

Two tall men in their twenties approached, both with unkempt beards. They didn't look particularly friendly. Lauren figured she might have been set up. She tried to remember if she had seen these guys when she was sitting in her car.

As they climbed the stairs, she looked at their hands. They both clutched paper bags from Five Guy's – a local hamburger joint.

Lauren put her hand into her own bag and gripped her Sig. She held firm, clutching the gun within the bag, as the two guys walked by. She didn't relax until the guys opened a door down the hall, entered the dorm room, and locked the door behind them.

Releasing the grip on her pistol, Lauren quickly pulled a pick from her bag to unlock the door. The door didn't take much working over. The fake brass lock and deadbolt gave way and Lauren slipped into the apartment.

Lauren took her first steps into the apartment slowly and quietly. She did not want to give advanced notice to anyone waiting inside for her. Yet she also wanted to be ready in case of an ambush. She put her hand back into her bag and gripped the handgun.

She closed the door, paused, and looked around. Other than a couch against the far wall, the living room was empty. No sign of anyone in the apartment.

She ventured down a short hallway. She passed a kitchen on the right and bathroom on the left, until she came to two doors. Lauren assumed that these doors led to the girls' bedrooms. But she did not know which one belonged to Gabriella and which belonged to the roommate.

She chose the door on the right. She opened it with her left hand, while still gripping her gun.

It definitely wasn't Gabriella's room.

The walls were decorated with pictures of young girls and an oversized teddy bear sat on a chair in the corner. A poster of Vincent van Gogh's *Still Life Vase with Fifteen Sunflowers* hung above the bed. A statute of the Virgin Mary was on the bookshelf. Lauren knew Gabriella had neither religion nor sunshine in her life.

She moved on to the bedroom on the left.

This is definitely Gabriella's room.

The room was relatively empty, aside from a bed, a desk with papers on it, and an old wooden bookshelf holding a few academic text books. A dark red cover was thrown across the bed.

The spartan bedroom was clearly deceptive. Lauren

knew there was more in here than it seemed.

Lauren had convinced herself that Gabriella was in South Bend to assassinate her. She came to this apartment to prove that she wasn't crazy. She was looking for weapons, a paper trail from Caracas, any personal details about her own life. Lauren needed credible evidence that she was in danger.

Under the bed she found a plain black suitcase. It looked like the type of suitcase that Latin American financiers of terrorist organizations use to exchange cash. She opened the case's false bottom but it was empty. She slid it back under the bed.

She moved the dresser two feet to the right. She ran her hands over the newly revealed wall. She felt a rough section about one foot up from the floor. She peeled back a strip to reveal a small hole in the wall.

She removed a small gun vault from the cavity. Judging by its weight, she figured it held one pistol. A pistol didn't concern her too much, so she put it back, reapplied the wall strip, and moved the dresser back into its place.

Squatting from the floor, she looked up at the ceiling tiles. She dragged the desk chair to the middle of the room and stood on it. Removing a ceiling tile, she put her hand into the roof and pulled down a black Adidas gym bag with a Notre Dame logo.

The bag was stuffed with wads of American dollars, possibly $100,000 or more. It would have made great spending money for Lauren and George. She could walk away with it now and know that Gabriella had no recourse. No foreign operative would be dumb enough to walk into the South Bend Police Department and file a stolen items report for $100,000 in cash.

Instead, Lauren stood on the chair and put the bag back into the ceiling. She wasn't there for money. She wasn't a thief or a crook. She had risked her life to protect innocent people around the world and to track down the worst of humanity. She was not about to go to the dark side any time soon.

Lauren moved on to Gabriella's desk. Two stacks of paper sat on each side. The first was a pile of essay drafts and reading assignments. Lauren flipped through the papers briefly and then put them down. None of it was noteworthy.

She turned to the second, smaller stack. At the bottom she found a document embossed with an emblem of the U.S. Secret Service. It was titled: "Visit by Former President Miller to South Bend, Indiana. Rally in Support of Congressman Michael O'Riordan. October 31, 2012."

She turned to the next page. It contained a detailed timeline of the former President's upcoming visit to South Bend. It outlined the timing and routes that Miller would take from South Bend Airport to Notre Dame's Compton Family Ice Arena, where the rally with O'Riordan was scheduled to take place. It also contained very detailed schematics of the two separate locations.

Lauren took the stack of papers and sat down in the chair.

Why would she need to know this?

How did she get her hands on such sensitive material?

What is she planning to do with it?

Lauren leaned back in the chair as she read the schedule. As she leaned backward, she heard the back right leg of the chair rattle, like it might fall off. She planted the chair back on the ground and flipped it upside down.

She unscrewed the leg from the base and turned it over. A 50 ml syringe and glass bottle dropped to the floor. Lauren picked up the bottle. The label read "Po-210."

Lauren had no background in chemistry. But she

was quite familiar with Radionuclide Polonium-210. The odorless and colorless poison had made its splash on the international espionage scene in the case of Alexander Litvinenko.

The former Russian KGB officer checked into a London hospital suffering from serious bouts of diarrhea and vomiting. He was unable to walk. He slipped in and out of consciousness. Three weeks later, he died.

British authorities investigated the case. They found enough polonium in Litvinenko's body to wipe out a small town of 10,000 people. All signs pointed to KGB agents, angered by Litvinenko's accusations that the KGB was forcing Vladimir Putin back into power. Whether they operated under direct orders from Moscow remained unclear. What British authorities did know was that the polonium, in that quantity, could only have been obtained from a state nuclear facility.

The willingness of Russian operatives to use polonium raised the stakes around the world. Intelligence agents became much more cautious in dealing with the Russians. No spook wanted to defend against a colorless, odorless, and lethal liquid.

Lauren wondered how Gabriella would have gotten her hands on the polonium. She suspected Syria. Russia had an interest in keeping the Middle East destabilized as a threat to the United States. Syria's President, Bashar Al-Assad, had been propped-up by Moscow for years. Russia and Syria would only give up polonium if they knew it was a big enough job. And that it would be difficult to trace it back to them.

So Gabriella has it – what's she planning on doing with it? What would be a big enough hit for the Russians and Syrians to trust in Gabriella?

With one knee on the ground, Lauren looked at the polonium and looked at President Miller's schedule.

That's it.

She's not here to kill me.

She would have done that already.

She's here to kill the former President.

Gabriella's audacity floored Lauren. She thought it was a bold move to strike a former American president on American soil. The blowback would be serious, but the damage would be done and Gabriella would recover her reputation in Caracas.

SLAM!

Lauren jerked her head up at the sound of the apartment door closing. She quickly put the polonium and the syringe back into the chair leg and screwed it on to the chair. She slid the chair back in place at the desk. Lauren grabbed her bag, pulled out her gun, and steadied herself.

She listened carefully.

Lauren could hear distinct movements – a jacket landing on the couch, a purse on the coffee table, a set of keys on the kitchen countertop.

The person walked toward the bedrooms.

Lauren raised her gun.

"Gabriella – are you home?"

The person's steps grew closer.

"You there, Gabriella?"

Lauren quickly lowered her arm. She slid her gun into her Kate Spade handbag. She stepped out of Gabriella's room smiling.

"Hi, I'm sorry to scare you… I'm Lauren. I'm a classmate of Gabriella's."

"Oh … Hi. Is she here?"

"Oh . . . no . . . She . . . uh . . . just left."

"Does she know you are here?"

"Oh yeah. Of course. She let me in. I just came over to borrow a book. She was rushing out and couldn't find it. But she said to just look myself."

"Sounds typical. She's always running off somewhere. Was she with her boyfriend?"

"Boyfriend?"

"Yeah, the Congressman. A creepy old guy who's always lingering around."

"Uh, yeah. They were off somewhere."

"It's so gross. Gabriella's a nice girl. I don't know what she is doing with that creepster," said the girl, rolling her eyes.

After discovering the polonium and the former President's schedule, Lauren knew exactly what Gabriella was doing with a man twice her age.

"So what book did you come to borrow?"

"It was . . . uh . . .," started Lauren. Her eyes scanned the bookshelf for any book that she could quickly make a connection with. "That's it," said Lauren, grabbing a book about Lebanon off of the shelf.

"Lebanon, huh?"

"Yeah, I was thinking about heading there for fall break and Gabriella said that she had a book I could borrow."

"Is it safe over there?"

Lauren looked down at the book, paused for a moment, and then looked up at the roommate.

"About as safe as South Bend," said Lauren, with just a touch of irony. "Well, I better get going."

"Do you want me to tell her anything when she gets back?"

"You don't have to. I will see her soon enough."

"Congressman, they're ready for you."

"Just give me one second," responded Mike O'Riordan gruffly

"Certainly, sir," said O'Riordan's Press Secretary, exiting the room and closing the door behind him.

O'Riordan lay sprawled on a couch in a backstage dressing room, drinking a bottle of water. His feet were up on a coffee table. Gabriella sat perched next to him. Her hand rested on his thigh.

The couple had spent the previous six hours at Gabriella's dorm room, slipping in and out of naps. All of the emotional ups and downs from the last two days had taken their toll. They were both struggling to find the energy for this debate.

O'Riordan had been scheduled to spend the afternoon prepping for the debate, instead of lounging in Gabriella's bed. His staff had wanted O'Riordan to rehearse his talking points. Advisors saw this debate as a final opportunity to hammer the campaign's narrative – that O'Riordan was a serious and credible family man, while Jimmy was a naïve, out-of-touch political climber.

O'Riordan, as he had confided to Jaworski, had a bigger weapon up his sleeve. He was so confident that it would finish Jimmy King that he didn't feel the need to prep for anything. Plus, he much preferred spending time with Gabriella.

The downtime with Gabriella had also given O'Riordan the chance to change the suit and tie that he had been wearing for the last two days. For tonight, he wore the standard federal government uniform – black suit, white starched shirt, red tie. The only flair came from his wrists.

O'Riordan sported a pair of antique cufflinks embossed with the figure of a matador. They had been a gift from Gabriella to stroke his ego. She told him that he carried himself like a matador – calm, confident, and one step ahead of enemies. The cufflinks, she said, were a reminder of what he was fighting against – hard charging and obstinate foes attacking from all angles.

He loved the cufflinks and her little soliloquy about why she bought them. It played into his romantic obsession with Latin America. He envisioned himself a modern day matador when he gave speeches on the floor of the House of Representatives or when he sparred with reporters at nationally televised press conferences. The cufflinks on his wrists signaled that he was prepared for a fight.

"Are you ready for tonight?" asked Gabriella.

O'Riordan nodded in response. He had a steely look in his eyes.

"Will you go through with the plan?"

O'Riordan nodded again.

O'Riordan and Gabriella were being held in a backstage dressing room at Notre Dame's DeBartolo Performing Arts Center, a $63 million state-of-the-art arena.

The debate had been initially scheduled for DeBartolo's intimate 80-seat Penote Performers Hall, a venue used predominately for classes and recitals. News about Mary O'Riordan and the close race between O'Riordan and Jimmy had bolstered interest in the event. Supporters in both camps sought tickets. The national media requested press credentials. The debate organizers – WNDU television station, the *South Bend Tribune*, and Notre Dame's Rooney Center for the Study of American Democracy – were forced to move to the 360-seat Decio Mainstage Theater.

"Sorry, sir, but they need you in the holding spot," said O'Riordan's Press Secretary, barging into the dressing room again.

"Okay, I'm coming."

O'Riordan stood up from the couch and started walking toward the door. Gabriella grabbed his hand as he walked away. He stopped and turned back towards her.

"The plan?" she asked.

For the third time, O'Riordan silently nodded his head.

He followed his Press Secretary through a maze of hallways. Pictures of famous entertainers that had graced DeBartolo's halls lined the walls. A television camera crew followed them to the edge of the theater's stage, where a woman in her mid-thirties wearing a television headset waited for them.

"Hi Congressman, I'm Shelley – an assistant television producer with WNDU. The Bears just threw a Hail Mary to send the game into overtime. The station wants to carry the debate live, immediately after the game is over, so we don't lose any viewers. An NFL overtime game could be over at any moment. That's why we want to hold you here. The station wants to be ready to go right away."

"How long do you want to hold me?" asked O'Riordan, with a hint of annoyance in his voice.

"It hopefully won't be any longer than five minutes."

"Fine," said O'Riordan, letting out an audible sigh.

"Can I get you anything?"

"No, I'll just wait."

O'Riordan stood by himself, listening to the noise of the crowd. It was a packed house and the energy in the room was audible. O'Riordan peered around the curtain and saw people standing in the aisles.

"And we're going to hold you right here because

the Bears game is just about be over."

O'Riordan turned to see the WNDU producer ushering Jimmy King to the side of the stage right next to him. The debate organizers hadn't thought to use two separate entrances for the candidates. The plan had been to usher them directly to the stage from their dressing rooms. They hadn't factored in the game running into overtime.

"Um . . . sure," said Jimmy as he looked over at O'Riordan.

O'Riordan took a long look at Jimmy.

It was the first time O'Riordan had come face-to-face with his youthful challenger. His initial reaction was amazement. He could not believe that Jimmy looked even younger in the flesh than he did on television.

This kid barely looks out of his teenage years.

The more he looked at Jimmy, the more his amazement turned to disgust. O'Riordan couldn't believe that he was losing to this kid.

I'm a fifteen term Member of Congress. I've brought home a lot of federal funding to this district. I've served the people of Northern Indiana well, and they pay me back by supporting this kid?

"Hi, I'm Jimmy," stated Jimmy, sticking his hand out in a matter-of-fact way.

O'Riordan took another long look at Jimmy, ignored his hand and turned his back to him. He folded his arms across his chest as a look of contempt crept over his face. He had nothing to say to the kid. He went back to staring at the stage. But now, he thought less about the electricity of the crowd than about how it was humanly possible that he was losing to this amateur.

The pair stood in silence

"The Bears just missed a field goal. The Eagles are about to get the ball," said the WNDU producer, appearing again and darting away quickly.

Jimmy saw an opening to sidle up next to O'Riordan. The two men stood shoulder-to-shoulder, without looking at each other. They both remained focused on the stage.

"You know . . . I'm . . . uh . . . real sorry about what happened to Mary," Jimmy stammered. His words hung in the air.

After a long pause, O'Riordan spoke up, without any hint of emotion.

"And why would you be sorry?"

"I . . . uh . . . I just feel bad, that's all."

"Why would *you* feel bad?" said O'Riordan, starting to get annoyed.

"I just feel bad. Okay? I didn't mean anything by it."

"Why would you apologize then if you didn't mean anything by it?" asked O'Riordan, continuing to needle Jimmy. O'Riordan knew that Jimmy was sincere, but he was using it as an opportunity to get inside his head.

"Hey I didn't have anything to do with what happened to Mary," said Jimmy, pushing back slightly.

O'Riordan had remained focused on the stage up until this comment. He turned toward Jimmy and leaned into Jimmy's face. Jimmy could feel O'Riordan's breath on his face.

"Look, I don't care whether you did it or not. But they'll care," said O'Riordan, pointing to the audience. "And that's all that matters."

"What?" said Jimmy, shocked by O'Riordan's comment. "You can't do that. You can't make people think I had something to do with Mary's attack."

"I can and I will," said O'Riordan, seething with anger.

"But that's a lie! That's not fair!" protested Jimmy, his voice growing shrill.

"That's not fair? That's not fair? I'll tell you what's not fair, you little turd. Some kid coming out of nowhere to lead in this election. That's not fair. This is my district, kid. I've represented it for thirty years. I've given everything I have to the people of Northern Indiana. I'm not about to lay it down and lose to you now."

O'Riordan's face was flushed red with anger.

"And I'll tell you something else," continued O'Riordan. "You had better drop out of this race . . ."

"Or else what? You're going to let people think that I attacked your daughter?"

"Eagles are on their five yard line. It looks like they are about to score."

The men turned to the WNDU producer as she darted in and out of the holding area again.

"I'm going out there tonight and telling everyone that you know I wasn't involved," said Jimmy.

"And who is the audience going to believe? Some kid who happened to be at the same bar as the victim on Friday night? Or a grieving father who has spent every waking minute at his daughter's bed side?"

"I'm asking for an apology too, for the cops harassing me this morning."

"You do that, and this morning will be nothing in comparison to what you will go through in the next few days."

"What I'll go through in the next few days? Are you threatening me?"

"You have a choice. You can get out of the race now and keep your name clean for a future run for office," said O'Riordan through gritted teeth.

"Or what?" asked Jimmy, naively.

"Or . . ."

The WNDU staffer barged into the holding area, cutting O'Riordan off.

"Hi. Game just finished. Bears won. We're going live in ten seconds. Congressman, you're on," said the WNDU producer, giving O'Riordan a gentle nudge onto the stage.

"Or what?" called out Jimmy, watching O'Riordan walk on to the stage and work the crowd, smiling and waving to people in the audience.

"Would you mind getting me a drink, Son?"

Father Finnegan sat on the couch in George and Lauren DeMarco's living room. He no longer looked like the disheveled drunk who had passed out on the floor the night before. His wet hair was slicked back. His crumpled and stained priest's uniform was in the washer and dryer. He wore a pair of George's Harvard boxing sweats. Father Finnegan appeared to have a fresh start.

After the roller coaster ride of the last twenty-four hours, George had figured that he needed a fresh start as well. He would only be able to help Father Finnegan if he was thinking clearly. The first thing he needed to do was clear the house of the priest's offensive smell.

Once George was able to get Jimmy King out of the house, he went to work. He rounded up a bar of soap, a wash cloth and a bath towel. He gave the stack to Father Finnegan with the polite suggestion that he might "feel better" if he had a shower and a change of clothes.

The priest didn't detect George's ulterior motives. Smiling, he grabbed the stack and thanked George for being such a courteous host. George, fighting back the overpowering smell, added that he would leave some clothes on his bed.

George hadn't intended to put the priest in a pair of Harvard sweat pants. But they were the only item in his wardrobe that would fit the priest's rotund frame. Father Finnegan hadn't protested. He rather liked the psychological boost from the athletic gear.

As Father Finnegan emerged from the guest bedroom in his new attire, George laughed. The stumbling drunk now walked with his chest puffed out. George admired the fact that this priest hadn't lost his sense of humor, despite all that had happened in the last day.

But Father Finnegan's request for another drink did not impress George.

"Um . . . Father . . . I . . . uh . . . don't mean to be rude, but don't you think you might want to lay off the booze for a night? You know . . . considering all that's been going on?"

George ventured cautiously. He didn't want to offend him.

"Son," began Father Finnegan, as he turned to look George in the eyes. "It's not the drinking that got me into this mess . . . it's the guilt."

George did not know how to respond. Judging by the look on Father Finnegan's face, George knew he was sincere. Why he felt so guilty or drank so much was beyond George. He wasn't about to psychoanalyze him now.

George hurried to the kitchen and pulled out a Coors Light can from the back of the fridge. It was the only alcohol he had left. He grabbed it, not bothering to ask if it would be acceptable.

The two men had been waiting for the start of the televised debate between Jimmy King and Mike O'Riordan. George didn't want to miss a second of it. He was hoping that one of the candidates might reveal something about the predicament Father Finnegan was in – either through a candid word or a gesture. George knew that it was no coincidence that he had been followed by the Colts' fans after taking in the priest. And when Jimmy King showed up on his doorstep, George was convinced that all of the events were somehow connected.

After Jimmy left, George had done some digging on him. George only vaguely remembered Jimmy from D.C.

He called a handful of trusted Harvard and D.C. friends to get a better sense of Jimmy's personality. They all had the same response – nerdy, awkward, ambitious, at times arrogant and dismissive of others.

Would this be the type of person to violently attack his opponent's daughter?

The question played on George's mind.

"What'd I miss?" asked George, handing the Coors Light to Father Finnegan on the couch.

"Football game just finished. Bears stopped the Eagles on their five. When they got the ball, the Bears quarterback threw on a toss into the back of the end zone. Looks like the debate will start at any minute."

George grabbed the remote and turned up the volume. As he did, a loud knock came from the front door.

The two men looked at each other nervously.

"Who do you think it is?" asked Father Finnegan.

"I don't know. But don't move or say anything," whispered George.

George didn't budge from the couch. He stayed focused on the TV. The football game ended. The broadcast switched live to DeBartolo. George tried not to let Father Finnegan's nervous face distract him.

KNOCK-KNOCK-KNOCK.

The knocks continued, louder and faster now.

Father Finnegan's face grew more worried. George kept staring at the television. A beaming and waving Mike O'Riordan walked on to Decio's stage.

KNOCK-KNOCK-KNOCK.

Louder and faster again.

George watched Jimmy King walk onto stage. The kid looked less confident and radiant than O'Riordan. George wondered whether their outward appearances had any connection to what had been going on.

KNOCK-KNOCK-KNOCK.

167

This final series of knocking broke George's concentration. He turned to Father Finnegan, put a single finger to his lips and walked quietly and slowly to the front door.

Approaching the window, the man behind the door caught George's eye. George had been spotted. He couldn't hide now. He had to open the door.

"Uh . . . can I help you?" asked George.

"Hi, I am with the Jimmy King for Congress Campaign. We're going door-to-door to tell people a little bit about Jimmy. You mind if I come in?"

The tall, muscular man with the buzz cut appeared to be in his late 30's. He sported a Notre Dame Starter jacket, a pair of blue jeans, work boots and a five o'clock shadow. He didn't have any materials identifying him with King. No fliers or bumper stickers. He didn't look like the little old, blue-haired ladies that made up Jimmy's core group of volunteers.

Running on adrenalin, George had somehow missed this fact. He was focused on getting rid of the guy as quickly as possible.

"Sorry, we're not registered to vote here," said George.

The man hesitated.

"Well, uh, you can pick up a registration form on Election Day. Please, it will only take a few minutes of your time."

George detected aggression in his voice. It finally set off an alarm bell.

"Sorry, we're not going to vote this year. Have a good night," said George, closing the door as he spoke.

The man wedged his foot into the door.

"I'm sorry. You're gonna have to leave now," insisted George.

The man didn't say anything. He pulled open his

jacket to reveal a Smith and Wesson .357 Magnum Revolver tucked into his waist. With his head, he motioned for George to back away from the door.

If he hadn't caught him off guard, George would have dropped him right there. George put his hands in the air and slowly stepped backward. The man followed George into the house. He closed the door behind him and locked it.

"What's going on?" called out Father Finnegan, still sitting on the couch.

The man pulled the gun from out of his waist. He pointed it at George, and then motioned for George to sit on the couch. George did not move.

"Sit," said the man in a terse tone.

George still refused to budge. He stood motionless in the middle of the living room.

"Don't give me no problems. I've only come for him," said the man, glaring at Father Finnegan.

George and Father Finnegan looked at each other. George calculated what moves he could make.

"Don't think about trying anything," warned the man again. "I only came for the priest. You don't need to be a hero."

How'd he know Father Finnegan, decked out in Harvard boxing sweats, was a priest?

George and the man stood face-to-face, about four feet from each other. The man continued to point the gun directly at George. Neither budged.

The room was silent, aside from the debate on the television. The cameras cut back and forth between Jimmy King, Mike O'Riordan, and the moderators. The crowd erupted in applause for O'Riordan.

George continued to stall. He did not want to give in to this guy. He wanted more time to see what connections there might be between the congressional candidates and this random man. He also wanted to figure out why this man, who claimed to be with the Jimmy King campaign, was demanding that Father Finnegan go with him.

"George, it's okay. You've done enough. Let me go with him," said Father Finnegan.

The man looked at Father Finnegan. George kept his eyes on the man and his gun. He kept his arms in the air.

RATTLE.

As Father Finnegan stood up from the couch, the sound of keys jangled at the door. The three men stood frozen as the keys entered the lock. Father Finnegan looked nervously again at George.

The man moved quickly to George and shoved him to sit down on the couch. He thrust the gun in Father Finnegan's face and signaled for him to join George on the couch. The man himself backed up to the wall. He stood out of sight from the front door. He motioned for the two men to be quiet.

All three men waited patiently.

"George! George!" said Lauren DeMarco, walking through the door. "You won't believe . . ."

Lauren stopped in her tracks as she entered the living room.

". . . what is about to go down," she said as her voice trailed off and she saw the man with the .357 Magnum.

She reached into her Kate Spade handbag.

The man put the barrel of the gun up against her head.

"Don't try anything."

Lauren calmly removed her hand from her handbag and placed it on the ground. She raised her hands in the air. She lowered herself slowly onto the couch between George and Father Finnegan.

"Let's go, Father."

Lauren turned to Father Finnegan with a curious look on her face. Then she turned to George. George continued staring at the man.

Father Finnegan exhaled deeply and stood up. He closed his eyes and bowed his head. To himself, he whispered a prayer to Saint Michael, the angel that led God's armies against Satan in the Book of Revelation.

"Saint Michael the Archangel, defend us in battle, be our protection against the malice and snares of the devil. May God rebuke him we humbly pray; and do thou, O Prince of the Heavenly host, by the power of God, thrust into hell Satan and all evil spirits who wander through the world for the ruin of souls. Amen."

"Time to go, Father."

The man grabbed Father Finnegan by the shoulders and forced him toward the door. He kept his gun pointed at George and Lauren. The pair remained on the couch.

"Don't worry . . . this will all be over on Tuesday," said the man as he backed away from George and Lauren.

The couple sat motionless on the couch, wondering what he meant.

The man kept his .357 Magnum pointed at them as he exited the house with Father Finnegan. He closed the door behind him on the way out and tucked the gun back into his waist.

George and Lauren jumped off of the couch and raced to the window. They watched as the man guided Father Finnegan down the block. A plain white van waited at the corner of Wakewa and Iroquois. The side door flung open and the man pushed Father Finnegan into the back of the vehicle.

George turned to Lauren.

"You've gotta go after him," said Lauren flatly.

Without saying a word, George grabbed his keys,

wallet, and cell phone and raced out the front door.

MONDAY

Chapter 23
Monday
5:00 a.m.

Father Finnegan yawned and rolled his head upward. His body clock told him to wake up, but his eyes were glued shut.

He yawned again, this time grimacing in pain.

With his eyes still closed, he counted the throbs that reverberated through his head. His stiff body made it a struggle to shift his weight around. He felt terrible.

He went to wipe the sleep out of his eyes. Trying to raise his right hand to his face, he discovered that his hands had been cuffed behind his back with duct tape. The discovery pumped a small amount of adrenaline through his body.

He forced his eyes open.

Where am I?

Pushing through the pain, Father Finnegan's eyes shifted around. He tried to take in his surroundings. In the darkness of the morning, nothing looked familiar.

He knew he was inside of a building. He heard the sound of rats scurrying around on the cold, cement floor. He could not determine anything more.

He was used to waking up in random locations. Usually, the local bartenders were good about ordering him a cab at the end of a long evening. Other times, Father Finnegan stumbled out before anyone could help him. Attempting to find his way home, he would inevitably get lost, pass out, and wake up at 5:00 a.m. in a location that was not Sorin Hall.

His first thought this morning was that it had happened once again. He figured he would dust himself off and get on his way home. But the duct tape and the dark room quickly told him that this was a different situation.

His second thought was that he had been arrested. When he discovered himself next to a bloodied and bruised Mary O'Riordan, he had anticipated being arrested at any moment. Being rescued by George gave him a temporary reprieve.

He had not expected George to keep him safe forever. The time simply allowed Father Finnegan to prepare himself mentally for the arrest. Now, sitting with his hands cuffed behind his back, he thought that moment had finally arrived.

As he struggled to decipher his surroundings, his fears slowly wore off. He was not in a jail cell. He was not even in a police department. He was in some kind of an abandoned building. More importantly, he did not know why.

What am I doing here?

He wracked his brain to remember the previous evening. He figured he had to have been drinking. That is what he did every night. So he thought about alcohol.

Coors Light. That's it.

He remembered that he had not gotten drunk. He only had one Coors Light.

So how did I end up here?

He remembered drinking the Coors Light in George's living room while watching the debate. He distinctly remembered the knock at the door. Then, one-by-one, the events of the previous night came back to him. He slowly replayed it all in his head.

First the knocks on the door. Then George talking to the person at the door. The unknown gunmen forcing his way into the house. The standoff between George and the gunman. Lauren's arrival and the continued standoff. Relenting to the gunman. Walking out of the house. Hurried pace down the sidewalk.

Shoved into the back of an empty van. Gun-man jumping on top of me. Wrestling me to the van floor. Smashing my head against the van's hard floor. Body bruised from the manhandling. Black sack thrown over my head. Hands pulled behind back. Duct tape wrapped around wrists. Smashed again as the gunman picked him-self up.

Van taking off. Someone other than the gunman driving. Driving only a short distance and then transfer-ring to another car. Driving around South Bend. Taking too many turns to count. Driving in the second car for a longer period of time.

Finally arriving at this location. No idea where I am. Still only the gunman and the other person. Can-not detect any other people. Taken inside of a building. Forced into a chair and left here alone. No sense as to whether anyone else was around or if left by self.

Father Finnegan groggily struggled to keep his eyes open. It took him several seconds to adjust to the morn-ing darkness. The black sack, which had been covering his face, now lay at his feet. Looking directly above, Father Finnegan could see the yellowish hue of the moon through a cracked skylight. It was strong enough to illuminate only parts of the building.

When his vision came into focus, he scanned the room. Off in the distance his eyes followed a trail of what looked to be conveyor belts. Through the empty darkness, he traced the outline of several levers that dotted the con-veyor belts at various intervals. It was enough to give him an idea of where he was.

What am I doing in a factory?

He had a hard time holding his head up as a result of the continuous pounding. Craning his neck to look around the factory exacerbated his pain. He was not a muscular man, but he was so sore he thought he could feel every muscle in his body.

His physical pain was not even as bad as his emotional pain. He had been in a fragile state for the last two days. He had tried to put on a brave show for George and Lauren. Inside, however, the worry and guilt had been eating away at him. The confusion from waking up in an unknown factory and not knowing why was the last straw.

Father Finnegan slumped over in his chair. He eyes welled up with tears. He had reached his breaking point.

When Father Finnegan had woken at 5:00 a.m. in the past, confused about his surroundings and struggling with a hangover, he never worried. He knew that each day provided a fresh opportunity to make amends with the Lord and atone for his sinful ways.

Today was different. He feared that he would not get that chance for redemption. He feared that his drinking may have done him in once and for all.

With those concerns at the front of his mind, he resorted to what he did every morning that he woke up at 5:00 a.m. He prayed.

This morning was easier than others to select his prayerful intentions. He prayed for help from the patron saint of lost causes, Saint Jude.

"Oh blessed Jude, who was with the Lord Jesus at the Last Supper, be with me during my final hours. Pray for my desperate soul so that I can atone for my wretched and miserable ways. Ask the Lord to shine his graces upon me and to save me from Satan's curse."

His voice trailed off at the end of his prayer. He listened intently for the movements around him. Above the sound of scurrying rats, he could sense that another person was in the room.

"Who's there?" he called out.

Father Finnegan squinted into the distance. He

179

detected a human in the shadows. It remained too dark to decipher the person's face. Slowly the person moved closer and closer.

"I didn't do it," insisted Father Finnegan.

The person crept closer.

"Please spare my soul," pleaded Father Finnegan, desperately.

The person stopped about five feet from Father Finnegan. With the illumination from the moon's hue, Father Finnegan was able to make out the man's face. He had not seen that face in years, yet he recognized it immediately.

"What . . . What are you doing here? I haven't seen you in . . ."

"Fifteen years," interjected Jaworski.

"You've got to let me go," begged the startled priest. "I didn't do anything to that girl."

"I know you didn't do it, Father," responded Jaworski.

The response confused Father Finnegan.

"So what am I doing here? You've got to let me go. You've got to help me clear my name."

"Not just yet."

"But if you know that I'm innocent, then you've got to help me."

"You've got to help me first," responded Jaworski.

"What do you mean?"

"You've been holding some information for fifteen years now."

"What?" responded Father Finnegan.

It took him several seconds but then he realized what Jaworski was referencing.

"I told the police everything I knew . . . I helped them find your son's body . . . I did everything I could."

"You didn't do everything, Father."

"What do you mean? I did. I swear to the Good Lord that I did."

"Not everything. You've got a name."

It dawned on Father Finnegan what Bob Jaworski sought. The initial relief from recognizing a familiar face now turned to defiance. Father Finnegan realized why he was in this situation and what he could to do get out of it. But he knew that he had taken a vow.

"I'm sorry. I just can't."

"Father, this can be real easy. You tell me the name and it's over. I know you didn't attack that girl."

"How do you know that?"

"A few of my guys were at the 'Backer on Friday night. We knew you were going to be there."

"So you set me up?" asked Father Finnegan in disbelief.

"They knew you would get too drunk and not remember a thing."

"What about the girl?"

"They had not planned on it being Mary. We had someone else in mind. But when she started talking to you, that's who they targeted. She put up a bit of a fight when she walked outside the 'Backer, even pulling a knife. My guys eventually got her under control, but not before getting stabbed in the abdomen."

"Is that why she looked all bruised and battered?"

Jaworski stood there, without responding or showing any emotion.

"So you're blackmailing me?"

"Father, like I said, this is real easy. You just have to tell me the name and its all over."

"And if I don't?"

"I'll personally drop you off at the South Bend Police Station and let the cops know that this is the alcoholic who attacked a congressman's daughter and went on the run."

Father Finnegan understood Jaworski's point. No one would believe that he was innocent. He did not have to look in a mirror to know that he was a pathetic site. The thought depressed him.

"I can't do it," replied Father Finnegan in a hushed tone.

"Father, you don't have much of a choice in this situation."

"I just can't," he softly insisted, while letting his head slump down again.

Jaworski stepped in from the dark shadows. He forced himself within inches of the priest. He made sure that Father Finnegan was looking him directly in the eyes and could see the anger in his face.

"Father, I'm not here to play games. I've spent the last fifteen years of my life trying to track down my son's killer. When they closed his casket, I made a vow that I would hunt down the person who did this and bring them to justice. Not a day has gone by in my life that I haven't thought about my son . . . that I haven't heard his voice in my ears . . . that I haven't seen his face smiling back at me. As a father, I am not going to let my son down."

"I understand your pain," replied Father Finnegan, honestly.

The death of Jaworski's son had inflicted an intense amount of distress on the priest. That distress was amplified by not being able to share all of the details of the murderer's confession. Despite his valiant attempts to wash away the pain with alcohol, it gnawed inside him each and every day.

"Then tell me who did it."

"I can't . . . I took a vow."

Father Finnegan's comment appeared to anger Jaworski even further.

"Since when did you become such a disciplined man?"

"You may not think that I am much of a man at all, but I am still devoted to the Lord. When I accepted my calling to the ministry, I took several vows. The Sacrament of Reconciliation is a sacred seal between the Lord and the members of his flock. I vowed to uphold that sacramental trust and to welcome the fallen back into the arms of the Lord."

Jaworski took a step back.

"Well Father, I just confessed how I got you into this situation. So looks like if you are not willing to share the information about my son, then I'm not willing to let you share the information about Mary O'Riordan."

Father Finnegan did not respond. He did not need to respond. He knew what Jaworski was implying by this comment.

"Like I said, this is real easy. You tell me who confessed to killing my son and I'll let you share my confession with the cops."

Father Finnegan continued to stare crestfallen at Jaworski. There was not much to discuss. Father Finnegan knew that he had made several vows in his life that he had broken. Every day he vowed not to drink alcohol, and the next morning he always woke up drunk.

This vow, however, was different. This was a vow that he had made with the Lord. And, despite his personal weaknesses, Father Finnegan was not about to betray the Lord's trust.

Father Finnegan remained silent as he listened to Jaworski talk.

"You don't have to make this decision right now, Father. I'll give you some time. But one way or the other, I'm going to fulfill that promise I made to my son."

BANG!

The slamming of the front door jolted Lauren awake. She deftly jumped off of the couch and on to one knee. She aimed her P239 at the entryway leading into the house.

"George?"

Lauren relaxed when she saw her husband step into the living room. She had been sleeping on the couch as a precautionary move. She wanted to be closer to strike if anyone approached the house. She had not expected George to wake her up.

"What's wrong?"

George did not respond as he threw his keys across the room in frustration. He did not need to say anything for Lauren to grasp his anger. She had seen several outbursts before to be prepared for what was about to come.

Lauren never faulted George for his emotional outbursts. She knew that it all stemmed from his tumultuous childhood. And, more importantly, there was nothing malicious about George. The outbursts only came about because of frustration.

Not bothering to pick up his keys, George slumped down into a chair in the corner of the living room.

"I drove all over town. No sign of the van, no sign of that gunman, and no sign of Father Finnegan," said George, the frustration oozing out with every word.

Lauren let him sit and defuse for a few moments before she spoke up.

"You did your best. It's okay."

"It's not okay, Lauren," insisted George, passionately. "I assured Father Finnegan that I would sort this all out. And I just let him get snatched like that, right from our own house?"

"It's not your fault."

"But it is. I made a promise. It was the least that I could do after everything that Father Finnegan has done for me."

"George, you got to go easier on yourself, how were you supposed to know that the priest was gonna be kidnapped?"

"I didn't even do anything. I just stood there and let that guy walk right out of here with him."

"What were you supposed to do? Take him head on when's got a .357 Magnum pointed straight at you? That would have been dumb. You definitely would have gotten yourself killed, Father Finnegan killed, and probably me killed in the process. Is that what you wanted?" asked Lauren, pushing back a bit on George.

George realized that she had a point. He had made the promise to Father Finnegan. But he never wanted to put his wife's life at risk.

"I just . . . I just wish that there was more I could have done."

"You still can. Remember what that guy said?"

George looked at Lauren curiously.

"He said that this will all be over on Tuesday," said Lauren, answering her own question.

"Yeah, what'd he mean by that?"

"I have no clue, but at least it buys you another day."

"You're right," said George, getting up from his chair. "I gotta get back out there."

"Easy, George . . . there's something that I need to tell you."

185

"What's that?"

"I heard on the news last night that the FBI is going to start investigating the case."

"Really?"

"They were saying that it's become a federal issue because it involves a Congressman's family member and they think it is tied somehow to the congressional election."

"So what does that mean exactly?"

"It means that you can probably expect a visit from the FBI."

"Seriously? How would they even know to come here?" asked George.

"They'll work it out eventually. And when they do, they'll want to talk to you," said Lauren, in a matter-of-fact tone.

"So what do I do?" asked George. He knew that she had dealt with FBI counterparts when she had worked at the Counterterrorism Center. She would have a better grasp of what the FBI agents wanted and how to remain calm giving it to them.

"Tell the FBI what they want to hear."

"And what's that?"

"Enough to give them some other leads. They need to cross you off their 'persons of interest' list so that they can move on to someone else."

"How exactly do I do that?"

"Just explain to them how you ran into Father Finnegan walking around the lake. Give a good description of what he looked like. Then tell them you went to Macri's, got a sandwich, and came home for the game. The priest didn't go into Macri's with you, right? So there must be some girl behind the counter or even some surveillance footage that can verify you were by yourself."

"Why don't I want to tell them the whole story?"

"Because otherwise they will keep you locked up

until they find Father Finnegan."

George nodded his head to signal that he understood.

"Listen, the only way that priest is gonna be found is if you are out on the ground. We ran into this all the time when I was in Iraq. Every wannabe terrorist tried to kidnap anyone affiliated with the West – journalists, aid workers, contractors, you name it. A lot of times we weren't successful. The times we did manage to get our hostage back, we had people on the ground that knew the hostage. We had people who could ID someone suspicious and either pinpoint a location or get that suspicious person to give up the location."

"So what does that mean for me?"

"First, you need to be fresh. It's been a long last two days and its going to be a long next two days ahead of us. Catch your breath this morning. Take a nap. Then second, get back out there. See if you recognize anything or anyone suspicious – that gunman from last night, the white van, a Harvard boxing sweatshirt in a bush – anything that might help."

"You want me to just drive around South Bend? What good will that do?"

"Don't just drive around South Bend aimlessly. Start with a lead. You said you ran into some guy in Father Finnegan's room that was wearing a Teamsters jacket, right? So why don't you go to the Teamster headquarters to see if you recognize the guy from Finnegan's room or the guy who showed up here last night."

"And what if I don't find anything?"

"You've got forty-eight hours until we are in serious trouble. Don't worry about anything before then."

"Serious trouble, huh?"

Lauren hesitated to respond.

"Let's not worry about that right now."

187

The pair stared at each other silently. The bond between them had grown intensely over the past year. Each of them drew on the other as a source of strength and inspiration. With the turmoil of the last two days, they had come to rely on each other even more.

"Hey what's all this 'we' business?" asked George, breaking the silence. "I thought you had issues of your own to worry about."

"George – I love you. I made a vow I'd be there whenever you needed me. I've been in these types of situations countless times. We'll figure this out together."

"Okay," said George. "But what about last night?"

"What do you mean?"

"When you came rushing in the door, you started to say something, but you were obviously cut off."

"Oh yeah . . . I . . . uh . . . think you have enough on your plate to worry about right now."

"C'mon . . . you can't do that."

"What do you mean?"

"You can't give me some pep talk about being there to support me and then let me feel like a ratbag for not supporting you," insisted George.

"Well . . . you don't have to worry about the Fox killing me."

"That's good news. Why aren't you happy?"

"I mean . . . at least she won't kill me for the time being."

"Okay, why not?"

"At least I don't think so."

"You don't think so?"

"I think she has a bigger target in mind than me."

"A bigger target? Why are you being so cryptic? Just spit it all out."

"George, I think she's here to kill former President Miller."

188

"Seriously?"

He watched as Lauren nodded in response.

"How do you know that?" asked George.

"Well, when I was in her apartment yesterday . . ."

"You were in her apartment?" interjected George. "What were you doing? How did you get in?"

"I broke in. How else do you think I do these things? But don't worry about that. No one saw me but two of her neighbors and her roommate."

"Wait, you're kidding me, right? You broke into her apartment and several people identified you doing it?"

"Not exactly. I mean . . . they didn't see me break in. The neighbors saw me outside the apartment."

"And what about the roommate?"

"She came home while I was in the Fox's bedroom."

George tried to suspend his whole disbelief about the situation. He did not like the idea of her running around South Bend, breaking into people's apartments. But again, he had come to trust and rely on Lauren. He knew she would not do anything stupid or at least nothing too risky.

"How'd you pull that one off?"

"I told her that the Fox let me in to get a book, but that the Fox had to leave."

"The roommate bought it?"

"Of course she did," said Lauren. "So anyways, before the roommate got there, I was searching the Fox's room. I wasn't looking for anything specific. I just wanted to look for any clues that confirmed she was here to kill me."

"But you didn't find anything specific?"

"Not specifically, no. What I did find was a vial of polonium-210."

"What's that?"

"It's a radioactive element that can be lethal when

you inject it into someone. It causes a really nasty death. And what's worse is that it is odorless and colorless, so tough to detect."

"That sounds like pretty serious stuff. How'd she get her hands on it?"

"Probably from the Syrians. The Russians used it to take out a journalist a few years back. Seeing as how Russia props up Syria and how Syria props up Hezbollah and how the Fox was in the thick of Hezbollah, that would be my most likely guess."

"So she could just get this stuff like picking up cough medicine?"

"Probably not that easy. Some higher-ups in Hezbollah and in Syria's General Security Directorate would have to vouch for her. And they wouldn't just turn it over for her to use on the playground. She'd have to do something big with it. And Russia would have to be able to distance themselves from her."

"What do you mean 'something big?'"

"So yeah, that's where President Miller comes in. The Fox had the line-by-line schedule for the former President's visit to Notre Dame tonight."

"He's coming for an O'Riordan rally, right?"

"Yeah, that's right, and the Fox had a detailed account of where the former President is supposed to be at each minute of his trip. She also had designs and schematics of all the buildings where he is planning to be – the new hockey arena, the airport. She knows every single step that he will take on this visit."

"So you really think she's going to kill the former President of the United States?"

"She's got the polonium. And killing the former President would be big. I just cannot figure out what else she would do with that stuff. Other than kill me . . ."

George gave her an annoyed look.

"C'mon, if she wanted to kill me and do it with po-lonium, she probably would have already done it by now," said Lauren.

George just shook his head in annoyance. He did not want to hear her macabre talk.

"I mean it. If she wanted to kill me, I'd be dead or she would have at least tried. She hasn't attempted any-thing and that's because I think she has a bigger fish in mind. This is the only thing that seems to make sense."

The couple sat there, letting the possibility of an as-sassination soak in.

"So what are you going to do about it?" asked George.

He looked her in the eyes. He watched as she stood up from the couch. She did not say a word, but he knew what she was thinking. And it was not the response that he wanted to hear.

"No. Lauren, you can't. We went over this already. You can't just whack her," pleaded George.

Lauren did not say a word as she walked upstairs to their bedroom. George followed after her. She started to get changed out of her pajamas and into jeans.

"Why don't you just notify the Secret Service?" insisted George.

Lauren stopped changing and turned around to face George.

"You do realize that the FBI is probably going to be here in a few hours?" asked Lauren, rhetorically. "One person in the family with federal agents crawling up their ass is one too many. If you expect to save Father Finnegan, then we don't need more attention from the feds."

George just stood there and listened quietly.

"Besides, as soon as federal agents start swarming, the Fox is going underground."

Lauren stopped talking to put on a fresh shirt. Now

fully dressed, she leaned in to George and softened her voice.

"George – she almost killed me once. You don't know what it's like to wake up every day and wonder if this is the day you will be assassinated . . . if this is the last day I will ever see you again. Whatever happens with the former President, she still wants to kill me. That's her only goal. Well, I'm sick of worrying about what ifs. I'm sick of worrying about her. I'm gonna finish all of this for good."

After a few seconds, he spoke up.

"So what can I do to help?"

"I'm up! I'm up!"

George flung his blanket off and swung his feet onto the ground. He rubbed his eyes and looked at his watch.

8:32.

I slept fourteen hours?

He stretched as a ray of sunshine came through the window and hit him on the face. He shielded his eyes from the brightness. He checked his watch again.

Oh . . . 8:32 a.m. I only slept two hours.

He stood up from the couch. He wore a pair of Harvard boxing sweatpants and a sweatshirt with a pair of white Nike ankle socks. He looked like Father Finnegan had looked the day before, albeit a younger, trimmer and sober version.

KNOCK-KNOCK-KNOCK.

"I'm coming," shouted George at his front door.

After he had spoken with Lauren this morning, he had curled up on the couch. Because he was so exhausted, he fell straight asleep. His plan was to blow off his morning classes to get some rest. He figured he would start looking for Father Finnegan again this afternoon. Those plans, like everything else that he had planned for this weekend, were thrown into disruption by whoever was knocking at the front door.

KNOCK-KNOCK-KNOCK.

"I said just a second," stated George firmly.

As he started to come to his senses, George steadied himself for whoever was behind that door. After last night's kidnapping, George did not want to be caught off guard. He ran to the kitchen and grabbed a knife.

He cautiously crept up to the front door. He held the knife behind his back, ready to spring into action. He slowly peered through the window to see who stood outside.

What's he doing here?

As George opened the door, Jimmy King pushed George to the side and stormed into the DeMarco's house, without even saying hello.

"They still believe it," said an exasperated Jimmy, as he paced around the room.

"What are you talking about?" asked George, not ready to handle another Jimmy King problem just yet and still hiding the knife behind his back.

"They still believe that I was somehow involved in this whole O'Riordan mess."

"What do you mean 'they still believe'? Who is 'they'?"

"People, George . . . people," said Jimmy, as he continued to pace around the room.

George took a deep breath. As much as he did not want to deal with Jimmy, or even had the patience to listen to him, he knew he had to address these problems now. The faster he got Jimmy under control, the faster he could get him out of the house. And the faster he got him out of the house, the faster he could get back to sleep.

"Okay, start from the beginning. What people think you are involved with Mary O'Riordan? Did someone say something to you?" asked George in a calm and soothing voice.

"George, people are talking. They're saying things. We've got to fix this mess."

George walked to the kitchen and put the knife back in the drawer. As he returned to the living room, Jimmy was still pacing and mumbling. George quickly lost his patience.

"Jimmy – calm down," said George sternly. "You gotta get yourself under control."

"You don't get it. It's my butt out there. Not yours."

George released a deep sigh.

He'll tire himself out, calm down, and be out of here shortly after that. Then I can get back to sleep.

"How come you aren't doing more to help me?" demanded Jimmy.

George was not sure if he was being serious, so he gave Jimmy a puzzled look.

"I thought you were going to help me resolve this situation. You told me you would help. You can't let me down George."

Apparently he is serious.

"I had to take care of some things," responded George.

"What could be more important than this election?"

You mean other than trying to find a kidnapped priest who may or may not be alive?

"I said, what could be more important than this election?"

Jimmy asking for the second time grated at George's nerves. George could deal with a wannabe politician, who was stressed out at the end of a long and tough campaign. He could not deal with a whiny and demanding kid pushing him around. It took all of his strength to keep his composure.

"What exactly would you like me to do?"

"Do whatever it is that you do," said Jimmy, without any hint of irony. "We need to start fighting back."

"It's not quite that simple. I can't just go around beating people up."

"Then why did you agree to help?"

195

•

George stood there thinking to himself that he really had not agreed to help. He had been forced into saying something by Jimmy, who was delirious yesterday and even more delirious today. George still could not believe that this was all happening.

"Look, Jimmy, I'm sorry if you thought that there was something specific I was going to do."

"Sorry? SORRY?" asked Jimmy, raising his voice. "I'M SORRY THAT I EVER TRUSTED YOU!"

George continued to stand in the middle of his living room staring at Jimmy. He did not know what had triggered this outburst or how to respond. He tried being calm. He tried being stern. He tried being apologetic. Nothing had worked.

Now he just wanted Jimmy out of his house. He did not want Jimmy as his problem anymore. He opened his mouth to tell Jimmy to leave when he saw Jimmy take a step back.

Jimmy looked startled. He slowly put his hands in the air. George turned to the front door to see what had startled Jimmy.

Staring back at George were two men in dark suits – an African-American male and a white male with a goatee. Both men were in their late thirties. They both had guns drawn. They slowly crept into the living room, not taking their eyes off George or Jimmy.

"Which one of you is George DeMarco?" asked the African-American.

Before the man had even finished his question, Jimmy was pointing at George.

George turned his entire body around to face the man. He sized them up and knew he was outnumbered and outgunned. He put his hands in the air.

"I'm George. Who are you guys?"

"FBI."

George's face gave a look of exasperation. He knew these guys were coming. But he didn't want to deal with them while Jimmy was still in the house.

"We heard shouting and the door was open so we came in."

George shot Jimmy an annoyed glance.

"You must be Jimmy King," said the African-American agent.

"I was just heading out," said Jimmy, as he started to walk toward the door.

"Not so fast," said the agent, thrusting the gun at Jimmy. "Why don't you both take seats on the couch."

"Can I see some identification, fellas?" asked George.

The two agents exchange glances with each other that said they did not want to be dealing with a law school student.

"Sure," responded the African-American, who did all of the talking for the two agents.

George waited as the men pulled wallets out of their inner suit pockets and opened them to reveal badges. George pretended to do a thorough inspection. He did this to buy some time to think and to assert himself before these agents.

"Okay, Agents Winters and Calvin. What can we help you with?"

"I think you know why we are here."

"No, why?" responded George as he shook his head no and feigned ignorance.

"George, where's Father Sean Finnegan?"

"I don't know," said George, which was an honest response.

"Okay then, when did you last see him?"

"On Saturday," responded George. He could feel Jimmy turn his head to stare at him.

"When on Saturday?" asked Agent Calvin.

"Around midday. I was walking from the law library to the parking lot. I ran into Father Finnegan walking around the lake. I said hello. He asked me how school was going. I told him that it was challenging but that I was enjoying it. Then I told him I had to get home to watch the game. I said goodbye and headed off."

George regurgitated this story just as Lauren had told him to say it. He gave enough description to make it sound plausible. Yet it was banal enough to keep the agents from asking too many questions.

As he told his story, he could sense Jimmy getting worked up next to him. He remained focused on the agents. He did not want to stoke Jimmy's paranoia further.

"And you haven't seen him since?" asked Agent Calvin in a skeptical tone.

"Nope," responded George calmly, with all eyes in the room fixed on him.

George sat on the couch, acting as nonchalant about the situation as he could. He stared back at Agent Calvin. The agent gave him a few seconds to see if he might add any details.

"Hmmm . . . okay. Now, Mr. King, what brings you by this morning?"

"Um . . . uh . . . George and I are old friends."

"You guys know each other from Harvard?" asked Agent Calvin, looking at George when he asked the question.

"Yes," responded George.

"No," responded Jimmy at the same time.

The two agents exchanged puzzled looks with each other. Then they exchanged skeptical looks with Jimmy and George. Jimmy tried to backpedal on the difference.

"We . . . uh . . . knew of each other. But we weren't exactly friends."

"When did you become friends?" asked Agent Calvin, again looking at George when he asked this question. This time around, George did not take the bait. He kept his mouth shut and let Jimmy answer.

"That was in D.C. When we were both working up on the Hill. I came by to get George's thoughts on my campaign."

Agent Calvin simply nodded his head in response. Agent Winters still did not say anything. He just sat there staring at Jimmy and George.

"So George is kind of like an unofficial adviser to your campaign?"

"Uh . . . yeah," said Jimmy as he perked up. "That's a good description."

"What kind of advice does he give you?"

George did not say a word. He let Jimmy handle these questions. He wanted to see if Jimmy could control himself or if the kid would reveal his paranoia to these FBI agents.

"You know, just various advice on messaging and outreach efforts."

"And what about Bob Jaworski? How long has he been an adviser to your campaign?"

Sitting on the couch, George thought he recognized that name. He racked his brain trying to figure out where he had heard it before. Then it dawned on him.

The man who was in Father Finnegan's room was named Jaworski. What's Jimmy's connection to this guy?

"Well . . . uh . . . he's not like . . . uh . . . a formal adviser."

"But he gives you political advice? What's a union hack doing with a rising star in the Republican Party?" asked Agent Calvin in a flatteringly tone.

"Bob Jaworski's son was my best friend."

"*Was?*"

"Yeah – Tommy. He passed away exactly 15 years ago tomorrow."

"What happened?"

"He drowned," said Jimmy without elaborating.

George could tell that there was more to the story. The vacant look on Jimmy's face fueled George's suspicion. Jimmy, however, did not seem too eager to share anything else.

"So Jaworski helps out with your campaign even though he is Chairman of the County Democratic Party?"

"He . . . uh . . . thinks of me as a son."

The arrangement surely sounded suspicious to George. No father let their son run for Congress in the other political party and remained involved in both parties' campaign efforts. It just did not add up. Despite the unseemly connection and Jaworski's presence in Father Finnegan's dorm room yesterday, George could not figure out what tied all of this together.

"You know where Jaworski is right now?"

Jimmy shook his head no.

"Well, when you run into him, let him know that we would like to talk," said Agent Calvin, as he handed Jimmy a business card.

The two agents stood up and headed for the door.

"If either of you has anything you want to share, don't hesitate to be in touch," said Agent Calvin.

The men exited the house, closing the door behind them.

So much for getting some sleep.

George did not know when Jimmy might run into Jaworski next. But he did know that it would likely lead him to Father Finnegan. And, as Lauren had pointed out, the sooner they found Father Finnegan, the more likely it was that they would find him alive.

With the clock ticking, George knew that he could

no longer let this paranoid kid out of his sight. He turned his head to Jimmy, who sat there looking stunned.

"Where's the next campaign event?"

"I'll take a small latte."

As the woman behind the counter took the money and got the coffee, Gabriella scanned the room. She stood at the counter of Greenfield's Café, in Notre Dame's Hesburgh Center, looking for an empty seat. She had just finished her first class of the day and she was expecting Michael to arrive at any moment.

She was not sure what to expect from him this morning. He had stuck to the plan at last night's debate. When given the opportunity to talk about Mary, he lowered his head and made his eyes well up. He spoke softly and lovingly about the daughter that "filled his heart full of love."

Gabriella watched as most of the audience's eyes also welled up with tears. She could tell that people felt sympathetic for O'Riordan. It worked perfectly until O'Riordan could not help himself.

In a grand sweeping statement, he announced that he would get back on the campaign trail today. He stood at the podium and declared that Mary "would have wanted nothing more than to see him win this election." And to fulfill the wishes of his daughter, he planned to resume his campaign tomorrow.

Gabriella did not think that this was the best move. By going out on the campaign trail again, he would subject himself to all types of questions. There was the potential for other issues to disrupt the narrative of O'Riordan as the devoted father who had not left his daughter's bedside. Gabriella believed that this narrative was strong enough to carry O'Riordan to victory. She wanted him to avoid any substantive issues.

She felt so strongly about this belief that she told him she would not go out campaigning with him today. He felt stung by the news. He pleaded with her to come. He told her how much he needed her to be there. Yet she stuck by her decision. She saw it as her opportunity to take a stand.

She also saw it as an opportunity to exert her control over O'Riordan. She thought that he would feel guilty for not adhering to her advice. She wanted to exploit that guilt to keep him mentally under her control. She knew he was a weak and desperate man. With her, he had more confidence. Without her, he would have to go back to throwing himself upon naïve graduate students. It was a future that Gabriella knew O'Riordan did not want to face.

Sitting with her coffee in the corner of Greenfield's, Gabriella also pondered her own future. Election Day was less than twenty-four hours away. Two-hundred thousand people were expected to vote in the district's election tomorrow. Those two-hundred thousand people did not know it, but they would decide whether Gabriella's career and, to a certain extent, her life got an extension.

Coming to South Bend was supposed to be an easy opportunity to revive her career. When she accepted the job, she thought that the risk would be relatively low. All that she had to do was keep O'Riordan happy so that he kept divulging classified information. She figured she would put in a few years of work to show the leadership in Caracas that she still had the skills and loyalty to be effective. Then she thought she could return to the Middle East, where the heart of the fight was taking place.

If O'Riordan lost tomorrow, it would shatter all those plans. If he was not in Congress, he had no intelligence to share. And if he had no intelligence to share, he was of no value to Caracas. Then Gabriella would be stuck in South Bend with an aging former congressman who carried no influence in D.C. At that point, she might have to consider disposing of O'Riordan in order to get herself out of South Bend.

That was not even the worst outcome. The worst outcome was SEBIN headquarters deciding that Gabriella was no longer of any value to them. She did not put it out of the realm of possibility that she would be taken out. She knew the leadership in Caracas could easily issue an order that she should not leave South Bend alive. The decision would become much easier to make if O'Riordan did not survive the election.

Gabriella figured the consequences of the election were too serious to be left in the hands of O'Riordan's campaigning ability. That is why she was angry that he decided to campaign today. It was why she wanted him to just ride the sympathy wave to victory.

Sipping her latte, another thought came to her mind. *When is Lauren DeMarco going to make her move?*

Gabriella came home last night and could tell that someone had been in her room. When she asked her roommate about it this morning, her roommate said that a classmate had come by to borrow a book. Without asking her roommate for any more details, she knew right away that it was Lauren.

She inspected every inch of her room. Nothing had been taken. Not the gun or the cash or even the polonium. Nothing had been left. Not a listening device or a camera.

Why would she break into the apartment, go into my room and not take or leave anything? Was she coming to kill me?

She was completely puzzled by Lauren's actions. If Lauren had wanted her dead, she would have been dead already. She might have been holding back because the death of a congressman's girlfriend, along with an attack on his daughter, would draw too much attention. But Gabriella believed Lauren had something planned, otherwise she would not have turned up in South Bend.

Right now, she figured the best course of action would be to keep tabs on Lauren. She had too much going on with the election and making sure that O'Riordan did not screw up on this final day. She did not have time to plan an extensive operation to take out Lauren and keep a distance from the hit. If she botched a hit and brought unwanted attention on O'Riordan's campaign, Caracas would surely signal for her end.

Gabriella was too smart and too ambitious to risk her future right now. She had waited several years to get back at Lauren. She could wait one more day.

"Are you still angry at me?"

Gabriella looked up from her latte to see Mike O'Riordan staring down at her with a sheepish look on his face. From his question and his body language, she could tell that she had the upper hand. She knew she could manipulate him to get what she wanted for tonight.

"You should have taken my advice."

O'Riordan slumped down into a chair opposite from Gabriella.

"What are you doing out campaigning? You had it wrapped up."

"Gabriella," he pleaded. "I'm sorry . . . I just . . . I . . ." O'Riordan's voice trailed off and then perked up again. "Did you see them last night? They loved me."

"They loved Mary. You should have kept the focus on her."

"No . . . it was me. They loved me. They've always loved me. You heard them. They wanted to see me in person. I had no choice. I had to say that Mary would have wanted me to keep campaigning. I had to give them what they wanted."

"Michael, you should have kept all the focus on Mary. You're risking too much by being out there campaigning yourself."

"Gabriella, I can finish this campaign and put away that little jerk for good. The people need to see more of me. The polls are closing. We are within the margin of error. I've got a few more events today to fire up my base of union supporters. Then tonight with former President Miller will seal the deal."

She glared at him with a peeved look on her face. She had made her point. She could have tried to make him feel guiltier, but his mention of former President Miller gave her the opening she wanted.

"Do you really think a man who is no longer in office can help you?" she asked, trying to act nonchalantly about the event.

"Oh of course! They love him here. These are his people. Blue collar, socially conservative Democrats have always been his base. Being on stage with him and getting his endorsement will surely put me over the top."

"What time is the rally?"

"The rally is scheduled for 5:00 p.m. so they can show it live on the local news broadcasts. But the President is scheduled to land at South Bend Airport at 4:40 p.m."

"And he goes directly to the hockey arena?"

"That's the plan."

"Do they put him in an armored limo?"

"Oh yeah. It's one of those bomb-proof vehicles."

"And he must have lots of security?"

"Yeah, he still has Secret Service agents who provide him protection. It's not as extensive as the current President, but it is still very secure. Why do you care about his security detail?" asked O'Riordan, curiously but not recognizing Gabriella's true motives.

206

"I just think that a man of your stature should be shown the same types of courtesy as this former President," responded Gabriella, without hesitation.

O'Riordan blushed at the thought.

"What is he doing after the rally?"

"He heads back to the airport. He's got more campaign stops to make before the election tomorrow."

"So he's only on the ground for a very short time?"

"Maybe no more than an hour.

Gabriella nodded in agreement to O'Riordan, while working through the timing in her head.

"So what time are you headed to the airport?" she asked.

"We are scheduled to head there shortly after 4:00."

"Where should I meet you?"

"Um . . . Gabriella, I've been meaning to say something to you about this."

"What is it Michael?" she asked curiously.

"Well . . . uh . . . see the former President's wife is friends with Helen. They got to know each other at the Congressional picnic hosted by the White House each summer. Members got to bring their wives to the picnic. When the President's people reached out to plan the trip, they said that Mrs. Miller was especially looking forward to catching up with Helen. So she's going to be with me for the evening."

Gabriella shot O'Riordan a look of disgust.

"Listen, I'm sorry, I should have told you earlier."

"So the wife you barely talk to gets to spend time with the former President and the woman you love does not?"

"I . . . I'm sorry"

She cut him off.

"Michael . . . I thought you loved me?"

"I do . . . I do . . . it's just one night. I'm sorry. I

should have told you earlier."

"Am I not good enough for you? Are you embarrassed to introduce me to the former President?"

"No, it's not that at all. Like I said, it is only because Helen and the President's wife are friends. I didn't want to jeopardize the trip by saying that Helen wouldn't be coming because I am about to divorce her to run away with my girlfriend. How would that look in an election where I've been campaigning as the family man?"

Gabriella released an audible sigh to let O'Riordan know that she understood the decision but that she did not accept it.

"Well, you can at least prove that you're not embarrassed about me by introducing me to the former President."

"I'm not embarrassed about you."

"Then here is your opportunity to prove it."

She showed no emotion as she issued this ultimatum to him. Even when his face seemed to plead with her for leniency, she did not react. She wanted that introduction. She just sat there quietly as she waited for his response.

"Fine, I'll talk to the advance staff. We'll try to position you in the holding room so we can have a few minutes alone with the former President."

"We must stand together in solidarity throughout the working world to fight oppression everywhere."

Bob Jaworski crept quietly into the back of the assembled crowd of workers at AM General's Military Assembly Plant. He listened carefully to every word. He did not make a sound or make his presence known. He did not want to interrupt Congressman O'Riordan's speech.

Jaworski had arranged for the congressman to tour AM General's plant as part of a campaign event. The plant manufactured the popular Humvee tactical military vehicles. Jaworski thought that it would provide the perfect backdrop for a campaign event. The all-American company and its red blooded, patriotic employees could hopefully provide some cover for O'Riordan.

Jaworski knew that O'Riordan came across as an effete intellectual who was more concerned with the culture of faraway places than with the interests of Northern Indiana's blue collar community. In these waning hours of the campaign, Jaworski wanted to distract any media from highlighting O'Riordan's Latin American romanticism. Placing O'Riordan on this factory floor was a step in that direction.

The optics looked great from the back of the crowd. O'Riordan spoke from a small, elevated platform, with an enormous American flag painted on the wall behind him. Next to the platform sat a newly finished Humvee, with a painting of a bald eagle clutching the American flag on its hood. Factory workers in the crowd wore blue jeans and hard hats, decorated with American flag stickers. The images evoked a real and strong America. Jaworski thought that he had coordinated a perfect event, except for what he heard coming out of O'Riordan's mouth.

Jaworski leaned in to a burly man, wearing a sleeveless Harley Davidson t-shirt, a pair of jeans, and steel-toed work boots.

"What's he been talking about?"

"I don't know . . . some stuff about plight of the worker across the world," responded the AM General employee in an annoyed tone.

Jaworski did not like the sound of that. He scanned the crowd to see if others seemed to share this burly guy's opinion. The lackluster aura signaled that something was not right. No one seemed to be waving flags or pumping O'Riordan signs into the air. A number of employees had blank or confused looks on their faces. Something had gone wrong.

Jaworski started to get angry. He had set up a perfect event for O'Riordan. All that the Congressman needed to do was come in, say the Pledge of Allegiance, promise to keep fighting for the American worker, and then get out. He knew O'Riordan had a tendency to give long-winded speeches. But this whole event could be sabotaged if O'Riordan decided to lecture the employees.

Even worse, O'Riordan would anger the crowd if he cut into their lunch hour. Like most factory workers in the area, these guys got to work at 6:00 a.m. and finished their day by 3:00 p.m. That meant that they were on lunch break by 10:30 at the earliest or 11:00 a.m. for the majority of the workers. O'Riordan already cut into the 10:30 group's time, and Jaworski saw some of those workers leaving the floor. The union boss was worried that an en masse walk-off would occur if O'Riordan did not end the speech soon. That would not be the optics that Jaworski wanted for this event.

Jaworski needed to get O'Riordan off the stage without making it seem like something was wrong. He quickly considered his options from the most sensible to the most drastic. He could tell the AM General floor manager to get up there and thank O'Riordan for coming. He could cut the audio to O'Riordan's microphone. He could shut down the power to the whole plant. He didn't want to do any of those things, but he would if he had to.

First, however, he wanted to try getting O'Riordan's attention himself. He stood a few feet behind the last of the more than one hundred employees gathered in front of the stage. Fortunately, Jaworski caught O'Riordan's eyes, just as O'Riordan began to talk about the Venezuelan citizens being exploited by CITGO and other multi-national corporations.

"Thank you for having me, don't forget to vote tomorrow, and viva la worker!"

Jaworski cringed. Rallies were supposed to end on a high note to motivate people to get out and vote. Here, no one was clapping or cheering or whistling. O'Riordan would be in big trouble tomorrow if Jaworski did not intervene.

The least he could have done was finish by saying 'God Bless America' and no one would have remembered his foolish rants.

Jaworski did not immediately approach O'Riordan. He waited until the factory workers scattered to lunch or back to their positions on the factory floor. Several recognized him and came over to pay their respects. Jaworski handled them all like a skilled politician, asking if they had gotten recent promotions, seeing if sick family members needed anything, and checking to see how their kids were doing in school.

Jaworski continued to hedge his bets. This was his base – not O'Riordan's. These factory workers and thousands of other Teamsters throughout the district would vote the way that he told them to vote. And tomorrow morning, he would make his decision known.

Although everyone assumed his support was behind O'Riordan, he could get out word in the morning – before the polls opened – and change the entire election. The reason he was waiting until tomorrow morning was because he had not expected the election to be this close. Quite frankly, he had not thought the kid would put up much of a fight. If it hadn't been so close, he would have thrown his weight behind O'Riordan earlier and been done with it. For his own survival, Jimmy's surge had caused him to keep his cards close to his chest. If it looked like Jimmy might pull out a victory tomorrow, he had no qualms about throwing his political machine behind the kid.

Jaworski did not feel wedded to O'Riordan. In fact, over the years he had increasingly grown to dislike the man. He hated O'Riordan's self-centeredness. He hated the way O'Riordan romanticized Latin American culture above Hoosier values. And he most definitely did not like O'Riordan's philandering ways.

Married for nearly thirty years himself, Jaworski had little respect for a man who had cheated on his wife multiple times with graduate students half his age. Jaworski watched O'Riordan around all these naïve students and thought it was pathetic. He saw the damage that these affairs had done to O'Riordan's family.

Despite the lack of respect, Jaworski had supported O'Riordan through all these years. He mainly stuck by him because no formidable challenger had ever sought to unseat O'Riordan. He was also dependent on the cash that O'Riordan funneled through the Teamsters. No one else had been offering to pay that kind of money.

This election gave Jaworski the sense that he might finally be able to dump O'Riordan. He was impressed that

Jimmy King presented a legitimate challenge to O'Riordan. And he appreciated that Jimmy was willing to pony-up the cash for his services. Heading into these final few hours, he wanted to make sure that whoever won the election continued to pay for his valuable services.

"Nice of you to show up," said O'Riordan sarcastically.

Jaworski could tell that O'Riordan had come a long way since he was begging for support on Saturday. Jaworski had no idea where O'Riordan had developed his newfound sense of confidence. He hoped that O'Riordan had not mistaken the public sympathy for his daughter as support for his campaign.

"You're not even going to tell me where you were?"

"I . . . uh . . . had to take care of something."

"What could be more important than this campaign?"

Jaworski stood there silently.

O'Riordan got right up in Jaworski's face.

"I've been there for you for years and you can't even support me in the final hours of this campaign?" asked O'Riordan rhetorically.

Jaworski looked around to see if any of the factory workers were watching this unfold.

"Why don't you look at me when I am talking to you?"

Jaworski could not believe the way that O'Riordan was acting. He grabbed O'Riordan by the arm. He forced him across the factory floor, out a pair of side doors and into the parking lot. Jaworski wanted to be out of the view of all the workers.

"Why don't you settle down. You haven't won anything yet," responded Jaworski forcefully, standing with O'Riordan in the empty parking lot.

O'Riordan backed down from Jaworski's face.

213

"What exactly were you saying up there?"

"I told them what they wanted to hear. I told them that I stood in solidarity with them and their fellow workers around the world."

Jaworski shook his head in disbelief as O'Riordan repeated his impromptu solidarity speech.

"These guys don't care about that kind of crap. They just want to make a few extra bucks and hopefully send their kids to college. You gotta avoid that Spanish garbage."

"It's Latin American, if you knew your geography."

"I don't give a rat's ass. You need to stop talking about it."

"Aren't you head of the Teamsters? I thought you were supposed to be concerned about the plight of the working man? The subjugation of the worker anywhere is the subjugation of the worker everywhere!"

"Organized labor exists to protect jobs. My job and the job of every dues paying Member. If they ain't paying dues, then we ain't busting our humps for them. So I don't work for the scabs crossing the picket lines here in Northern Indiana or the Mexicans trying to make an extra peso."

"I was talking about Venezuelan oil field workers. That's Latin American."

"Venezuelan, Latin American, Chi Chi's Mexican Grill . . . who gives a crap. You need to quit talking about it."

Jaworski stared down O'Riordan.

"And what do you propose that I talk about?"

"You see any of my guys, you just tell them that you are going to keep fighting for Hoosier values and that you are out there to support patriotic American working families."

"You keep referring to them as *your guys*. If they are *your guys*, then why isn't this election wrapped up by

214

now? Why do I have to go to these stupid factories and pretend to be interested in how a tank gets made?"

It took every ounce of self restraint for Jaworski not to deck O'Riordan. In any other situation, he would have leveled an arrogant jerk like O'Riordan. He was dying to teach the politician a lesson.

"They are my guys. Don't you worry about that."

"Well then why do I need to be here to kiss their butts?"

Jaworski still could not believe O'Riordan's arrogance. He just did not seem to realize that, if Mary had not been attacked, this election would not have even been close. Sympathy for Mary was the only thing keeping him in this race.

"Listen, you've only got a few more events to go, then the rally tonight, and then the election tomorrow. Just make sure you don't talk about any of that Spanish solidarity crap again."

"Aren't you coming to these events?"

"I've got stuff to take care of for tomorrow."

"I'm starting to think that you've been playing me all these years. Why do I even bother paying you? You talk about turning out the vote and other 'stuff to take care of' but I've never actually seen you make a difference."

Is he serious? Does he forget the reason why I don't tell him what I do?

Jaworski thought O'Riordan was no longer just arrogant, but actually losing it. Throughout the years Jaworski never told O'Riordan a single thing about what he did with the embezzled cash or how he bought votes. The whole point was to keep the congressman in the dark. If any investigations started, O'Riordan could plausibly claim that he knew nothing.

The situation with Mary and Jimmy King breathing down his neck must be making him crazy. How could a man standing for election to Congress be on the verge of losing his mind?

Jaworski did not know how to respond, so he stood there unresponsive, just staring at O'Riordan.

"Just keep one thing in mind, it's my name on that ballot. Not yours. No one's voted for you fourteen elections in a row. It's me they've been voting for. Me," said O'Riordan as he jabbed two thumbs into his own chest.

Jaworski continued to stand there without saying a word. He thought how easy it would be to walk away now and not look back. He could wash his hands clean of O'Riordan forever and never have to put up with his antics ever again.

"So tomorrow, if I win, once again, I'll know that I did my job on the campaign trail. But if I lose, I'll know that you never had any influence. That you never made a difference in these campaigns. And I'll know that I wasted money on you for years."

Still Jaworski stood there not saying a word.

"So it's up to you to decide whether you finally deliver an election."

Jaworski took his time responding. He wanted to let O'Riordan know that he was now and had always been in control.

"Don't you worry about a thing," said Jaworski confidently. "I'm gonna finish all of this tomorrow."

"I need a name, Father," shouted Bob Jaworski.

Jaworski walked in as the priest was slumped over in his chair. He could not tell if the priest was sleeping or if he was unconscious. He shouted to get Father Finnegan's attention.

Jaworski also shouted because he was still fuming about his conversation with O'Riordan. He already had enough to worry about in these final hours. O'Riordan, acting like a spoiled Hollywood starlet, did not make things any easier. Shouting helped release some of his frustration.

Standing over the incapacitated priest, Jaworski tried to put aside any thoughts about O'Riordan or the equally delirious Jimmy King. Tomorrow's election was an afterthought to what he had been planning for a while. The fate of the two candidates meant nothing compared to the fate of the person he was trying to track down.

Jaworski hoped that Father Finnegan was ready to talk. He knew that the priest was withholding the identity of his son's killer. Friends in the South Bend Police Department, who had investigated the death, told Jaworski that Father Finnegan heard the killer's confession, which is why he was able to help them locate the body. Jaworski wanted them to force the priest to release the killer's name, but they said they were powerless to make that happen.

Jaworski even went to the District Attorney, who he had helped get elected. The DA knew that the Catholic vote was more important than the union vote and declined to prosecute the priest. Father Finnegan had kept his mouth shut for all of these years.

After an initial grieving period, the anger slowly built within Jaworski. Every morning for the last fifteen years, the union boss had listened to his wife say the rosary on her knees beside their bed. His heart would sink as she would ask God to watch over their son in heaven, and then cry. With each cry, Jaworski thought about the sight of his son's lifeless body being pulled from the river. While most men would have become numb to the tragedy, it ate away at Jaworski.

He reached his boiling point earlier this year. After his wife went through her morning routine, she picked up the *South Bend Tribune*, saw a picture of Jimmy King on the cover announcing his candidacy, and she broke down. At that moment, Jaworski broke down too. He knew it should have been his son on the cover. If he had kept his son safe, he knew the kid would have gone on to great things. At that moment, Jaworski committed himself to avenging his son's death.

That is why Father Finnegan was tied up in an abandoned Studebaker factory. Jaworski thought that he could blackmail Father Finnegan into releasing the killer's identity. It was a simple trade – the killer's identity for Jaworski's statement to the police about Mary. He knew most men would have jumped at the chance to win back their freedom. Jaworski understood that the priest held himself to a different standard, but he thought that there was a small chance the alcoholic might take the offer.

If Father Finnegan remained defiant, Jaworski intended to apply as much physical pressure as necessary to help Father Finnegan reach his breaking point. As a devout Catholic, it was not behavior that Jaworski was proud of. Like most Catholics, he had a reverence for priests, even the alcoholic ones.

But Jaworski justified the potential torture, in his own mind, as a necessary part of enacting justice. His own emotional and mental anguish, which had been building over the years, colored any concern he had for anyone else. If torturing a priest is what he needed to do to get the killer's name, then he would find Father Finnegan's breaking point.

Before Jaworski set to work on Father Finnegan, he gave the priest time. Jaworski hoped that Father Finnegan would reveal the name without having to smash any of the priest's bones. Having watched Father Finnegan for a while and seen his weakness for alcohol, Jaworski did not think that it would take long for the priest to break.

Jaworski put his hand underneath Father Finnegan's chin and lifted the priest's head. The union boss looked him in the face, but the priest's eyes struggled to maintain contact.

"You hear me, Father? All I need is the name and then you get to go home. You'll be cleared of any wrongdoing. And you never have to worry about this again."

Struggling to respond and laboring with each breath, Father Finnegan eventually spoke up.

"I'm sorry, Son, but I've already told you: I took a vow."

Jaworski kicked the priest's chair in anger, sending Father Finnegan tumbling to the ground. Jaworski stood there for a few seconds with a deadly stare on his face. As Father Finnegan let out a loud groan, Catholic guilt seeped into Jaworski's body. He went over and helped the priest back to his feet.

"Father, I'm not joking around. I've suffered for too long."

Father Finnegan let out several coughs before summoning the strength to respond.

"If you have pain in your life, Son, you should take refuge in our Savior, the Lord Jesus Christ."

"Every day for the last fifteen years I've gotten up

and prayed. And every day I've asked Jesus to take away my pain. But the pain is still with me, and it's even worse than fifteen years ago."

"In John, we hear Jesus say 'I am the light of the world: he that follows me, walks not in darkness, but shall have the light of life.' Jesus' light is there to welcome you. But you must embrace Jesus with all of your heart. He died to give us salvation. If you believe in Jesus, know that one day all of your sins will be forgiven and your pain will be washed away."

"Is that what you've done, Father?"

"Yes . . . I made a commitment to serve the Lord."

"And what have you gotten in return?" inquired Jaworski.

"Eternal salvation," said Father Finnegan emphatically.

Jaworski scoffed at the response.

"From what I hear, you still have your fair share of problems," said Jaworski, trying to guilt Father Finnegan.

"That's true, my Son. I do have my own problems. I know that. It's part of being human. We are natural sinners. That's why I pray to the Lord for forgiveness for my sins, for the courage to resist temptations, and for guidance in a better way of life."

"And do you think he's listening?"

"Of course. He listens to everyone."

"Even the drunks?"

"Especially the drunks."

Father Finnegan's quick response made Jaworski pause for a second.

"Well, I don't think he's been listening to me because my pain has only gotten worse."

"You must have faith. You must trust in the Lord with all your heart."

"I'm done trusting. I've suffered for too long. It's

time that I handled things my way."

"We all battle with demons, my son. Keep in mind the words from Isaiah. 'Woe to those who call evil good and good evil.'"

"What's that supposed to mean?"

"You may think that you are avenging the death of your son. But by inflicting pain on others, even those who have committed a mortal sin, you are just doing the devil's work for the devil."

Jaworski face tightened when he heard this comment. He cocked back his arm and smashed his fist into Father Finnegan's face. The priest's head snapped back and then forward. When the priest's head flung forward, Jaworski punched him again right in the middle of the face. Jaworski raised his fist to punch Father Finnegan a third time. He caught himself when he saw blood streaming down Father Finnegan's nose.

Jaworski took a deep breath himself. He shook the hand that he had used to punch Father Finnegan and stretched the fingers. Then he grabbed the priest's head and steadied it.

"Just give me the damn name, Father."

"I . . . uh . . . I'm sorry . . . I just can't."

Crack.

Jaworski punched Father Finnegan again.

"It doesn't need to be like this. It's just a name. Nothing more than that," insisted Jaworski.

Father Finnegan dropped his head. Jaworski lifted it up and punched Father Finnegan one more time. This punch landed straight on Father Finnegan's cheek. Jaworski knew that he would have shattered the priest's cheekbone, if it weren't for the priest's puffy face cushioning these blows. All those years of drinking provided one physical benefit, thought Jaworski.

After the punch, Father Finnegan dropped his head

again. And again, Jaworski lifted it up. He went to punch Father Finnegan but stopped. If Father Finnegan was not going to give up the name right at this moment, there was something that Jaworski wanted to get out of the way.

"So you can't tell any other person what someone tells you in confession?"

A dazed Father Finnegan struggled to respond, so Jaworski shook him.

"You hear me? I asked if it's true that you can't talk about what's said in confession."

"That's right. The sacramental seal is inviolable," mumbled Father Finnegan.

"Well, here's another confession for you. I am going to kill whoever is responsible for the death of my son. You can give me one name and it ends there. But if you don't give me any name, I'm gonna track down each and every possible suspect and take care of them one by one. Everyone will experience the pain that my son went through. I'll start with you, Father. And then everyone after you will be on your conscience."

Jaworski had worked himself into a fury. By the end of his comments, he was shouting at Father Finnegan. Images of his son's short life flashed in his head.

Tommy's birth. Tommy's first day of school. Tommy playing Little League. Tommy's body being pulled from the river. Taking the lifeless body from the cop's arms. Clutching the boy, falling to knees, and sobbing.

The priest did not seem to be paying attention to Jaworski's rant. He was slumped over in his chair, his head hung low, and drops of blood fell from his nose, splattering all over George DeMarco's grey Harvard boxing sweats.

Jaworski took a few steps back from Father Finnegan. He was breathing deeply and his pulse was racing. He felt as if his body had finally succumbed to the anguish, which he had been battling for years. Jaworski knew that there was no turning back now.

Standing there breathing deeply, he heard Father Finnegan mumbling to himself. Jaworski inched in close to listen to what the priest was saying.

"Be strong in the Lord . . . Put on the whole armor of God so that you may be able to stand against the wiles of the devil . . . Put on the breastplate of righteousness . . . And the shield of faith . . . and the helmet of salvation."

Jaworski was amazed that the priest could find the solace to pray at this moment.

"Where does that come from?" asked Jaworski.

Father Finnegan's head remained dropped down. He did not make eye contact with Jaworski and it took the priest several seconds to respond.

"Saint Paul's letter to the Ephesians," said Father Finnegan, without lifting his head.

"I hate to say it, Father," started Jaworski, preparing himself to unleash more physical pain on the priest. "But you are going to need more than the Armor of God to defend yourself here."

Father Finnegan paused before responding.

"It's not for me, my Son . . . it's for you."

"So that went well," said George, as he and Jimmy climbed inside George's Jeep Cherokee.

Technically, George was not lying. The event had gone well in comparison to the previous three campaign stops of the morning. But none had gone exactly as planned.

The parade of problems started on a visit to the Mishawaka Wal-Mart. No one from the campaign called ahead to notify Wal-Mart that they would be in the parking lot greeting voters. It made for an embarrassing scene when Wal-Mart security told them to stop harassing the customers and asked them to leave.

Next they went to a meet and greet at the Recreational Vehicle and Manufactured Housing Heritage Foundation and Hall of Fame in Elkhart. The Hall employee who was supposed to coordinate the visit got the dates mixed up. She thought Jimmy was scheduled to come next Monday. When Jimmy insisted on talking to some of the employees, people refused to get off phone calls or to stop playing solitaire on their computers. George counted a grand total of seven people that Jimmy actually spoke with.

At the third stop, a visit to the St. Joseph County Republican Women's weekly coffee meeting, elderly women harangued Jimmy with all kinds of questions. None of the questions related to the campaign. Most wanted to know why he was not married and, since he was not married, why he did not become a priest. George cringed for Jimmy when a ninety-one-year-old woman, who thought she was whispering to her friend, announced at the top of her voice, "I think he's a homosexual." Jimmy never recovered after that comment.

The final fundraising luncheon at the South Bend Country Club had gone slightly better. Jimmy had expected 150 to 200 people to be in attendance. Exactly thirty-three people showed-up. Of those thirty-three, only twenty-four had paid the $100 per person suggested contribution.

Most campaigns never fundraise this late in the election cycle. Most are focused on get out the vote operations. Jimmy did not have that luxury. His campaign had been increasingly running a debt. The campaign's debt stood at $217,000 this morning – a significant number when you consider that O'Riordan only raised $500,000 for his last re-election and Jimmy had no personal assets to finance the campaign.

Since the election was so close, Jimmy had authorized campaign expenditures – yard signs, radio buys, mailers – without concern for his finances. He had convinced himself that there was a large universe of potential donors whom he had not solicited. He thought that these people had only recently started paying attention to the campaign, and they would be eager to support his potential victory.

As it turned out, that universe was much smaller than Jimmy anticipated. The luncheon's numbers started dwindling over the weekend, as more information about Mary O'Riordan and the subsequent investigation came to light. A large block of potential donors dropped out this morning when the polls showed O'Riordan surging and likely to win re-election. George saw the color leave Jimmy's face when they walked into the country club's ballroom and scattered amongst circular tables sat a third of the crowd that had been expected.

Personally, George did not care how many people actually showed up. He was only interested in one per-

225

son. Bob Jaworski. George kept an eye out for Jaworski at each campaign stop. He had only seen Jaworski's face once – yesterday morning at Father Finnegan's room – but he had not forgotten it. The burly union boss would have been easy to spot in these sparse crowds. Yet there was no sight of him at all. And at the fundraising luncheon, again, Jaworski was nowhere in sight. George started to think that attaching himself to Jimmy was going to be a dead end.

"It wasn't supposed to end like this . . ." said Jimmy, as his voice trailed off.

George thought the same thing. When he told Lauren that he would take care of the situation, he had meant it. George intended to bring Father Finnegan back to safety and to clear his name. He had not anticipated that he would spend almost an entire day driving around with no leads in sight.

"So where to now?" asked George.

"Back to campaign headquarters. I have to thank some volunteers."

George reversed out of the parking spot, exited the country club and started in the direction of downtown. The pair did not exchange any words as George drove for several blocks. George silently replayed Jimmy's comments in his head.

It wasn't supposed to end like this.

George thought about the comment some more. This time, however, he did not think about Father Finnegan. He thought about Jimmy.

What did he mean by that comment? How was it "supposed to end"?

George looked over at Jimmy sitting in the passenger seat. He decided he had to pry a little. He felt that he had developed enough of a rapport with Jimmy to push him on some questions. And, more importantly, at this point he had nothing else to lose.

"So do you think things would have been different if you had not run into Mary on Friday night?"

Jimmy showed no reaction to the question. George waited for a response. Jimmy sat there motionlessly for nearly a minute before he quietly spoke up.

"I didn't even talk to her for that long. We went to high school together and of course with her dad and the campaign, I felt like I should at least say hello. Then she flipped out on me. She started railing about politicians. I didn't know how to react so I just walked away. I wish I had never even said anything to her."

While trying to keep his eyes on the road, George watched for Jimmy's reaction. Growing up, George had been around a few Brooklyn hustlers. He could always tell when they were trying to pull a fast one over you. He didn't think that Jimmy was hiding anything about seeing Mary on Friday night. But George still had a hunch that Jimmy was not as innocent as his boyish face appeared.

"Well, you still have an entire day before the election. Couldn't that Jaworski guy help you out? Isn't he some local power broker?" asked George, feigning ignorance about Jaworski and trying to draw Jimmy out on their relationship.

"You think the Democratic Party Chairman wants to help the Republican candidate?"

"I thought those FBI guys this morning said that he was already helping you out?" asked George, pushing back on Jimmy.

"Look, between you and me, he has helped me out. But all that he's done is offered campaign advice. Nothing more than that," said Jimmy, sounding defensive to George.

"So can't you get him to do more than that? He obviously feels indebted to you for some reason since he's even agreeing to help you out in the first place."

"I was best friends with his son. He's treated me

like a son for years. That's all there is to it."

"If he's treated you like a son, wouldn't he do whatever it takes to help you win?"

"What are you saying?"

Jimmy turned his head and gave George an annoyed look.

"Nothing," said George trying to deflect Jimmy's suspicion. "I'm just trying to figure out ways we can get you the votes tomorrow."

George kept focused on the road. He avoided eye contact with Jimmy. He knew his comments about Jaworski touched a nerve. Now he had to figure out why.

The previously sullen and quiet Jimmy squirmed in his seat.

"Headquarters is up there on the right. You can double-park behind that white van out front and drop me off."

White van?

There it sat.

Parked right outside Jimmy's campaign headquarters was the white van that George had spent nearly a day looking for. This white van had "King for Congress" posters affixed to the side. While the van that Father Finnegan had been pushed into had been plain white, George knew this was the same van because of an odd dent above its back right tire. The dent had an outline like the shape of Florida.

How long has it been parked here? If I had come here last night, would I have saved myself an entire day of wandering aimlessly?

George pushed those thoughts out of his head. He told himself that now was not the time to worry about what could have been. He finally had a lead.

"Is that a campaign van?"

"Uh . . . um . . ." stammered Jimmy.

George tried to remain calm and indifferent to Jimmy's response. He wanted to know why the van sat in front of Jimmy's headquarters. He wanted Jimmy to keep talking.

"Well, if I tell you this, you can't tell anyone else."

"Oh course," responded George, now even more interested to know about the van.

"You promise?"

"Yeah, definitely, it stays between me and you."

Just spit it out already.

"So I wasn't completely honest about Jaworski earlier . . ."

"What do you mean?"

Jimmy paused. George waited anxiously.

"Well . . . uh . . . he's had some of his Teamsters doing odd jobs for the campaign. Jaworski knew we were strapped for staff and cash."

"What kind of odd jobs?"

"Making get out the vote calls, stuffing envelopes, you know, the regular volunteer things."

George did not believe him. He could tell by Jimmy's reticence that there were other things going on. Union stooges did not do volunteer work for a Republican campaign without some serious financial incentives.

"What's so secretive about that?"

"George – union members helping out a Republican? In South Bend?" said Jimmy, sounding incredulous. "If any of the other Teamsters found out those guys were helping me, they'd be completely ostracized from the union. And Bob Jaworski would go down with them."

"And you want to protect Jaworski?"

"I've got no other choice. He's helped O'Riordan get re-elected for years. Without his support, I'll never win."

"Well it doesn't look like his support has done much

good for you," said George. He knew there was more to the relationship with Jaworski that Jimmy was not volunteering. He pushed Jimmy to divulge those details.

"Bob Jaworski is a good man. He's been there for me time and time again," said Jimmy, refusing to disclose exactly how Jaworski had been helping his campaign.

Jimmy opened his passenger side door and got out of the parked Jeep. He stood on the curb with the door open.

"Listen, I appreciate all of your help today. But I don't want to waste any more of your time. I'm sure you have to get back to class or reading or your wife."

George recognized he had pushed too far. He regretted it immediately. He needed a recovery. The white van stood two feet from him. He had to find out who drove this van last night.

"Jimmy, it's not over. The polls showed you guys tied. You can still win this thing," insisted George.

"Being tied with O'Riordan still means losing by 10,000 votes. Thanks for being so optimistic. Maybe in two years, right?" said Jimmy as he closed his door and walked toward the entrance of his headquarters.

George knew he had to keep on digging. He jumped out of his car. He followed Jimmy behind the all-glass storefront. He paused as soon as he entered the headquarters.

He scanned the crowd for a suspicious face – Jaworski, the gunman from last night, the two young guys at the 'Backer. He did not recognize anyone – none of the suspicious characters from the last two days and no one who looked like a baseball bat wielding Teamster thug. The dozen or so volunteers scattered about the open room consisted of suburban housewives, senior citizens, and college kids. They were the only people with the time to volunteer in the middle of a workday.

Right inside the door, Jimmy stood next to a table lined with telephones. An elderly man and two Saint Mary's freshmen sat on fold-out chairs at the table. Jimmy stopped talking to them when he saw George enter the room.

"George, I appreciate the support, but really, you should go home."

George scanned the crowd for a second time before responding.

"Oh yeah . . . I . . . uh . . . do you have a bathroom I could use?"

"Yeah, it's in the back. Go through that back office and you'll see it."

"Thanks."

George slowly made his way to the back of the room. He sized up every volunteer he passed. He tried to remember if he had seen any of them before. None appeared familiar.

Coming to the back office, he found the bathroom located in the far corner. He went in and closed the door. It was nothing more than a closet. A leaky toilet sat against the back wall. A puddle of water streamed out toward the sink, covering three-fourths of the tiled bathroom floor. The sink hung on the right side, just inside the door, and an oval mirror hung on the back of the bathroom door. George squeezed his shoulders through the doorframe, just fitting inside the bathroom.

He stared at himself in the mirror.

Who are these unions thugs? Where are they? How do I get Jimmy to talk?

He turned on the tap and splashed some water on to his face.

Where is Father Finnegan?

BOOM!

George heard a loud blast, followed by shattering

glass. The floor rumbled underneath his feet. The light bulb dangling above his head flickered. Female shrieks broke the post-explosion shock.

George turned to rush out of the bathroom, but slipped in the toilet water puddle. Unable to control his momentum, George smashed his forehead into the mirror and tumbled to the floor.

Although George opened a deep gash of dark red blood over his left eye, his adrenaline kept him moving. He hurried into the main office of the headquarters. He noticed immediately that the white van lay on its side, partially inside of the headquarters. It appeared as if an explosion sent the van tumbling through the headquarters' storefront windows.

Where's Jimmy?

George moved slowly toward the front of the headquarters, where a crowd encircled a man on the floor. George heard one of the Notre Dame students yelling into his cell phone about needing an ambulance as soon as possible because "he might die on us." The group stood right where George had seen Jimmy talking to the campaign volunteers. George feared the worst.

Jimmy?

A wave of relief washed over him when he peered through the crowd and did not see Jimmy. The elderly man lay collapsed on the ground with his hand in a fist over his heart. George watched him for a nearly a minute and the old man did not move once.

So where's Jimmy?

George left the group and headed to where the front entrance had stood only minutes earlier. He ducked under shards of glass and stepped out on to the street. There he found Jimmy standing on the sidewalk. Jimmy looked away from the headquarters and appeared indifferent to the chaos going on around him.

"Jimmy! Jimmy! Are you okay?"

Jimmy did not respond to George's questions. He did not even turn around to see George hustling toward him.

"Jimmy – you okay?" George asked again.

George came face-to-face with Jimmy. He looked Jimmy up and down to see if Jimmy had any injuries. George saw no cuts, bruises or scrapes.

Jimmy simply stood there with a smirk on his face.

George thought he might be in shock, so he asked again.

"Jimmy, are you okay?"

Jimmy continued to look out, with a smirk on his face. He finally spoke up.

"It wasn't supposed to end like this . . ."

Where are you?

Lauren DeMarco sat on a couch in the atrium of the Hesburgh Center for International Studies, asking herself where the Fox was hiding. She wore blue jeans, knee-length boots, and a Polo down feather jacket to protect against the November chill. A navy blue Notre Dame hat, pulled low on her head, obscured her eyes from the passers-by. A notebook sat in her lap, with a textbook and her Kate Spade handbag on the couch beside her. She tried hard to blend in with the numerous undergraduates, graduate students, and academics traversing about the atrium.

She found it odd to be back in this setting. Only two days earlier she had been here when her encounter with the Fox upended her quiet married life. At first she was startled to see the Fox. But then she quickly realized that God was giving her a second chance to finish what she should have finished in Lebanon.

From her perch on this couch, she kept tabs on the Fox. She watched her go to classes, attend a lunchtime lecture on international conflict and inter-faith cooperation, and join her Congressman boyfriend for a coffee in Greenfield's, the Center's local café. Each time the Fox walked by, Lauren drew her handbag, with the P239 stashed at the bottom, into her hands.

She would have preferred to finish the job in an abandoned parking garage or deep in the woods of a state park or any other place where dozens of potential eyewitnesses were not lurking about. The Secret Service agents and South Bend cops scattered across campus, preparing for the former President's visit, complicated things even further. If she attempted it right here, she might not make it off campus.

She pushed those thoughts to the back of her head. She would figure something out after the fact. She always did. For now, however, she had to stay focused on the Fox.

Lauren had been sitting on this couch all day. After yesterday's revelation, she knew she could not lose the Fox before former President Miller's arrival. So she followed the Fox to class first thing in the morning. Since the Fox was in the Hesburgh Center all day, Lauren remained inside the Hesburgh Center all day as well.

This stakeout was not as tedious as the time that she spent sixteen hours inside of a Mumbai snake charmer's oversized basket, but it was still a stake-out after all. And Lauren never liked stakeouts. This former Harvard lacrosse player much preferred running, jumping, fighting, shooting weapons, and doing any physical activity other than sitting around all day and waiting.

Needless to say, she was glad when George called. It gave her a break from the monotonous task of surveillance. Yet it still made her look like she belonged amongst all the other smartphone-addicted students.

"I'm in the Hesburgh Center. I've been here all day following her. It shouldn't be much longer though. President Miller's plane lands at the airport in about forty-five minutes. Her class just finished and she should be headed to the airport."

"Are you okay?"

"Yeah, I'm fine. Why?"

No response came from the other end.

"George? Are you there?"

"Lauren, there was an explosion."

"Are you okay?"

"Yeah, I'm fine."

"Are you sure?"

"Yeah, I'm okay."

"What happened? Where were you?"

"At Jimmy's headquarters I went there with Jimmy after his fundraising luncheon. When we rolled up the white van that carried away Father Finnegan on Sunday night was parked out front."

"The same white van? How'd you know?"

"It had the same dent over the back right tire. I mean, how many of these types of vans are around South Bend?"

"So what happened?"

"I went inside to use the bathroom. All of a sudden there's a loud blast, the building shakes, and I hear screams. I go rushing out and the van has come through the front windows. Some old volunteer is having a heart attack. Medics came but I don't think he's gonna make it."

"What was it like?"

"What?"

"The explosion? What was it like?"

"It wasn't a good feeling if that's what you're asking."

"No I mean. What was the blast like? How strong was it? Did it go up or did it go out?"

"Strong enough to shake the building and send a van through the front windows. Why?"

"George, car bombs are Hezbollah's weapon of choice in Beirut. Ever since the 80's, it's been how Hezbollah sends a message. During the more tense times, there was one going off every few weeks. It's damaging both physically and psychologically. Walking past a truck or van you never knew if it was just making local deliveries or if it had a more damning purpose."

"You think Hezbollah has taken its proxy war to the streets of South Bend?" asked George, in disbelief.

"Not Hezbollah, but Hezbollah's friends."

"Hezbollah has friends in South Bend?"

"I'm looking at one right now," said Lauren, as she watched the Fox emerge from a classroom with a group of other graduate students. As she spoke, she pulled the Notre Dame hat lower over her face to make sure she was not detected.

"You mean the Fox?"

"George, who else could it be? She spent years in Beirut working closely with Hezbollah foot soldiers. She'd be familiar with all kinds of explosives and that includes the car bomb."

"But why?"

"Don't you see who that car bomb was directed at?"

"Jimmy?"

"Exactly. George, if she kills Jimmy, it makes it a lot easier for boyfriend to get re-elected."

"Wait, first you said she was here to kill you. Then you said she was here to kill the President. Now you say she is here to kill Jimmy?"

Lauren did not respond.

"Lauren, is there anyone in South Bend she isn't here to kill?"

Lauren detected sarcasm in George's voice.

"Listen, George, you may not believe me, but it's not a coincidence that she is here. I know this woman. I studied everything about her. She does not do anything by coincidence."

"So what is she going to do?"

"I am going to find out soon enough. George, she looks like she's about to move, so I gotta get going."

"Wait, what am I supposed to do?"

"Hang in there, you're getting closer."

"Getting closer?"

"You said you found the white van, right?"

"Yeah, it was parked outside Jimmy's headquarters and now it's lying on its side in the entryway."

"Well, there's got to be some clues on that van. See if you can find anything inside of it – an ID, a receipt, a hamburger wrapper – anything that identifies who was driving it."

"Lauren . . ."

"What?"

"I don't want anything to happen to you . . . I love you."

Lauren did not speak as the words sunk in.

"I know, George. I love you too. You don't worry about a thing. I'm gonna take care of her before anything else happens," responded Lauren. "George, she' moving. I gotta go."

"Wait, when am I going to see you again?"

"I don't know . . . George I gotta go. Don't let Jimmy out of your sight," said Lauren.

She pulled the cell phone away from her ear. She heard George say "Be safe" as she ended the call and put the phone in her bag. She gripped her gun to reassure herself that she was ready to go. She stood up from the couch, leaving the notebook and textbook behind.

She followed as the Fox walked toward the parking lot. The space in the Hesburgh Atrium did not allow her much of a distance. She held back and tried to blend in to a crowd of students shuffling between classes. She watched as the Fox looked straight ahead, without turning around.

"Lauren?"

Lauren ignored the voice calling out her name from behind. She continued following the Fox into the parking lot.

"Lauren DeMarco?"

Lauren kept her eyes fixed on the Fox, but she stopped walking.

"Lauren is that you?"

Standing still in the atrium, Lauren watched the Fox slowly turn around to look back at her. Watching the Fox's eyes come into sight, Lauren relinquished her position. Lauren spun around to see who had called out her name and to avoid being spotted by the Fox.

"Lauren, how are you?" asked Henry Sullivan.

Lauren hesitated in responding to the Kellogg Institute Director, whom she had met on Saturday. She was only focused on the Fox.

"I'm . . . uh . . . good. How are you?"

"I'm well. Everyone enjoyed meeting you on Saturday."

"Oh . . . yeah. Me too. It was great to meet everyone," responded Lauren, trying to keep the conversation as short as possible. She knew that every second she spent with Sullivan put another few feet of distance between her and the Fox. Her posture revealed that sentiment as well. She kept one foot at a short distance behind the other one, so that she could quickly catch up to the Fox.

"Well, have you had the chance to speak with Gabriella?"

"Um . . . no . . . why?" Lauren asked nervously. She pulled her bag up to her waist and reached inside. She gripped her pistol. She cautiously looked over her shoulder.

"Hmmm . . . I don't know if I want to spoil her surprise."

Lauren looked at Sullivan curiously.

"What do you mean surprise?"

"I'll let Gabriella tell you herself. She was here just two seconds ago." Sullivan looked around the atrium. "Gabriella! Gabriella!" Sullivan called out and pointed toward the doors that led to the parking lot.

Gabriella was pushing the doors open. She paused

and looked back. Sullivan waved to her.

"Gabriella!" he said once again, motioning for her to come over.

Lauren did not turn her head. She knew that it was the Fox alright, but Lauren did not want the Fox to realize that it was her. She kept her eyes fixed on Sullivan's face, so she did not see Gabriella simply stare at Sullivan for one second before heading out into the parking lot.

She knew, however, that something was not right. She saw Sullivan's face contort into a puzzled look. She watched as he stopped waving at the Fox mid-motion. She resisted the urge to look, but she tightened her grip on her gun. She was ready for this moment.

"I guess she's got some place she needs to be," said Sullivan as he shrugged his shoulders.

Lauren eased her finger off the pistol's trigger.

"I . . . uh . . . actually have some place to be as well," said Lauren, starting to slink away.

"Oh, yes, of course, I must let you go. But I just wanted to tell you again how much everyone enjoyed meeting you. And . . ."

Sullivan paused with a mischievous smile on his face.

Just get it out already!

"We thought with your background and experience that you would be a perfect fit for the two institutes. We want to get you involved in a project with Professor Derring."

"Oh . . . uh . . . that's great, but I really got to go," said Lauren, taking another step backward.

"Don't you want to know what the project is all about?"

Not really.

"Uh . . . sure."

"We thought it would be an interesting project to

look at the role that women can play in peacebuilding and preventing terrorism in Beirut. With your background and Gabriella's background, we thought you two just had such a great head-start on the project. We really want to tap into your networks and your experiences."

"Oh . . . yeah . . . that'd be interesting. For sure."

Lauren was slowly creeping backward where she now stood about five feet from Sullivan.

"And we thought that you and Gabriella are such a great pair together. You two seem to have such a great rapport and just get along like you're old friends. Plus, we thought you are both great warriors for peace!"

Lauren now stood about fifteen feet from Sullivan and she kept tip-toeing backward.

"Women preventing terrorism in Beirut, huh? Sounds great. I . . . uh . . . actually have one idea already on how to make that happen. I'm gonna go track down Gabriella to unload all these ideas on her . . ."

Where'd she go?

Lauren cautiously raced out of the Kellogg Center, gripping her gun and ready to pull it from her bag in a second. She did not want to lose the Fox. She also did not want to walk into an ambush. She knew it would not look good to get into a shootout only a few hundred yards from the hockey arena, so she kept a tight grip on the weapon and prepared herself.

Exiting the Hesburgh Center's eastside entrance dumped her into Notre Dame's main parking area. She scanned the rows and rows of cars. Dozens of vehicles and hundreds of people were streaming in for the rally with former President Miller.

Lauren looked for that lithe body, flowing brunette hair, and fashionable Latin American attire. Fortunately for Lauren, the Fox could be easily distinguished from the average Midwesterner.

There she is.

Lauren spotted the Venezuelan weaving in and out of cars. The Fox was walking in the direction of the hockey arena. Lauren released the grip on her gun and took off. She moved quickly and, just like Gabriella, weaved in and out of parked cars and people streaming to the arena. She managed to do so without running and without drawing any attention to herself. It was an old spy's trick to be in a hurry and yet still blend into the surrounding environment.

Dodging parking cars and families unloading from minivans, Lauren never took her eyes off of the Fox. She made up ground easily. Covering half of the parking lot,

Lauren finally got close enough to take a clear shot.

But she purposefully held back. She gave the Fox enough distance so as not to be detected. Lauren followed Gabriella intently, sticking to her every move.

Where is she going?

The Venezuelan abruptly stopped moving in the same direction as the streaming crowd. Lauren stood firmly, watching the Fox turn to the right and head to the southernmost edge of the parking lot. She saw Gabriella pull a set of keys out of her handbag, which was slung over her shoulder, and approach an old Saab. She continued to stare as the Fox unlocked the car, carefully placed her bag on the front passenger seat, and climbed into the vehicle.

Where is she headed?

Watching Gabriella get into this car, Lauren could not understand what the Venezuelan was doing.

Why isn't she going to the rally?

While keeping an eye on the Fox, she looked around at the rest of the crowd.

Why did she all of a sudden change direction? Did she get spooked by security? Was she working with someone? Did she get tipped off that it was not safe? Who's helping her? Was the Fox's cover blown? Is my cover blown?

Lauren's eyes darted around. She looked in all directions. She tried to see if there was someone who looked suspicious – anyone who could have signaled to the Fox not to go into the arena. She worried that the Fox might be working with someone she had never seen before. She wondered if she had been set-up. The thoughts raced through her head. Lauren gripped her pistol again, just in case.

She also did not let the old Saab out of her sight. She watched as the Fox backed out of the parking spot and slowly maneuvered through the crowd and the cars looking for parking spots. Keeping one eye on the crowd around her and another on the Fox, she thought about why Gabriella would be driving away from the arena.

Is she planning on taking out the President remotely? Is one of the vehicles packed with explosives? Is there another car bomb about to go off?

That last thought made Lauren extremely nervous. She had seen the damage that a car bomb could do in Beirut. She knew it would be an ugly scene.

There are at least several thousand people in and around the hockey arena.

She felt momentarily paralyzed. She knew that she could not just go up to the Secret Service and tell them that there was a bomb planted in a car. That was the surest way to get detained and effectively sideline her from catching the Fox. She also knew running around and telling people to go home or go anywhere but the arena was not a credible choice. Again, it was a sure way to be detained.

Watching the Fox creep through the parking lot in the Saab, she had to make a decision. She could stay here and try to clear the area or warn security about the possibility of a bomb going off. Or she could follow Gabriella, wherever it was that the Venezuelan was headed. She paused for only one second.

She had to follow the Fox.

She had more of a chance of locating any bomb and bringing the Venezuelan's reign of terror to an end if she could capture Gabriella once and for all.

She sprinted back to her car. Running through the parking lot, she passed dozens of people headed to the rally. A little girl, about two-years-old, holding her grandmother's hand, waved and smiled at Lauren. The kid's gesture made Lauren feel immensely sorry and guilty for letting it get to this point. If she had taken out the Fox earlier, all of these people's lives would not be at risk.

She got to her sold BMW and turned around. She spotted the Saab still trying to maneuver through the parking lot. She fished through her purse for her keys, found the pair, went to unlock the driver's side door, and then hesitated.

What if it's my car that she rigged?

Lauren thought that it was a real possibility that this could still be a set up. Although her car was parked too far from the arena to damage the building and hurt anyone inside, it still made sense. What better way for the Fox to take out Lauren *and* terrorize people by detonating a bomb in Lauren's car. Lauren took a step back from the car.

With her adrenaline racing and the Saab pulling away, Lauren dropped to the ground. She did a quick scan of the underside of the vehicle. She did not notice any extra wires or anything that looked out of place. She popped open the trunk quickly – nothing in there either.

Lauren knew it was not the most effective inspection. But she had to get going. She could not let the Venezuelan slip away.

She unlocked the driver's side door and climbed in. She threw her bag on the passenger's seat and stuck the key in the ignition. She paused. She knew that if she turned on the car, it would trigger any bomb and she'd be dead. She said a quick prayer.

Dear God, please protect me and get me through just one more time.

Here it goes.

Lauren smiled as the BMW roared to life.

But the smile disappeared just as quickly as it had arrived. If it was not her car, Lauren thought that there might still be another car out there with C4 plastic explosives packed into it. She had to get Gabriella in her own hands and force a confession about any bomb plot.

Lauren cut through the pedestrians and the traffic

245

pouring into the parking lot. Moving as quickly as possible to get out of the crowd, she knew every car had to get on to Angela Avenue to get anywhere. She had lost track of the Saab, so she tried to figure out where the Venezuelan might be headed.

Where is she going? She lives on the other side of campus. Why is she headed out this direction? Is she headed to a safe house? Is she trying to get out of town?

That last question triggered Lauren's memory. In the chaos of worrying about a bomb threat, Lauren had forgotten that former President Miller was scheduled to arrive at any minute. From yesterday's apartment break in, Lauren knew that Gabriella had all of the details about the former President's arrival.

She must be headed to the airport.

Lauren came to the intersection of Angela Boulevard and Eddy Street. She turned right. She headed west to the airport.

There's the Saab.

Pulling up to the intersection at the traffic light at Notre Dame Avenue, Lauren spotted the Saab four cars in front of her. Her hunch had been right. As the light turned green, Lauren kept at a safe distance. She kept her car tucked directly behind the Dodge Caravan in front of her.

Several cars continued to provide a buffer between Lauren and Gabriella as they approached the intersection at Michigan and Angela. Lauren thought that the way to the airport was straight ahead, continuing along Angela Boulevard, but the Fox put on her left blinker and turned south on to Michigan Avenue. Lauren knew she could not lose Gabriella, so she turned south on to Michigan as well. Driving along Michigan, she watched as the side of the road signs advertised downtown South Bend and its various attractions.

This isn't how you get to the airport. Why is she

headed downtown?

Lauren continued to tail the Fox from a safe dis-tance. As the cars made their way over the St. Joseph River and into downtown, Lauren increasingly got the sense that the Venezuelan was not headed to the airport. But she could not figure out where she was going instead. Lauren's confusion grew as she watched the Saab turn off Michigan and on to the campus of Memorial Hospital.

Where is she going?

Lauren followed the Saab, turning off downtown South Bend's main thoroughfare. She scanned the sur-rounding area. The hospital's campus seemed relatively quiet. Lauren still did not know why the Fox had turned off here, but she watched as the Saab pulled up to the four-story parking garage, took a ticket from the automatic dispenser, waited for the gate to lift up, and then drove into the garage.

What's she doing here? Is she going to dump the Saab for a new car? Is she leading me into a trap?

Lauren knew the risks of following the Fox into a parking garage. She would be in a very tight spot. There would be only one entry and exit point. It would make things very difficult if she walked into a trap. She likely would have to shoot her way out.

With one hand on the steering wheel, she reached over to her bag. Trying to drive and keep focused on the Saab, she fished around until she got her grip on her gun. She pulled the P239 out of her handbag and readied herself.

She pulled up to the ticket dispenser and paused. She stared into the darkness. The hospital's parking garage shut out the light like every other parking garage she had ever been in. Yet here, the darkness represented more than just a structural design. She knew she was driving herself into an unknown situation – a situation where the Fox had the upper hand.

247

Lauren tightened her grip on her gun. She took the ticket from the dispenser. She grabbed the steering wheel and drove into the parking garage.

Here we go.

Where are you?

Lauren braced herself for where and how she was going to find the Fox.

She eased down on the gas. Her BMW crept along the first floor. She had rolled down all four windows to be able to hear everything around her. The open windows also provided an unobstructed view, if she had to start shooting from within the car.

Rolling slowly and quietly across the parking garage's first floor, Lauren saw no sign of the Fox or the Saab. Not all of the spots were taken, so she questioned why the Fox had avoided the first floor. She took each corner cautiously, not wanting to be caught in a hail of bullets. But three corners and three times she came into nothing – just the abyss of the parking garage. She decided to make her way to the second floor.

Her head whipped side to side as she moved stealthily up the ramp. The only thing worse than being gunned down from the front, she thought, was being caught in a crossfire of bullets. But again, she got to the top of the ramp without anyone in sight.

She took the second floor as cautiously as the first. Rolling, along she took note of the empty spots, the quiet solitude of the garage and the different cars. Toyota Carolla. Dodge Durango. Chevy Silverado. But no Saab. She came to the second ramp and approached it without hesitating.

There are only two levels to go. Where is she?

Lauren's heart started beating faster. She took the

corners even slower than she had on the first two. The anticipation grew and grew, only to drop off each time she rounded a corner and found nothing. She came around the third corner to the side with the hospital entrance and listened.

There she is.

She heard a car door close right across from the third floor entrance – about 15 yards from where the BMW stood. She slammed down on the gas and then stopped just as soon as she had started. She raised her gun, aiming through the window.

"DON'T SHOOT!"

A balding man in his early forties, dressed in a white buttondown and Dockers khaki pants thrust his left arm into the air. His right arm was held down tightly by a pregnant woman dressed in a pair of Juicy Couture velour warmups. She was breathing heavily and moaning. The man cowered backward, shielding his wife in the process.

Lauren quickly realized that this was not who she was looking for. But she did not bother to apologize. Her steely glare remained fixed on her face. And she quickly jerked her head around, so as not to be blindsided.

With the BMW stopped right in front of the hospital's third floor entrance, she looked through the double set of sliding glass doors. In between the first and second set of doors, Lauren saw a pair of elevators. Her head spun just in time to catch a mane of flowing, dark brunette hair duck behind the closing doors of the second elevator.

There she goes!

Lauren quickly pulled the BMW into the handicapped parking spot next to the entrance. She leapt out of the car, tucked her Sig Sauer into the back of her jeans, and ran into the hospital. She stood at the elevator as she watched the numbers light up. The second elevator did not stop until it got to the first floor. Lauren found the stairwell right inside the second set of doors and raced down the stairs. She ran and skipped down steps until she came to the first floor.

Arriving on the first floor, she steadied herself. She readjusted the gun in the back of her jeans. She tossed her head to let her hair fall into place. She casually opened the door and walked out on to the hospital's first floor.

Lauren looked to her right and saw the main entrance to Memorial Hospital. She looked to her left and saw a large lobby with a scattering of sofas, chairs, and coffee tables with old *People* magazines. Up on the right was the conference room where O'Riordan had held his Sunday press conference. Further down the hall, the hospital split into two separate wings – one on the right and one on the left.

Lauren did not see the Fox. She looked to her right toward the front entrance. She did not think the Fox would have come down the elevator only to walk out the front door.

She's here for a reason.

Lauren turned to her left and hustled down the hallway. Coming to the split in the hospital, she read the signs on the wall. *Children's Unit* was painted on the left side of the wall, along with an arrow pointing left. *Patient's Rooms 100 to 150* was painted on the right side of the wall, along with an arrow pointing to the right. Lauren chose to go right.

"Can I help you?"

A Polish-looking woman in her early sixties, wearing hospital scrubs, sat behind the nurses' station. She looked at Lauren curiously. Lauren looked down the hallway, saw nothing, and then looked back at the nurse. She stepped up to the nurses' station.

"Uh . . . yes, hi. I was looking for a friend of mine. Woman with dark, brunette hair. She told me to meet her down here, but I already forgot the room number."

"She's in Room 103, but I can't let you go down there. The wing is only open right now to family. So unless you're family, I can't let you down there."

"Oh yeah, I'm family," said Lauren, as she started to slowly back down the hallway.

"You got some ID to prove it?" asked the nurse skeptically.

"Um, I left it in the car, but I'll only be one second. I just need to give her something," responded Lauren.

By this point, Lauren was already several steps away from the nurses' station. She continued to walk backward, putting more distance between her and the nurse. She watched the nurse stand up from her chair, looking annoyed.

"Hey. HEY! You can't go down there! I'm calling security."

Lauren turned her back to the nurse and sprinted the ten feet to Room 103. She pulled her pistol from the back of her jeans. She put it in her right hand and extended her arm. She slowly turned the doorknob with her left hand, ignoring the nurse shouting at her and telling her not to enter that room.

Lauren opened the hospital door slowly to find Mary O'Riordan. The congressman's daughter lay in a bed in the middle of the room, with a variety of instruments attached to her body. Lauren watched as the young woman's chest slowly heaved up and down with every breath.

Lauren saw no sign of the Fox. The room appeared to be empty. There was a bathroom, however, inside the room and the bathroom door was closed.

Lauren took a step inside the hospital room. Just as she did, Gabriella slammed the door into Lauren's arm, sending her gun flying to the floor. Lauren recovered her balance to see that the Venezuelan had been hiding behind the door. The Fox leveled her fist squarely into Lauren's face and jammed her knee into Lauren's stomach. The former CIA operative was caught off guard, and she doubled over in pain.

As Lauren fell to the floor, the Fox jumped over her and began to run away. Lauren reached out, grabbing the Fox by the bottom of her jeans. She tripped Gabriella, sending the Venezuelan tumbling to the hallway ground. A needle flew out of the Fox's hand. Lauren looked up only to have the Fox kick her in the face, splitting her lip open. Lauren's head snapped back, and she watched as the Fox got up, picked up the needle, and ran down the hallway.

Momentarily stunned, Lauren leapt back on to her feet. She retrieved her handgun from within the hospital room and took off down the hallway as well. By this point, a hospital security guard had arrived on the scene. Lauren saw the old nurse at the nurses' station point to her and tell the security guard, "That's the one!"

As the security guard approached Lauren with his arm raised and hand extended to her, Lauren grabbed his hand, twisted his arm, and brought the man down to his knees. Then she took off running. She headed back toward the main entrance of the hospital.

Rounding the corner, she saw a family of four and a pair of elderly women walking through the lobby. Beyond these folks, Lauren saw the Fox head into the stairwell. Lauren quickly raised her gun, but she hesitated. She did not think she could squeeze a decent shot in between these people without risking it. She hesitated for only a second. Yet it was enough time for the Fox to slip away.

Lauren chased after the Venezuelan. She raced into the stairwell and up the stairs. She climbed the first flight of stairs, the second flight, and the third flight, following the Fox back to the third floor. Emerging from the stairwell, Lauren turned left and saw no sign of the Fox inside

253

of the hospital. She turned right and ran into the parking lot.

Just as she came into the garage, she saw the Saab. She fired twice. The shots shattered the passenger window, behind the driver. They narrowly missed Gabriella's head.

Lauren pulled out her keys, jumped into her BMW, and floored it. She followed the Saab down to the first floor. Arriving at the exit, she ignored the parking attendant waiting to take her ticket and continued speeding out on to the street.

As Lauren emerged from the garage, she found the Saab turning north on to Michigan Avenue. Lauren followed her. This time she made no effort to conceal the fact that she was tailing the Fox. She stuck closely to the Saab as it headed north on Michigan, and then turned east on to Angela Boulevard.

The drive gave Lauren a moment to catch her breath. She looked in the rearview mirror at her split lip. A trickle of blood came down her chin. She pulled a tissue out from her bag and tried to stop the bleeding. Staring at her bloody face in the mirror, she wondered what had just happened.

Why did she need to visit Mary O'Riordan? Wasn't she supposed to be at the airport waiting for the President's arrival? Why would Mary O'Riordan take precedence?

And, more importantly, where is she headed now?

Why is she heading back to Notre Dame?
How is all of this connected to the former President's visit?

Lauren tried to process what had just happened. She had no clue why the Fox went to the hospital. She wished that she had taken out the Venezuelan in the garage. Now she worried about what the Fox might do next. She followed closely behind Gabriella, as the Venezuelan drove toward Notre Dame's parking lot.

Driving back on campus, she encountered several South Bend and Notre Dame police officers managing the traffic flow. It made Lauren realize that she had to be more careful in the use of her Sig. In this setting, as soon as she fired a single shot, she was likely to be swarmed by the various law enforcement officials.

She had been driving with her left hand, while holding the gun in her right hand. Needing to be more discreet, she lowered the pistol and slid it back into her handbag.

Lauren watched as the Fox settled the Saab into a parking spot and then hustled out of the car. The two stared each other in the eyes until Gabriella broke away and headed toward the hockey arena. Lauren quickly found a spot herself, grabbed her purse, and followed after the Fox.

As she approached the Compton Family Ice Arena, Lauren paused. Two lines of people snaked into the front doors. The Venezuelan stood in the middle of the left-hand line. At the head of these lines, uniformed security ran people through magnetometers and inspected bags, as South Bend and Notre Dame police and Secret Service agents milled about.

Lauren pulled her handbag in tight, clutching her handgun from the outside and wondering how she would get past security. She checked her watched. 4:49 p.m. The former President was scheduled to appear at 5:00 p.m. She had time to run back to her car, but she feared that the Fox might slip out of sight. More importantly, she needed to have the gun with her inside the arena. She looked around the building to see if there might be another entrance, and then she saw what she needed.

Emerging from a handicapped parking spot was an elderly woman, likely to be in her mid-80's, pushing a more elderly man, probably in his early-90's, in a wheelchair. The woman was impeccably dressed in a maroon blazer, adorned with a gaudy gold brooch. She had a scratch of pink lipstick over her pursed lips and her hair dyed lavender. The man wore a houndstooth blazer with a blue and gold striped tie. A baseball hat, which covered his bald head, read "A New Deal – FDR in '32!"

Lauren hustled over to the couple. She extended her right arm with her hand open.

"Here, let me help you with that."

Both the man and the woman looked up and smiled generously.

"Oh thank you so much," said the woman.

No – thank you.

Lauren grabbed a hold of the man's wheelchair and slid her handbag on to the handles.

"We are just such big fans of President Miller. Can you believe that he has come to visit us? This is going to be such a memorable visit."

If only they knew.

Lauren guided the old man and the woman into the line. She scanned the crowd, and she saw the Fox going through the metal detector. Lauren got a bit anxious. She did not want to let the Fox out of her sight.

While waiting for the line to move, Lauren saw a teenaged campaign volunteer approach the couple and waive them to the front of the line. Lauren followed the elderly woman's lead.

"Mayor & Mrs. Trapinski. How are you? Here, come with me," said the teenager.

"Oh thank you so much. We would have been here sooner, but Frank could not find his lucky blue-and-gold tie," said the elderly woman.

"I always wear this tie on the eve of an election," chimed in her husband, waving the tie in the teenage volunteer's face.

Lauren did not know who these people were nor did she care. She just wanted to get past security and get inside the building. She tried to hide her anxiousness and smiled politely at the volunteer as he sized her up.

"Well, you made it just in time. Come on, let's head inside."

The teenager flashed a laminated badge to security.

"They're with the campaign," he said, motioning to Lauren and the elderly couple.

"Everyone still has to go through the mags," responded a weathered-looking security guard, in his late 50's, with a white handlebar mustache. The security guard pointed to the large magnetometer metal detectors. He motioned for the three of them to walk through.

"No problem," responded the volunteer cheerfully as he guided Lauren and the elderly couple back into the front of the line. The campaign volunteer stood on the other side of the magnetometers. "I'll wait for you here. You just walk on through."

Lauren wondered if she should turn around now. It would look suspicious to pull back this close to the entry. But it would look a lot worse to go through and have her

Sig P239 handgun discovered. She saw the Fox fading into the heart of the arena and knew she had to get in there.

Lauren quickly decided to push forward. She figured that, if she got caught, she would politely explain it all to the Secret Service. Her hope was that if she could not take out the Fox, at least the Service might detain the Venezuelan.

The elderly woman went first. She hobbled along, taking her time. Lauren felt as if thirty minutes had passed before this woman made it completely through. Nothing happened. The woman waited on the other side, smiling back at Lauren and her husband.

Get ready.

Lauren pushed the wheelchair forward.

BEEP-BEEP-BEEP-BEEP.

The magnetometer lit up and made a beeping noise. The commotion drew the attention of the five different police and Secret Service agents standing guard. Lauren's pulse was racing, but she steadied herself. She smiled politely at the security guard, and did not make eye contact with the police and agents.

"You go through one more time without him," said the security guard with a stern look on his face.

"Sure."

Lauren walked back through the magnetometer. She turned around to face the guard. She waited for him to motion her through.

The security guard held her there. He took out his hand-held metal detector. He ran it over the elderly man sitting in the wheelchair. Lauren tried to avoid looking at her handbag, still hanging on the wheelchair's right handle. She did not want to draw any attention to the bag or its contents.

Nothing.

No lights.

No beeping noise.

Then the security guard turned his attention back to Lauren.

"That's quite the fat lip for a pretty lady," said the security guard, oozing sleaziness.

Most women would have slapped the security guard right there. Lauren knew better. She had dealt with sleazier men than this guy. One time, trying to leave the airport in Tripoli, Libya, a Libyan customs agent asked her about her sexual habits. Lauren, playing it cool, flirted with the agent long enough to walk two duffel bags, stacked with classified information about Libya's nuclear program, right underneath the guy's nose. She pulled the same routine on this American sleazebag.

"You should see how *he* looks," said Lauren, giving the guy a wink and a sly smile.

"Alright," said the security guard, chuckling and turning red. "Come on through."

She casually walked through the magnetometer.

Nothing again.

No lights.

No beeping noise.

"You enjoy the rally, ma'am," said the security guard, smiling again.

Lauren thanked the security guard and winked one last time. She noticed that the police and Secret Service were paying attention to her. But they were staring at her, as all men stare at attractive women. Lauren knew they were not suspicious looks, so she grabbed the wheelchair and followed the teenage volunteer into the arena. As soon as the group got beyond the view of the security at the entrance, Lauren grabbed her handbag off the wheelchair.

"I have to go meet a friend. Enjoy the rally," she said, turning her back to the elderly couple and the teenage volunteer. She did not even wait for a response. She hurriedly walked into the arena.

She found the nearest entrance into the rink area and rushed in. She stood at the top of a flight of stairs that led down to the floor of the arena. Looking down, Lauren noticed that the ice rink had been removed for the event. A stage had been constructed at one end. A man in a suit stood at a single podium in the middle of the stage. Lauren listened briefly as the man shouted about the one-percent ruining Saint Joseph County and not paying their fair share.

Lauren scanned the crowd. Several hundred people stood on the floor of the arena, looking-up at the stage and applauding sporadically to the man's ramblings. Another thousand or so sat in chairs around the bowl of the lower level. Lauren had no clue where the Fox was located, if she was even in this part of the arena at all. She did not stop scanning the crowd.

"Please join me in welcoming our great Congressman – Mike O'Riordan," bellowed the man on stage.

Lauren snapped her head toward the stage. A roar went up from the crowd. The people in the lower level chairs began to stand on their feet. More people standing made Lauren nervous that the Fox would blend in more easily.

She continued to keep her eyes on the stage. She tried not to be distracted by Fleetwood Mac's "Don't Stop Thinking About Tomorrow," which blasted over the PA system. When she saw Mike O'Riordan emerge from a curtained off area on the floor of the arena, she scrutinized the entourage around him. She strained to see if the Fox was in the group or lingering behind the curtains. She did not immediately see that flowing, dark hair, so she turned her attention back to the stage.

She watched O'Riordan climb a small set of stairs on the far side of the stage. He waved to the crowd in the upper rows. He pointed to a few people down in the front rows. Then he walked over to Lauren's side of the arena.

Lauren noticed him take an extra long time to smile, wink, and mouth something to a person standing in the first row of the lower level section, where Lauren stood. Lauren got up on the tips of her toes. She peered down the section to see who attracted O'Riordan's attention.

I got you.

Lauren reached into her bag and wrapped her fingers around her pistol. She began to walk down the section. As most of the people in the stands listened to O'Riordan give his stump speech, Lauren kept her focus on the section's first row.

She slid into the sixth row of seats, on the opposite side of the stairwell. She positioned herself with a clear view of the dark brunette standing five seats into the first row. She held her bag in her left hand and gripped the Sig Sauer inside the handbag with her right hand.

Lauren sat in that sixth row patiently. She never took her eyes off of the dark brunette. While others around her laughed, cheered, and applauded various lines in O'Riordan's speech, she paid no attention. She waited and waited and waited, until approximately seventeen minutes into the speech.

"*Now, without further adieu,*" shouted O'Riordan.

When Lauren heard this, she tightened her grip on her Sig. She squared her legs in the direction of the dark brunette. She took a deep breath through her nose.

This is it. Get yourself ready.

"Ladies and Gentlemen, please welcome my good friend and a great former President – President Miller!"

TUESDAY

CHAPTER 34
TUESDAY
5:00 A.M.

"Ugggh."

Father Finnegan groaned as his internal alarm clock went off. It was a whimpering groan, barely audible. He was so overcome by the pain that even his voice had been broken.

He had experienced a rough night many times before. On any given morning, he knew he might wake up with some kind of unidentified drinking injury and not remember how it happened. Most of the time it was minor cuts and scrapes from falling on the ground or walking through bushes. Sometimes these cuts were deep gashes. On an icy February night, Father Finnegan walked across campus with a Cabernet Sauvignon bottle in hand. Slipping on a patch of ice, the bottle shattered as he hit the pavement, requiring thirty-two stitches to keep his hand from falling off.

Worse than that was the time that he came across some of his Sorin Hall residents walking home in an April rainstorm. It was around 2:30 a.m. on a Saturday morning. Father Finnegan was strolling leisurely. As the kids ran past, trying to get out of the rain, Father Finnegan told them not to be in such a rush. He said that they should enjoy God's beautiful treasures. Then he broke out into "Singin' in the Rain," and started to recreate the movie's famous dance routine. When he jumped up to kick his legs together, he could not quite recover his balance. He came down hard on his left knee, shredding his ACL in the process.

The kids rushed over to help him up. Father

Finnegan just lay on the ground, laughing. He was so drunk that he did not realize he would need a couple of surgeries and several months of rehabilitation to learn how to walk properly again. It was only one of many body parts that had broken down under the stress of so much drinking.

Sitting duct-taped to this chair, Father Finnegan wished he had been drinking. His body ached all over. An unimaginable pain shot through his arms and legs any time he tried to move them. His face throbbed from Jaworski's repeated punches, convincing him that he had shattered his cheekbones. If he had been drunk, he thought, he would not be feeling any of this terrible pain.

For Father Finnegan, this should have been a morning to celebrate. It was the first morning in fifteen years that he had not woken up drunk or intoxicated. In fact, it was the first time in fifteen years that he had gone an entire day without having a drink. Most individuals that struggle with addiction would have killed to have a breakthrough like this one.

Instead, Father Finnegan felt miserable. The immense physical pain had something to do with this feeling. The emotional pain, however, had a greater impact.

He worried about how much longer he could withhold the name that Jaworski wanted. He knew that he had taken a vow to protect the confidence of the members of his flock. At one point in his life, he would have died before revealing anything told to him in a confessional. But years of drinking had chipped away at his resolve. And now, with Jaworski certain to unleash another beating at any moment, Father Finnegan did not know how much longer he could hold on.

For inspiration, this morning's prayers came from Psalm twenty-five, verses sixteen to twenty:

Lord, look toward me, and have pity on me, for I am alone and afflicted. Relieve the troubles of my heart, and

*bring me out of my distress. Put an end to my affliction and
my suffering, and take away all my sins. Behold, my enemies are many, and they hate me violently.*
*Preserve my life, and rescue me; let me not be put to shame,
for I take refuge in you.*

"Time to get up, Father. The day is ticking away."

Father Finnegan did not bother to open his eyes.
Nor did he lift his head. He recognized the voice immediately. But he was not eager to see Bob Jaworski. He was
not ready for what he knew was coming.

When Father Finnegan did not respond, Jaworski
walked up and put two fingers on the priest's neck. He
searched for a pulse. Father Finnegan continued to sit in
the chair, slumped over. He was not dead yet.

"Listen, Father, I've already told you this. We can
do this the hard way or the easy way. Either way justice is
going to be served," said Jaworski, in a matter-of-fact tone.

Jaworski stepped back two feet to inspect the priest.
Still Father Finnegan did not respond.

"Okay, if that's how you want it to be."

Jaworski walked back to Father Finnegan. He lifted
up the priest's head and steadied it. He raised his right arm
and slapped Father Finnegan with a swift, hard backhand.
The slap jolted Father Finnegan's eyes open. Jaworski
grabbed the priest's head again to steady it.

"You hear me?" asked Jaworski, raising his voice
this time.

Jaworski bent his knees so that he was eye level
with the priest. Father Finnegan's eyes were open, but he
did not respond. Except for a single tear trickling down his
face, Father Finnegan continued to show no emotion.

"I know you're in a lot of pain and I don't want to
be doing this. But your pain and my pain will go away if
you just start talking."

Still, Father Finnegan did not respond.

Jaworski took a step back from Father Finnegan. He pulled back his right arm and cracked the priest in the face. The punch sent Father Finnegan's head flying backward. It split open his lip. A stream of blood poured down the priest's chest.

Jaworski walked away from the deflated priest. He shook his right hand to get rid of the pain from the punch. Standing with his back to Father Finnegan, he looked down at his thick, swollen knuckles. While he was inspecting his hand, he paused.

Father Finnegan mumbled something inaudible.

"What'd you say?" asked Jaworski as he turned his attention back to Father Finnegan.

With his head still hanging toward the floor, Father Finnegan mumbled again. Jaworski cocked his head and closed in on the priest. He squatted like a baseball catcher to look Father Finnegan squarely in the eyes, but the priest's eyes remained closed. Jaworski stood there, as the pressure built in his knees, waiting for Father Finnegan to repeat himself.

"I had just finished the 6:00 a.m. mass," said Father Finnegan, speaking faintly.

Jaworski strained to hear him.

"I help out over at Little Flower. I'm up early, so I usually take the 6:00 a.m. mass on the weekdays. It's the same routine every morning. I get there and open up the church at 5:30. I say a brief mass and then touch base with some of the regulars. After people clear out, I always head to the confessional."

Father Finnegan paused to catch his breath. It was a struggle to speak each word. But he was compelled to tell Jaworski the entire story before the Lord called him home.

"Who was it?" demanded Jaworski.

"Most days I sit there by myself, asking God's forgiveness for my many failings. That day did not seem to be

269

much different. I sat there for a good ten, fifteen minutes by myself. Just as I was getting ready to leave, someone entered the other side of the confessional."

"Who was it?" demanded Jaworski again, this time with more intensity.

Father Finnegan did not respond to Jaworski. He did not bother to open his eyes. He continued talking.

"I settled back into my seat and said 'Good Morning,' to break the ice. The person on the other side said nothing. I figured I should just give the person some time."

Father Finnegan paused again without saying a word.

"There are two types of people that come to confession. The first are the 'Guilters.' These are the people that feel guilty about every little bad thing they have done or even think they have done. They'll sit with you forever telling you they cursed when they touched something hot or sped through a yellow light or saw a naked person on TV. They won't feel absolved until you give them a few 'Hail Mary's' and 'Our Fathers' to recite.

This was not my gentleman. He was one of the others. These people come in with a real heavy heart, something serious on their minds that they just want to unload. They seek God's forgiveness and want to know that everything is going to be okay. With these types, you have to give them some time to feel comfortable. You want them to set the tone."

"WHO WAS HE?" asked Jaworski, this time shouting.

Father Finnegan just sat there with his head hung low, not looking at Jaworski. He continued to struggle to get out the words. The priest summoned all of his remaining strength and poured out his heart one last time.

"We sit there for a few minutes not saying a word. Finally the gentleman opens up. He starts by telling me that I can convey everything he says to the police to help them find the body. I had no clue what he was talking about. I usually don't get to the papers until after mass. I hadn't seen the news. I hadn't heard anything about a kid. But I tell him that I understand and will respect his wishes."

"What'd he tell you?" asked Jaworski, more anxious now than angry.

"He says the kid . . ."

"That's my son you're talking about it. Not just some kid."

"I'm sorry," said Father Finnegan, honestly feeling remorseful. "So he just says that the police can find your son buried underneath a rock pile in the Saint Joseph River. The body . . . I'm sorry . . . your son is right near the entrance to River Bend historic district, off of Riverside Drive."

"What else?"

Father Finnegan hesitated.

"What else did he say?" asked Jaworski angrily.

"He said 'I'm sorry.'"

Father Finnegan sensed that Jaworski had backed away from him. At this point, Father Finnegan opened his eyes. He saw the change in the union boss's demeanor. He could tell that Jaworski's anger had been overtaken by grief. He had presided over plenty of funerals to recognize a bereaved family member.

"What did you say to the guy?" asked Jaworski solemnly.

"Nothing. He left before I could make any sense of what was going on. I sat there for about ten minutes thinking it all through. Then I left the confessional, got my jacket from the sacristy, and drove downtown to the police station. I'm in a bit of a shock as I walk through the door. One of my parishioners is a police officer. He sees me and comes over. I ask if there is somewhere private we can talk. And I tell him exactly what the man had asked me to tell the police."

Father Finnegan ended the story at that point. He remembered seeing Jaworski as they pulled Tommy from the water. He did not need to remind the grieving father of that moment.

He did not need to remind himself of that moment either. The images had been flashing through his head for the last fifteen years. No number of open-casket wakes prepared Father Finnegan for the shock that came from witnessing a ten-year-old's body dragged from the water. Seeing Tommy in that state caused Father Finnegan to do some serious questioning of his own faith.

Right now, however, Father Finnegan felt some relief. He knew it was tough for Jaworski to relive the story. Yet he thought the moment provided some release. In turn, he hoped Jaworski might reconsider any revenge plans he had for him or anyone else. He prayed that Jaworski might finally let him go.

"So who is this guy?" asked Jaworski, dropping his solemn tone and closing in on the priest's face.

A hint of anger and rage could be detected at the back of Jaworski's voice.

Father Finnegan did not respond, but he did dismiss any hope that Jaworski would let him go.

"I said, did you ask this guy his name?" demanded Jaworski, as he shook Father Finnegan.

Father Finnegan continued to sit collapsed in his chair, not showing any emotion. All that talking had drained Father Finnegan. He breathed heavily. He still did not lift his head.

"No, I didn't," said Father Finnegan, using every ounce of energy to respond.

"Guy's sittin' inches from you. Just confesses to killing my son . . . MY SON," repeated Jaworski, in an even louder voice. "He tells you where he's hidden the body and you never once ask his name?"

"No."

"So you have no clue who this guy is?" asked Jaworski, continuing to raise his voice and tightening his grip on Father Finnegan's shoulders.

"Oh no . . . I know exactly who he is."

"I was worried about you."

"Sorry, my phone died and I left the charger here," said George, as he entered his living room.

Lauren stood in the living room. She held her Sig Sauer P239 in her right hand, as her arm hung by her side. She wore pajama pants and a Notre Dame t-shirt.

She slept upstairs last night. But she awoke when she heard George entering the house. She raced downstairs, with her gun, not expecting it to be her husband.

"Where have you been? What's been happening?" asked Lauren, anxiously.

"I've been at Jimmy's house all night. I just came home to shower and change clothes," said George. He looked as if he needed a shower and change of clothes badly. His clothes from the day before were covered in soot from the explosion. Flecks of dirt littered his short, cropped hair. Dry blood crusted over on his forehead.

"All night?"

George nodded his head and walked into the house. He put his wallet and keys on the dining room table. He found a cell phone charger sticking out from an outlet on the kitchen wall, plugged in his phone, and sat it on the kitchen counter.

"Why all night?"

"Cause you told me not to let him out of my sight," responded George. "So after the cops investigated and the fire department cleaned things up and the EMTs took care of the volunteers, we headed to Jimmy's parents' house."

"He still lives with his parents?"

"Yeah, over in the Sunnymede area."

"What'd his parents say?"

"Nothing really. A couple of academics who seemed oblivious to what was going on. It was almost as if their son was organizing the neighborhood kids for a game of capture the flag, not running for the United States Congress."

"So where is he now?"

"He's still at his parents' place."

"You left him there by himself?"

"Yeah, but don't worry, the cops are with him."

"The cops? What are they doing?"

"Providing a security detail. Even though the FBI determined that the explosion came from an old gasline and not from a car bomb, apparently they still thought Jimmy should have some kind of security detail. The local South Bend cops said that the FBI and the Capitol Hill Police requested it. They said something about the threat level."

"What do you mean 'something about the threat level?'"

"I don't know. They just spoke in vague terms. They didn't exactly give me a full briefing."

"You don't remember what they said?"

"I remember a lot of what they said. FBI spent a good thirty minutes interrogating me. I just don't remember what they said about the threat level."

"They *interrogated* you?"

George simply nodded his head.

"What'd they ask?"

"A lot. It was those same agents that came by the house yesterday – Winters and Calvin. They asked all of the same questions they asked yesterday. I guess to check for inconsistencies."

"But what specifically did they ask?"

"First they wanted to know everything in my background – where I was born, who are my parents. Stuff like that. I asked them why they needed any of this stuff and then they got more specific. They wanted to know what I was doing with the campaign, how I knew Jimmy, everywhere I'd been the last few days."

"What'd you tell them?"

"The truth."

"You tell them about Father Finnegan?"

"I told them the same thing that I told them yesterday."

"What'd you say?" asked Lauren.

"I said: 'I told you this yesterday.' And then repeated what I told them yesterday."

"So they don't suspect anything?"

"I don't know."

"You don't know?"

"How am I supposed to know? They didn't exactly tell me what they suspected or what leads they had or what they needed to follow up on."

"How'd it all end?"

"How'd what all end?"

"The FBI's questioning. How'd it end? They tell you that you were free to go or that they were going to be keeping an eye on you or anything like that?"

"They didn't get the chance. Jimmy came over in the middle of it and told them not to worry about me. He told them I was with him. So they stopped asking me questions."

"They just stopped?"

"Yeah, just stopped asking me questions right there. But they spent some time talking with Jimmy about giving him a security detail."

"What'd he think about it all?"

"The security detail?"

"Everything. The kid's gone through a lot in these

last few days. He must be pretty upset?" asked Lauren.

"Not at all," said George, as he shook his head back-and-forth to signal that Lauren's presumption was wrong. "He's in a great mood – best mood I've seen him in the last two days. That's why I didn't sleep last night. Jimmy was too excited. He was acting like a little kid on Christmas morning. He wanted to talk non-stop."

"About what?"

"About everything, but mostly politics. He talked about voter turnout for today. He talked about the themes he wanted to highlight in his victory speech. He talked about what committees he was interested in."

"So he's convinced he'll win?"

"Definitely. It's quite the turnaround from the last couple of days. When he showed up on Saturday, he was scared out of his wits. Really worried that the cops thought he had attacked O'Riordan's daughter. His only concern was staying out of jail, not winning an election. Even yesterday, his heart did not seem to be in the campaign. We went to several events where the turnout was really low. He'd walk out of every event looking like someone had just shot his dog in front of him. There was no fight to him. He was completely deflated."

"And now he thinks he'll win?"

"Now he thinks he could have out-campaigned Kennedy in 1960."

"What a strange turnaround."

"It's been bizarre to watch the complete transformation. Since the explosion, he's had a whole new attitude."

"He's not scared about another attack?"

"Not at all. It's almost as if he was glad that the explosion happened."

"But didn't you say that some staffer died?"

"An elderly volunteer had a heart-attack and died on the way to the hospital."

"And Jimmy didn't express any concern?

"Lauren, the kid didn't even seem to notice."

The pair stood in their kitchen, staring at each other. George could tell that his wife found this entire situation as odd as he did. George had spent hardly any time with Lauren over these last few days. He hoped this gave her some sense of all that he had been going through.

"How are you holding up?" asked Lauren.

"I'm tired. I'm stressed. I'm pissed. These last several days have been a lot. What else do you want to know?"

"You didn't find out anything more about Father Finnegan?"

"No," responded George angrily. "Just that white van outside Jimmy's headquarters. He said it belonged to a few union guys that helped out around the campaign. But he was real cagey about it all. Wouldn't explain who these guys were or what exactly they did for the campaign. I got nothing."

"What do you think?"

"I don't know. They could be real muscle. Or they could be your regular campaign dirty tricks unit – stealing opponent's signs, cutting the microphones at events. Those type of activities. Nothing malicious, just dirty. But I don't know. I didn't meet these guys nor do I have a good enough sense of the political landscape to really know how rough it is."

"So what are you going to do?"

"Get showered, change, and head back out there. There's a whole schedule of events for today. He's going to be at St. Joe's High School in about thirty minutes to greet voters. He wanted me to meet him there."

"You're gonna go?"

"I don't want to. I'm exhausted. I missed the entire day of classes. I nearly lost my life. But I don't think I have a choice. There's still no sign of Father Finnegan and Jimmy and this Jaworski fella seem to be our only leads."

"Well, hang in there, I know it's been tough, but you still got time. That guy who snatched Father Finnegan said that it would all be over today, right?

"Yeah, one way or another, I guess . . ." responded George, not wanting to specifically talk about what might happen to Father Finnegan if George did not find the priest.

"How are you holding up?" George asked his wife.

"I didn't sleep a wink," said Lauren.

"But I thought nothing happened?" asked George.

"Nothing at all. I was ready, too. I had a perfect line of sight. I could have taken her out before she had the opportunity to move. But nothing happened."

"Nothing happened?" asked George, now taking control of asking questions.

"Well, not nothing. But I mean nothing in the sense that she made no moves that indicated she was going to attack the President. It was actually the exact opposite. She clapped and cheered and laughed along with the rest of the crowd. She did what any good foreign operative does – she blended into her surroundings."

"I thought you said she was supposed to be with O'Riordan?"

"Well, she wasn't. She had a seat in the first row of the lower level. But O'Riordan came out on stage and waved and mouthed something to her."

"What'd he say?"

"I couldn't pick it up from where I was standing."

"How'd she respond?"

"I couldn't see her face. But she was clapping and cheering along with everyone else in the section. It was quite the show of devotion."

"So why don't you think she was backstage with him?"

279

"I don't know. Maybe it was a political decision. Maybe it was because she was running late."

"Running late?" asked George, inquisitively.

"That's right. She stopped at the hospital before the rally to visit O'Riordan's daughter."

"How do you know?"

"I was there."

The expression on George's face said he was partly annoyed that she had done this and partly curious about what happened.

"I was at the Kellogg Center when she finished with classes, and I tailed her. At first, I thought she was headed to the airport to meet former President Miller on arrival. Instead, she headed downtown to Memorial Hospital. So I followed her into the hospital. She made a brief visit to the daughter's room and then left."

George paused before responding. He was processing it all in his head.

"Lauren, you know the daughter died, right?"

"What are you talking about? When?"

"Last night. Jimmy got tipped off by a reporter and then we saw it on the eleven o'clock news."

"What'd she die from?"

"I think that they said she died from causes related to the injury. They said that she had been stabbed in the abdomen and had lost a lot of blood as a result."

"What time was this?"

"I don't know exactly. A few minutes into the eleven o'clock news."

"No, I mean what time did she die?"

"I think they said something like five o'clock."

"Something like five o'clock?"

"I don't remember the exact time of death. Why does it even matter what time it was?" asked George.

"George – we were at the hospital a little before

five."

"Yeah, you already told me that. That's why I thought it was weird she went to visit a dead person."

"George, she wasn't dead when I saw her."

"You saw her?" asked George, skeptically.

"Yeah, she was attached to various machines. She looked like she was sleeping, not dead."

"Well maybe she died after you guys left."

"George, it's too much of a coincidence."

"What are you saying? That the Fox killed O'Riordan's daughter? Lauren, I think you're too obsessed with this woman.

You thought she triggered a car bomb in downtown South Bend. It turned out to be an old gasline that hadn't been updated since the 19th century.

You thought she was going to assassinate the former President. But then she said that she sat in the stands applauding at every cheesy line like a teenage groupie at a rock concert.

Now you think she killed her lover's daughter in some kind of Stephen King fantasy fiction?

Lauren – I know you guys have a past. But maybe it's time to put that past behind you. Why don't you call those FBI agents that have been hounding me and let them handle it?"

George's plea to Lauren stemmed partially from his concern for her safety. It also stemmed from his personal frustrations. The last several days had upended both of their lives. He never thought he would think this, but he wanted a return to the normal law school routine.

Despite the plea, Lauren did not respond. She walked upstairs. George followed after her.

"What are you doing?" asked George.

Lauren changed into a pair of jeans. She slipped on a tight sweater over a camisole. Her handbag sat on a chair in the corner. She grabbed it, pulled out her gun, and tucked it in the back of her jeans. She hustled downstairs. George went downstairs as well.

"Lauren," said George, grabbing her arm and looking her right in the eyes. "Where are you going?"

"George . . . I've got her now."

"Hi, I'm Jimmy. I'd love to represent you in Congress. I hope that I can count on your support."

Jimmy King stood just outside the entrance to the gymnasium at Saint Joseph's High School. The gym served as one of the county's many polling locations. An overnight winter storm blanketed the ground outside the gym with snow and ice. Jimmy wore a navy blue topcoat to fend off the cold. The large coat hung loose on Jimmy, accentuating his boyishness.

As each voter approached the gym, Jimmy thrust out an open hand to welcome them. He wore a glove on his left hand and nothing on his right hand. He insisted on making a personal, physical connection with each voter. He looked each person in the eye, flashed a full smile, and repeated these short, three lines over and over. Despite the frigid temperatures and the drafty coat, Jimmy radiated warmth.

It was a complete change from yesterday morning's disappointing campaign events. At each stop, Jimmy could tell that there was no momentum behind his campaign. No one wanted to donate. No one wanted a photo. No one even wanted to stop and talk.

The gasline explosion turned everything around. Jimmy sensed it right away. A surge of phone calls to campaign headquarters offering to donate or volunteer confirmed his suspicions. The polls released this morning, showing a dead heat between Jimmy and O'Riordan, signaled to the country that Jimmy might win this thing after all.

To capitalize on this surge in the polls, Jimmy strategically chose to stand at this polling location. He spent last night going over the population demographics of the congressional district and the corresponding polling locations. Jimmy thought his base of support came from young professionals and retirees. He needed a very strong turnout from these two core constituencies in order to win. Saint Joe's gymnasium covered a precinct with that exact demographic.

Jimmy chose to be here so early in the morning for another strategic reason. He wanted the optics of him greeting these voters to spread throughout the district. He hoped it would generate enthusiasm amongst these constituencies, resulting in more voters getting to the polls.

He also wanted to send a message to his rival's base of support. Democrats in the district traditionally do not start to see their votes come in until the late afternoon or early evening. Union members need to be on the factory line before the polling places open, so they always wait until later in the day when they are off work. Jimmy thought that these reliable Democrats might be discouraged from voting if they saw and heard reports of a heavy turnout against their man O'Riordan.

Based on the first hour that the polls had been open, Jimmy felt good about his decision. A steady stream of voters made their way to the polling booths. Jimmy repeated himself over and over with each individual voter, not once showing any sign of being tired or bored by repeating himself so frequently. A pack of television cameras and still photographers, kept in a holding area twenty yards from the gym's entrance, captured him courting voters.

Jimmy knew the press was watching his every move, and like a high school drama student he played up to the cameras. He gestured and posed in an attempt to project himself as the next great American statesman.

Jimmy's security detail helped with the image. After the explosion, the South Bend Police told Jimmy that the FBI and Capitol Hill Police wanted him covered. Although many public officials hate the restrictions of a security detail, Jimmy jumped at the opportunity. He knew that the security would add gravitas.

On this final day of campaigning, two burly uniformed officers accompanied Jimmy everywhere that he went. And Jimmy took full advantage of them. He carefully positioned them in spots where the media would be sure to capture the detail.

Jimmy coordinated another stage prop for the cameras. A dozen St. Joe's students milled about in "Jimmy King for Congress" shirts, waving homemade posters, and chanting "Jimmy, Jimmy, He's Our Man. If He Can't Do It, Nobody Can." The noisy teenagers created an atmosphere of excitement. Jimmy fed off the adoring students' attention, cracking jokes about the school cafeteria's infamous meatloaf and dispensing advice on how to get into Harvard. The students hung on every word.

Jimmy went through St. Joe's as number one in his class all four years. Back then he did not think that his peers gave him the proper credit for his academic achievements. He steamed every time a St. Joe athlete's picture appeared in the *South Bend Tribune*. He complained about every announcement promoting the next school play. He thought more attention should be given to his perfect SAT score.

Today, however, Jimmy felt invigorated by the students' presence and the underlying message. He knew that the St. Joe's administration would not have permitted students to campaign on school grounds, unless the administration tacitly supported the candidate. Since St. Joe's was the most prestigious school in South Bend – the place where every Notre Dame professor sent their kid to be educated – he knew the South Bend establishment could be coming around on him. Years of craving recognition might finally be fulfilled.

"This is great, huh?" said Jimmy, whispering into George DeMarco's ear.

He did not wait for a response. He kept extending his arm to shake hands or delicately squeeze a forearm in a show of appreciation. He hugged elderly women and thanked them for their prayers. He grabbed a nine-month-old baby from its stroller and held the baby in his arms, smiling for the cameras. He displayed the ease of a natural politician and he knew it.

"Hi! I'm Jimmy King."

"I know," responded an attractive woman in her mid-thirties, with a firm handshake.

"Well, can I count on your support today?"

"I'm actually not voting."

"It's not too late to register," said Jimmy. "You can request a ballot inside. You just need to show them a driver's license."

"No, it's not that I'm not registered. I vote in D.C."

Jimmy stopped shaking the woman's hand and pulled back. He gave her a curious look.

"What's a D.C. voter doing in Northern Indiana on Election Day?" asked Jimmy, knowing that there was a specific reason the woman turned up at this polling place.

"I'm Allison Fratelli."

Jimmy knew the name as soon as she said it. Fratelli had earned a reputation around D.C. politicos for being a tough, thorough, and unrelenting investigative journalist. Around the Hill, staffers nicknamed her "The Breaker" for the number of scandals she broke about members of Congress caught up in prostitution rings, kick-back schemes, drug busts, and every other crime of moral turpitude. The name also suggested that she had a not-too-subtle ability to bust the ego and testosterone of every puffed up male Congressman. The party caucuses warned incoming members not to get involved with Fratelli unless they were looking to get seriously burned.

Jimmy flashed his wide grin.

"How can I help you, Allison?"

"I'm with the *Washington Post*, and I just wanted to get a few minutes with the Comeback Kid," said Fratelli, batting her eyes and smiling flirtatiously.

One of the burley South Bend cops stepped in between Fratelli and Jimmy, knocking George DeMarco out of the way in the process. He blocked Jimmy completely from Fratelli's view.

"Ma'am, I'm afraid you'll have to take your place with the rest of the journalists," said the cop, extending an arm toward the press pack gathered twenty yards away.

Fratelli took one step backward. She folded her arms on her chest. She did not say anything.

"It's okay, Mike," said Jimmy, putting a hand on the cop's shoulder. "We'll just be a few minutes."

The cop moved out from in between the aspiring politician and the investigative journalist. Jimmy did not stop smiling at Fratelli as this unfolded. He was glad to see Fratelli. *The Post* would not bother sending her out here on Election Day if they did not think that he was going to be important someday. He knew he was destined for greatness, and now the D.C. insiders were paying attention. All the signs pointed toward a victory today. Not even a Fratelli hit piece could derail things.

Besides, he did not fear Fratelli. He had heard the warnings about dealing with her. But he thought those were mostly geared toward dopey politicians who did not have his sterling academic credentials. He graduated from Harvard. He was a Marshall Scholar. He had spent time in D.C. He knew how the game was played.

"The Comeback Kid, huh?"

"It's quite an incredible story. You were on no one's radar a few months ago. Yesterday people had you left for dead, both literally and figuratively. I get a call in the middle of the night from my editor telling me to get to South Bend because the Comeback Kid is going to pull things out. You know how tough it is to find a last minute flight to South Bend?"

Jimmy laughed and blushed, believing every word she said.

"Well, we're glad you made it."

"I had to get out here to see the next John Kennedy for myself."

Fratelli's quip made Jimmy blush even more. He dropped his head and shook it in disbelief. He loved John Kennedy.

"So what do you want to talk about?"

"Um . . . is there some place where we can talk quietly?"

"Sure, let's head inside," said Jimmy. He nodded his head as if to convey that he understood the significance of this interview. "George, why don't you join us. Allison, do you know George DeMarco?"

"I don't. Hi I'm Allison. What do you do with the campaign?"

"George has been my right-hand man," said Jimmy confidently acting like the two were best friends. "He's been an instrumental part of this remarkable campaign."

George did not say a word, but walked with Jimmy, Allison, and the two South Bend cops inside St. Joe's. Jimmy led the group down the hallway to an office with a sign reading "Principal Krystal." He opened the door to a secretary sitting behind a desk in the middle of the room.

"Mrs. O'Leary, how are you?" asked Jimmy, giving the sixty-year-old secretary a hug.

"Jimmy, it's great to see you. I voted for you first thing this morning. We're all just so proud of you."

"Aw, thanks, Mrs. O'Leary. It means so much to have your support," said Jimmy. "Say, would it be okay if we used Principal Krystal's office for a few minutes? Ms. Fratelli is here from the *Washington Post* to do a feature on me."

"Of course, he's at a meeting in the teacher's lounge, so the room is all yours," said the secretary, opening the door to the principal's office and showing them inside. One of the cops waited outside in the hallway, while the other remained staked out in the secretary's foyer.

Jimmy walked over to the desk and sat down. Fratelli sat in a chair in front of the desk. George took a seat at a coffee table in the corner.

"So, what do you want to talk about?" asked Jimmy, leaning back in the chair and putting his feet up on the desk.

"Well, I was hoping that you could walk me through your campaign up until now. It's really been quite impressive how you've managed to run such a spectacular campaign despite everyone writing you off."

"You know, I don't pay much attention to the doubters. I personally have never had any doubt that we would win this thing. From day one, I knew that if I got out there and I met with the people and they had a chance to hear my message, they'd know that I offered a fresh, new vision for this country."

"I have to ask this, but did you think that Mary O'Riordan's attack and death helped you at all? It seems as if it may have distracted Congressman O'Riordan."

"The attack on Mary was a horrific tragedy and my sympathy and condolences go out to the O'Riordan Family. With that being said, it is a completely distinct issue from the campaign. We are going to win today in spite of Mary's death, not because of it."

"And what about yourself? How have you managed to stay so focused with everything going on, especially with yesterday's explosion and the death of your campaign volunteer?"

"I think it's a testament to my discipline and my focus that I've been able to run such a positive and successful campaign, despite the swirling distractions."

"Everything that's happened in this campaign has been quite remarkable. I don't think I've ever seen anything quite like it. How do you explain all of these events?"

"What do you mean 'explain?'"

"I mean there's just been so many extraordinary events happening – Mary's attack and death, the missing priest, the explosion – and throughout all of this you've managed to go from zero name recognition to neck-and-neck with a fifteen-term incumbent. Don't you think that it's a bit odd that, one, all of these things happened and, two, that you've come out stronger in the polls?"

"I'm not here to explain this unfortunate series of events. I've just stayed focused on delivering a positive message and a fresh vision for the people of Northern Indiana."

"So you're saying that these events are completely unrelated to the campaign?"

"I cannot explain why or how so many terrible events keep plaguing the people of Northern Indiana. But I vow to fight for them every day," said Jimmy, ignoring the gist of the question.

"And what does Bob Jaworski think about these events?"

Jimmy paused, but kept smiling. The question caught him off guard. Yet he wanted to maintain a cool façade for Fratelli.

"I'm sorry, but I don't speak for Mr. Jaworski," responded Jimmy, not knowing where she was headed with this line of questioning.

"Wasn't his son your best friend growing up? Don't you stay in contact? Has he given you any advice or guidance about the campaign?" asked Fratelli.

"I haven't spoken with Mr. Jaworski in a long time," responded Jimmy, this time more forcefully.

"What do you think he would say about your campaign?"

The smile disappeared from Jimmy's face. He was starting to get angry. He did not want anyone asking about his relationship with Jaworski until this election was long over.

"I'm sorry, you're going to have to ask him these questions," said Jimmy, glaring at the woman.

"Would you mind putting me in touch with him?"

Jimmy stood up from behind the desk. He walked over to the door and opened it.

"Thanks for your time. We've got to get to another campaign event. Mike, would you mind escorting Ms. Fratelli back to the press pool?"

Jimmy exited to the hallway. He forced a smile back on to his face to show the reporter that he could not be rattled. On the way out, he gave Mrs. O'Leary a hug and thanked her again. He did not make eye contact with Fratelli as the police officer escorted her out.

"Greg," said Jimmy to the other South Bend cop. "Would you mind getting the car ready? We've got to get over to Clay High School."

The cop turned and headed back to the exit through the gymnasium. George began to follow the cop. Jimmy stopped him. He waited until the second police officer turned the corner and was out of sight.

"You drove yourself, right?" asked Jimmy.

"Yeah, the car's parked out in front of the gymnasium," responded George.

"Get your car, don't let the security detail know, and meet me at the faculty parking lot in the back of the school."

"Why? Where do you want to go?"

"The Grotto."

"Why the Grotto?"

"I've got to go talk to Jaworski."

"Great morning to be alive, isn't it?"

A tall and skinny, fifty-year-old man, dressed in cold weather running gear, ran past Bob Jaworski. He shouted this question and flashed a wide smile without breaking his stride.

Jaworski hastily pulled away from looking out on Saint Mary's Lake to see the runner coming down the path. The runner caught Jaworski by surprise. For one thing, the below freezing temperatures, the biting wind, and the icy ground made it a difficult day to be out walking, let along running.

The runner also startled Jaworski because the union boss had been lost in his own thoughts. Fifteen years ago, on this date and at this time, Jaworski stood by helplessly as the police pulled Tommy out of the Saint Joseph River. As he walked along the path this morning, he thought about Tommy and nothing else.

After being shaken from his thoughts, Jaworski continued walking along the lake path. He stopped when he came to an opening directly across from the Grotto. On warmer days, a collection of ducks and geese milled about, waiting for families with young kids to come by and feed them. With today being so cold and dreary, no ducks, geese, or families hung around. Jaworski stood there by himself as the images and emotions from fifteen years ago ran through his head.

He and his wife had been annoyed when Tommy did not arrive home for dinner. At first, they told themselves he went to dinner at a friend's house and forgot to call home. When the dinner hour came and went, the Jaworskis began calling around to Tommy's friends, starting first with Jimmy King. As each phone call ended with a "No, we haven't seen Tommy," Jaworski became angry and his wife became nervous.

Jaworski put in a call to one of his buddies, Police Chief Ralph O'Halloran, to see if the cops on the beat could ask around. O'Halloran assured Jaworski that Tommy was probably just off goofing around and that they would find the kid. As the night progressed and O'Halloran had nothing to report, Jaworski hit the streets himself. He feared the worst, so he talked to every lowlife that ventured out only after midnight – the pimps, the prostitutes, the drug dealers. No one had seen or heard anything about Tommy.

Jaworski arrived back at his house as the sun came up. Sitting down with a cup of coffee, he and his wife looked optimistically at one another when the phone rang. Jaworski put down the coffee and grabbed the phone. O'Halloran's words echoed in his ears.

Bob, come meet me on Riverside Drive.

From O'Halloran's tone, Jaworski knew it did not sound good. He tried to stay positive. He hoped that he would be reunited with his son.

Arriving on the scene to an array of cops, firefighters and EMTs caused any optimism to quickly dissipate. Jaworski rushed out of the car. He saw a rescue diver from the fire department emerge from the water. The diver carried Tommy's limp, blue body in his arms.

Jaworski barreled through the crowd, racing to get to the river's edge. He grabbed his son from the firefighter's arms. He clutched the boy tightly to his chest.

He refused to believe that Tommy was gone, pulling the kid in even closer. O'Halloran put a hand on Jaworski's shoulder, telling him to let go. Jaworski remained with a steadfast grip. He knew that once he let go, it meant that he had to let go forever. Jaworski stood there in the cold November air, clutching Tommy and letting the icy water soak his clothes.

Looking out on Saint Mary's Lake, Jaworski could feel that icy water from fifteen years ago. If Tommy had been alive, some warmth would have radiated off his body. But it was cold water then and it was a wave of coldness that washed over Jaworski now. He tried his best to fight back tears.

He stared down into the water. That did not help. Glimpses of Tommy's face, with his sunken eyes and bluish hued skin, stared back at Jaworski. He could not shake that image from his mind.

He closed his eyes and let the tears stream down his face. He stood there for a few minutes, letting the wind whip across his face. Taking a deep breath, Jaworski wiped the tears away and walked the thirty feet to the Grotto.

Jaworski visited Notre Dame's replica of the grotto at Lourdes, France, each year on the date and time of Tommy's death. He came to the Grotto for the same reason that Notre Dame students came to the Grotto – comfort and inspiration.

Jaworski wanted God to take away Tommy's pain, his wife's pain, his pain. He wanted God to forgive him for not being there to keep Tommy safe. And, most importantly, he wanted God's help in bringing justice to Tommy's killer.

Jaworski took out a pack of matches and lit one solitary candle. The candle stood out amongst the dozens of unlit candles. Its flame illuminated the Grotto on this dark and windy morning. Jaworski walked behind the metal banister and lowered himself on to the kneeler. He closed his eyes and hung his head.

Kneeling in this serene atmosphere, Jaworski found himself humbled by the moment. He did not have the

strength to talk directly to God. His Catholic guilt made
him ashamed of how he had treated Father Finnegan. But
he wanted forgiveness, so he started by talking to the Virgin
Mary.

Hail Mary, full of grace . . .

As he prayed silently to himself, Jaworski sensed
another person approach from behind. He did not turn his
head to see who it was. Nor did he open his eyes when the
person joined him on the kneeler. He continued to pray.

"Guess who just had an interview with the *Washington Post*?" whispered the person next to him on the kneeler.

Jaworski stopped praying. He recognized the an-
noying, whiny voice immediately, but he kept his eyes
closed. He did not want to give Jimmy the satisfaction of
garnering his attention.

"*The Post* sent their toughest reporter out to do a
profile on me. Apparently, I'm the talk of Washington. No
one can believe the remarkable job I've done. Everyone
had me written for dead. Now, the polls show me surging
and people just can't stop talking about me. They're calling me the 'Comeback Kid.' I'm like Clinton in 1992."

Jaworski did not respond.

"But I'm smarter than Clinton, I know how to
handle the media traps. This reporter wanted to get me
talking about O'Riordan's daughter or Father Finnegan or
yesterday's explosion – anything to try and dig some dirt.
But I knew what was coming. You should have seen me – I
was so on-message."

Jaworski ignored Jimmy's ramblings and went back
to praying.

"She even tried to bait me on you."

Jaworski stopped praying.

"She tried so many different angles too. She asked
'What does Bob Jaworski think about these events?' 'What
type of advice is he giving you?' 'When did you last talk to

him?'"

Jaworski could no longer ignore Jimmy. He opened his eyes, but he kept them focused on the Grotto and avoided eye contact with Jimmy. He waited for Jimmy to explain what he had said to the reporter.

"She's the toughest journalist in Washington, but I was ready for her and I totally outsmarted her. I can't wait to see the fawning profile in tomorrow's *Post*. That town's not gonna know what hit them when I arrive."

"What'd you say to her?" grumbled Jaworski.

"What?"

"What'd you tell this reporter?" asked Jaworski in a harsher tone.

"Nothing. She tried, but like I said, she got nothing out of me."

"What did you tell her specifically?"

"I told her we had not been in touch. I said I don't speak for you. And I said that if she wanted your thoughts, she'd have to speak with you directly."

Jaworski did not respond. He closed his eyes again and dropped his head.

"Don't worry about it. She does not suspect a thing and I didn't give her anything to suspect. We're good – just relax."

Jaworski still did not respond.

"Besides, as long as you keep your guys under control this afternoon, I'm gonna win this thing. It's gonna be huge news and I'm gonna have huge clout. Then there's no way they can touch me. I'll be the Teflon Congressman, just like Clinton. And if they try to attack me, I'll rally the base against some hack journalist in the mainstream media. It'll make me a legend. The 'Comeback Kid' alright . . ."

Jaworski remained quiet. He sensed Jimmy's excitement, but he did not indulge him. He had other things on his mind than Jimmy's election prospects. He kept his eyes closed and head low even as Jimmy inched closer.

"C'mon, Bob, you don't have to worry about a thing. I'm gonna win this election. We should be celebrating already. No one believed in me and I did it. I did it! I showed them all."

Jaworski did not respond.

"C'mon, let's go celebrate!" said Jimmy, as he gave Jaworski a playful punch in the shoulder.

The kid's arrogance was out of control. He was totally consumed with the thought of becoming a congressman. He no longer deferred to Jaworski as a fatherly figure. Jimmy now saw himself as the authority figure.

"I'd appreciate some privacy," responded Jaworski. "I'm trying to pay my respects to my son."

"You can do that any time. You don't get to celebrate an epic election victory every day."

Jaworski opened his eyes and lifted his head. He stared down Jimmy. He did not need to say anything. The look in his face conveyed it all.

"Let's go, you can do this tomorrow," insisted Jimmy, not picking up on Jaworski's body language.

Jaworski rose from the kneeler. He towered over Jimmy. He poked his finger into Jimmy's chest.

"You'd better get out of here," said Jaworski, not mincing his words.

Jimmy put his hands into the air and came to his feet so that he was eye level with Jaworski.

"Okay, okay. I'm going . . . But just so you know, at some point, you'll have to give this up . . . Tommy's dead and he's not coming back," responded Jimmy, flippantly.

A bolt of rage shot through Jaworski's body. His face turned beet red. He grabbed Jimmy's overcoat with his left hand. He delivered a crushing blow to Jimmy's face with his right hand. Jimmy's head snapped back and his body fell limp under the force of the punch. Jaworski held Jimmy up by the overcoat.

"Get over it . . . there's nothing you can do for him now," mumbled Jimmy through his now bloodied mouth.

Jaworski delivered another shattering punch. Jimmy hung like a rag doll, held up only by Jaworski's tight grip. Jaworski turned away as Jimmy coughed up blood all over and tried to speak again.

"Besides . . . Tommy's death . . . it was an accident."

Disbelief swept through Jaworski. He could not believe what Jimmy had just said. He let Jimmy go to get more information from him.

As Jaworski placed Jimmy's feet back on the ground, Jaworski lost his grip on the ice. He slipped, falling forward on top of Jimmy.

Jimmy fell backward, as Jaworski's momentum came crashing down. The collision swept Jimmy's legs from underneath him. Jimmy dropped until the metal railing in front of the Grotto broke his fall.

CRACK!

Jimmy's head split open on the railing, as he continued plunging to the ground. The collision caused a six-inch gash in the back of Jimmy's head. Blood gushed like an open fire hydrant. It flooded the ice around the Grotto.

Jaworski lay face-first on the ice as Jimmy's blood rushed toward him. He lifted his head to keep the young man's blood from running into him, and then he scrambled to his feet.

He took several steps backward from Jimmy's body. The blood flowed around his Timberland work boots. Jaworski put his hand to his forehead as a sense of astonishment overpowered him.

Jaworski continued taking slow steps backward until he stood almost twenty-five-feet from Jimmy's body. He paused there to see if Jimmy showed any sign of life. The gushing blood made it all the way to where Jaworski stood. Jimmy still did not budge.

Jaworski stood, shocked, until a car passed by almost two minutes later. At that point, Jaworski realized he needed to get out of there. He turned around and hurriedly started walking.

As he walked along the path that snaked around the lake, he stared down at the ground in disbelief. So many emotions and thoughts ran through his head that he remained lost in his own world. Nothing distracted him – not the birds flying overhead, not the cars driving along the lake road, not even the person who bumped into him on the pathway. He tried to get his head around why and how Jimmy had killed Tommy.

He knew that there were only three people who could answer those questions. The first one died fifteen years ago. The second one lay, likely dead, back at the Grotto. And the third person was currently duct-taped to a chair in an old Studebaker factory.

Jaworski made his way to the parking lot. When he arrived, he climbed into his Dodge Ram 1500 and raced the ten minutes to the old factory. As each second passed, the anger in Jaworski grew.

Arriving at the shuttered Studebaker facility at a screeching halt, Jaworski flung open the driver's side door. He charged to the factory door. Storming inside, he pulled out a Smith & Wesson .357 Magnum Revolver and jammed it against Father Finnegan's head.

"WHAT HAPPENED?" demanded Jaworski.

Father Finnegan sat, collapsed in the chair, not responding.

"TELL ME WHAT HAPPENED," repeated Jaworski, shouting even louder than the previous time.

Father Finnegan still did not move.

"Fine then," said Jaworski, as he took a step back.

He raised the .357 Magnum and fired. The shot shattered Father Finnegan's right kneecap. Father Finnegan released an agonizing scream.

"Father, I know Jimmy King killed Tommy. He confessed to me a few minutes ago. Now he's face down in a puddle of his own blood. He's dead. You can tell me everything that he told you . . . And if you don't want to tell me, I'll make sure that you join Jimmy."

Jaworski placed his gun against Father Finnegan's left kneecap.

"It . . . *cough* . . . wasn't . . . *cough* . . . Jimmy," mumbled Father Finnegan.

Jaworski raised the gun from Father Finnegan's kneecap to his temple.

"What are you talking about?" asked Jaworski.

"You've killed the wrong man . . . *cough*."

"WHO WAS IT?!" shouted Jaworski, tightening his grip.

". . . *cough* . . . it was Michael O'Riordan."

Where the hell am I?

George parked his Jeep Cherokee next to the Dodge Ram 1500 and stared at the old factory in front of him. The building looked like it had been abandoned years ago. Graffiti littered the walls. Several windows were missing or had been shattered. Weeds sprouted-up through the cracks in the pavement. It seemed to be an odd location for Jaworski to visit on Election Day.

George did not expect Jaworski to come to this place. In fact, he did not know what to expect. He simply knew that if he wanted to find Father Finnegan, this might be his only opportunity. Lauren was right that sticking to Jimmy King would lead to a breakthrough.

Starting the day, George thought Jimmy might not provide any help. He spent the last two days with the kid with nothing to show for it. Driving to campaign events and surviving a gas explosion seemed to have been a waste of time.

George realized now that those events helped him bond with Jimmy. The chaos of the last several days gave George the opportunity to be tested and trusted. If George had not been there by Jimmy's side, Jimmy may not have asked George to drive him to Jaworski.

When Jimmy asked for the ride to the Grotto, George's fatigue suddenly vanished. He thought he might actually find Father Finnegan before the day ended. It was the break that he had been waiting for.

Although Jimmy told George to wait in the car, George knew he could not let Jimmy out of his sight for too long. He had to follow Jimmy. Even if he could not get close enough to hear the conversation, George needed to see how the two interacted. He figured he could leverage the interaction to get some information later on.

Bumping into Jaworski on the path along the lake startled George, who had been walking with his head down so as not to attract any attention. After the bump, George continued to keep his head down and he walked a few more paces so that Jaworski would not recognize him. As he walked, he wondered why the meeting had ended so quickly and why the two had even met in the first place.

Then George decided that this was his moment.

Running into Jaworski could be a huge step forward in helping him find Father Finnegan. He had been looking for Jaworski since encountering him in Father Finnegan's room two days ago. Now George had found him, and he did not want to lose him again.

George knew Jimmy would be angry about his decision to follow Jaworski. He had been around the kid enough over these last two days to get a sense of Jimmy's temperament. He figured he would catch a tongue lashing from Jimmy at some point.

It did not matter. George's only priority through these last two days had been to locate Father Finnegan, not get Jimmy elected to Congress. If it meant finding Father Finnegan, George would be more than happy to leave Jimmy stranded at the Grotto.

Sitting in his Jeep Cherokee, outside this run down factory, he did not know if Father Finnegan was inside. What he did know is that Jaworski could be at a number of places on Election Day. If the union boss and Democratic Party Chairman came to this factory, then there must be some important reason. And George knew the only way to find out that reason was to follow Jaworski inside.

George climbed out of the Jeep and made his way

across the parking lot to a side entrance. He picked up a lead pipe that he found lying in the parking lot. He wanted to be prepared for whatever he was walking in to. He quietly opened the door and snuck inside.

He surveyed the old factory. He listened carefully. He heard a person groaning in pain.

George walked quickly into the bowels of the building. He listened as the groaning became louder and louder. He followed the person's groans until it led him to an open area in the middle of the factory. He paused, standing behind a conveyor belt.

Father Finnegan!

George could not believe his luck. The groaning pains came from Father Finnegan, who was still collapsed a chair, blood flowing down his right knee. George watched as Jaworski jammed a gun against Father Finnegan's head and shouted at the priest. Watching this scene sent a surge of adrenaline through George.

Here we go!

George charged at Jaworski and Father Finnegan. As Jaworski turned to face George, George swung the lead pipe. He smashed Jaworski's hand, sending the gun and George's lead pipe both skidding across the floor. Jaworski lunged at George, who deftly avoided him. As Jaworski hit the ground, George stepped up and bashed him twice in the face with solid right hand blows, leaving Jaworski writhing on the ground in pain.

George grabbed the back of Father Finnegan's chair and dragged him behind an enormous vat. He wanted to be out of Jaworski's sight, in case the union boss fired off a round. He watched as Jaworski struggled to his feet, picked up his gun, and stumbled out of the factory.

"FATHER! FATHER!" shouted George, lightly shaking the lifeless priest. "Hang in there, Father. We're gonna get you out of here, okay?"

George inspected the priest and it did not look good. Father Finnegan bled profusely from the knee. The priest was fading in and out of consciousness. George presumed that Father Finnegan had suffered internal damage as well. The priest needed to get to the hospital.

George went to work. He took out his house keys and used them to cut through the duct tape that had kept Father Finnegan locked in the chair. He threw the old, heavy priest on to his back. He held Father Finnegan in place by gripping the priest's arms, which draped over his shoulders. He used all his might to walk to the parking lot and then dumped Father Finnegan in the back of his Jeep.

"Hang in there, Father. I'm gonna get you to the hospital."

"It's over, George," coughed up Father Finnegan, slumping over again just as fast as he had spoken up.

"Don't even think like that. You're gonna be okay, just hang in there."

George felt somewhat guilty lying to the priest. George did not actually know whether it would be okay. Father Finnegan was in bad shape. But George had nothing else to tell him.

George had to say something to keep the priest alive for just a few more minutes. George could not let the priest die on him now. He had risked his own life trying to find Father Finnegan. He was only a few minutes away from the hospital and, hopefully, from saving Father Finnegan's life.

George raced back in the direction of downtown South Bend. The Jeep weaved in and out of traffic, passing cars as fast as George could pass them. George ignored most street signs and flew through red lights. He kept an eye out for a police car, an ambulance, a fire truck, any emergency vehicle that might help him get to the hospital faster. He had spent the last several days avoiding government officials, but he realized that now he had no choice. He needed all the help he could get to make sure that Father Finnegan lived.

"You're doing great, Father. We're almost there. Just hang in there."

No response came from the priest.

"Hey, Father Finnegan. Stay with me. Almost there!"

George glanced quickly into the back to see Father Finnegan rolling around with the twists of the road.

"Hey, Father!"

"You've done your part, son," mumbled Father Finnegan. "The pain is gone."

George looked back again at the priest, thinking that he might lose Father Finnegan at any moment.

"Stay with me Father!"

The Jeep flew at 70 mph through the streets of South Bend. As the car raced, so too did George's thoughts. He tried to figure out what exactly was going on.

What did the union boss have to do with all of this? Why was Father Finnegan locked-up in that warehouse?

"Hey, Father!"

George looked again in the back of the Jeep. Father Finnegan did not move. George knew the priest was not in any shape to be answering questions, but he needed to find out what had just happened. With Jaworski still on the loose, George did not know who might be next.

Pulling up in front of Memorial Hospital, George threw the car into park. He jumped out of the front and dragged Father Finnegan out from the back. He slung the priest's arms over his shoulders and stumbled into the entryway of the hospital.

"HELP! SOMEBODY GET ME A DOCTOR!" shouted George repeatedly in every direction. "We're here, Father. Hang in there. We're gonna take care of you.

HELP! SOMEBODY!"

Several nurses, a security guard, and a doctor came rushing down the hallway. One of the nurses pushed a stretcher. George kneeled next to Father Finnegan, gripping the priest's hand.

"What happened to him?" asked the doctor.

"He's been attacked. Please you've got to help him."

"Okay, let's get him on the stretcher and get him to the closest room."

Everyone grabbed a different limb and, as the doctor counted to three, the group lifted Father Finnegan onto the stretcher. A nurse started pushing the stretcher down the hallway. George ran alongside. The group turned a corner and came to an empty room. The nurses started attaching an IV and other medical instruments to Father Finnegan's limp body.

"Are you his family?" asked the doctor.

"I'm a family friend."

"I'm sorry, but you will have to wait in the waiting area. We had a security breach earlier today and only family is allowed in the rooms. We'll be out to keep you updated," said the doctor, as he ushered George out of the room.

The security guard gave George a look indicating the seriousness of the doctor's statement.

"Um . . . yeah . . . sure, no problem. But I need to ask him one thing," said George, running back to Father Finnegan's side. "Father, wait. What was Jaworski doing? Where is he?"

Father Finnegan struggled to lift his head. He mustered all the energy he had to push his eyes halfway open. It was enough for George to make eye contact. Father Finnegan coughed and then cleared his throat, straining with every movement.

"Jaworski knows that it was O'Riordan," said Father Finnegan, as he collapsed back on to the hospital stretcher.

George remained fixated on Father Finnegan as the security guard gently pushed George out of the room.

O'Riordan?

George kept watching Father Finnegan, even as one of the nurses came over to close the door. The security guard stood outside the door and motioned in the direction of the waiting room. George started walking in that direction. The security guard accompanied him. As he walked, he did not know what to make of Father Finnegan's final comments.

What did O'Riordan do that Jaworski now knows about it?

George paced and thought about it some more.

There's only one way to find out.

George started walking out of the waiting room.

"Um, where are you going?" asked the security guard.

"I've . . . uh . . . got to move my car," responded George, without looking back at the security guard.

He picked up his pace. His walking slowly turned into a run. As he barreled around a corner, George bumped into a nurse pushing an elderly man in a wheelchair.

"Hey watch-out! Why don't you look where you are going?" said the elderly man.

"I'm sorry about that," responded George, lost in his own thoughts about what all had just happened.

"George? George is that you?"

"Oh . . . Hi. Mr. Canton, what are you doing here?" asked George, recognizing his neighbor.

"I was driving home two days ago from Martin's when a couple of young jerks in a truck plowed into me. They just shot straight through the stop sign. Can you believe it?"

"Are you okay?" asked George.

"Yeah, yeah. The doc put in a new hip and said I should be walking again in a few weeks. But I'll tell you . . ."

Mr. Canton's voice began to rise. George, realizing that his neighbor was okay, started walking away again. He kept nodding his head as Mr. Canton shouted at him.

"These kids these days . . . they don't have any respect for adults!"

"You're right, Mr. Canton," said George, about fifteen feet from his neighbor and getting farther away with each step. "I'll come visit you later this week."

Without looking back, George turned and ran down the hallway. He raced through the hospital, dodging doctors and visitors. He made it to the entrance, clearing the hospital's glass sliding doors, and found his car right where he had left it.

"GEORGE!"

With his adrenaline pumping furiously, George did not immediately recognize the sound of his wife's voice. He remained nervous about running into Jaworski when he least expected it. He ducked behind the hood of his car out of precaution.

"GEORGE!"

Lauren?

George recognized the voice the second time around and rose slightly above the hood of the car. He scanned the parking lot just beyond the entrance. He saw Lauren racing towards him.

"Lauren?" asked George, skeptically.

"George! What are you doing hiding behind the car?"

"Lauren, I found him."

"Father Finnegan?"

309

"That's right. I found him tied up in an old factory on the south side of town. You were right, Lauren. It was Jaworski."

"That's great news!"

"Not yet. He's in pretty bad shape. The doctors are working on him right now."

As he caught his breath, George changed his tone.

"How did you know we would be here?" asked George.

"I didn't. I came to follow up on something from yesterday."

George gave Lauren a concerned look.

"Don't worry about it. You've got other things on your mind. What are you doing now?"

"I gotta go find Congressman O'Riordan."

"I said that I did not want to be interrupted. What part of that do you not understand?"

Michael O'Riordan sat on a folding chair in a small holding room, located off a ballroom at the South Bend DoubleTree Hotel. He looked up from drinking his espresso and reading a day-old copy of the Caracas-based newspaper *Ultimas Noticias*. He gave his Press Secretary a disgusted look.

Gabriella Silva stood next to him. She was rubbing his back. She stopped momentarily when the Press Secretary came into the room.

The pair had been camping out in this room all morning. Next door, volunteers decorated the ballroom with balloons and *O'Riordan for Congress* signs. The DoubleTree's main ballroom was scheduled to be the site of O'Riordan's Election Night celebrations.

It had become something of a tradition for O'Riordan to host his victory parties at this hotel. Over the years, however, as O'Riordan's general popularity amongst his constituents shrank, so too did the number of attendees. The ballroom was no longer host to the South Bend Democratic Party's legendary raucous, boozy and music-filled parties.

At the start of today, it did not look like it would be much of a celebration at all. O'Riordan studied all of the overnight polls as soon as he woke up. Most showed him either tied with Jimmy or leading by a percentage point or two. On their face, the polls read as if O'Riordan still had a shot to win the election. O'Riordan's years of political intuition told him otherwise.

O'Riordan sensed that he was headed for defeat today. He had hoped that former President Miller's visit might provide a small enough bounce to get him across the finishing line. He felt good immediately after the rally. He thought they had a decent turnout, not great, but not a complete disaster. He knew former President Miller could charm a crowd. But when he was greeting people after the event, all that O'Riordan heard about was the explosion at Jimmy King's headquarters.

Rally attendees of all ages wanted to know what O'Riordan thought about the explosion. Some people asked if he had been in touch with Jimmy. Others expressed concern that another explosion might occur at any moment. Still others just came up, shook his hand, and spoke about what a tragedy it was.

Based on these interactions and O'Riordan's experience at other campaign events that night, O'Riordan knew that Jimmy had the momentum going into the final day of the campaign. It had nothing to do with platform or policy proposals. It had everything to do sympathy and personal feelings. O'Riordan had been a politician long enough to realize that these things sometimes sway elections, but he refused to accept it. He still clung to his belief that Jimmy was a kid who had no business taking away *his* congressional seat.

With defeat sure to come, O'Riordan's campaign aides proposed events to preserve O'Riordan's reputation. They especially wanted him to be out in the district, personally thanking voters for the years of support. O'Riordan, however, quickly dismissed this suggestion.

He was too bitter about the campaign and too bitter about losing to someone like Jimmy King. He would give a concession speech, something along the lines of not having O'Riordan to kick around anymore. But he would not do anything more than that – no calling voters to get them to the polls, no media interviews, and no thank yous.

Instead, O'Riordan chose to hide out in this small holding room all day, stewing about the campaign. He was in no mood to deal with the reporters staked out at his home or the ones that had finally learned about Gabriella and had positioned themselves outside her apartment. This holding room allowed O'Riordan to minimize the distractions. It had no television, no radio, and no computer, just a couple of chairs, a coffee table, and a small loveseat sofa. He sent word to his campaign team not to disturb him and Gabriella. The room provided a solitary retreat from the emotional rollercoaster of the last several days.

O'Riordan sat in this room all morning and fumed about the likely election outcome. Gabriella's gentle back-rubs could not soothe him. He could not understand why his decades-long career would end like this. He resented the people of Northern Indiana for making this decision. He could not think about anything else, not even his own daughter's death.

O'Riordan had learned about Mary's death last night, after the rally finished. O'Riordan had accompanied former President Miller back to the airport. As he stood on the tarmac, waving goodbye to the former president, a campaign staffer came-up. The staffer politely interrupted O'Riordan to tell him the news. As he digested the news, O'Riordan stopped waving. He dropped his face into his hands and cried.

The news caught O'Riordan off guard. He knew Mary was in a delicate situation. But he remembered the doctors telling him that she would make a full recovery and return to a normal life. He could not understand what would have gone wrong. He did not know why things had all of a sudden changed. Most importantly, he wished that he had been there to say goodbye. Guilt began to creep into O'Riordan's conscience.

Still standing on the South Bend Airport tarmac, the roar of former President Miller's private plane drowned out O'Riordan's thoughts. He looked away from the staffer and back to the former President, now sitting at the window in the first row of a Gulfstream. O'Riordan began waving again.

As quickly as that, O'Riordan's focus returned to the campaign. He stopped feeling guilty and started thinking about how his daughter's death might affect the campaign. He wondered how he might subtly use this event to his own advantage and whether there was even any time left to effectively use it.

Despite a willingness to exploit his daughter's death for his own political advancement, O'Riordan never got the chance. Mary's death came too late in the campaign to be a game changer. A few sympathetic voters moved back into O'Riordan's camp, but not enough to overcome Jimmy King's momentum. A majority of Northern Indiana voters had solidified their support behind Jimmy King and this made all the difference. O'Riordan knew that he was headed for defeat today.

Mary's death and the lack of any tangible political benefit from it only fueled O'Riordan's resentment. He could not understand why Jimmy King had garnered so much support. He compared the two tragedies in disbelief.

That kid went through a gasline explosion outside his headquarters. No one got hurt except for an old man who had a heart attack.

I lost my daughter. I'm never going to see her again. How come that does not resonate more?

O'Riordan's bitterness and resentment grew the more that he thought about these contrasting situations. He was visibly angry when his Press Secretary came into the holding area. He was not in the mood to be dealing with any other people.

"I'm sorry, Congressman. I know you said that you didn't want to be disturbed but I thought you might want to hear this news."

"What could honestly be so important?"

"Sir, Jimmy King has apparently died."

"What?" asked a startled O'Riordan, standing up to look his Press Secretary in the eyes.

"Um . . . there are reports that he was found outside the Grotto. Apparently he slipped on the ice and cracked his head on the banister. Initial press reports say he died before paramedics got him to the hospital."

"Are you positive?" asked O'Riordan, growing more serious.

"I just got a call from a beat reporter over at the *South Bend Tribune* asking me if we had any comment about it."

"What did you say?"

"I said that I needed to check with you before we released an official statement."

"Well, before you say anything, double check with a real journalist that it actually happened. Call someone from *MSNBC* or *The New York Times*. Then we'll work on a statement."

"Yes, sir," responded the Press Secretary, as he exited the holding room and closed the door behind him.

O'Riordan collapsed on to the chair in disbelief. He had been annoyed by Jimmy's presence in the campaign. He wanted to beat the kid and beat him badly to send a message. But he never wanted Jimmy to die. In a soft moment of humanity, he was shocked that both his daughter and his opponent had died within nearly twelve hours of each other. This was not the way he expected the campaign to end.

"Congratulations, Mr. Congressman," said Gabriella, as she came over and gave him a hug.

O'Riordan did not respond. He sat there frozen, staring at the ground.

"You did it. I'm so proud of you," said Gabriella, squeezing him again.

O'Riordan continued staring at the ground as he spoke up.

"He's dead, Gabriella. I don't believe it."

"You don't have to worry about that. It's all over," responded Gabriella, as she stopped hugging him so as to look him in the face. "You won. That's all that matters."

"But he's dead," said O'Riordan, staring at Gabriella with a shocked look on his face.

"It's not your fault that he died. You had nothing to do with his death. It was an accident."

"I know . . . but . . . I can't believe that he is dead."

"You can't worry about it. You need to be strong. You did it."

Gabriella grabbed O'Riordan by the shoulders and stared into his eyes to convey her message.

"The people will be looking to you for leadership. You need to be strong for them. You need to guide them out of this darkness. You are the liberator, remember?"

O'Riordan looked up at Gabriella. Her comments made sense. Regardless of what had happened up until this point, O'Riordan knew he was the Congressman for this district. With Jimmy King's death, he would remain the Congressman for this district. It was times like these, he thought, that the people needed his leadership. He rose from his chair as Gabriella took a step backward.

"You're right. I did it."

He grabbed her by the hand and pulled her in close toward him.

"We did it," said O'Riordan softly. "Thank you, Gabriella."

He embraced her in a tight hug. The embrace offered a release for O'Riordan. Gabriella had been by his side for these tumultuous last four days. He relied on her for more than she realized. She had reinvigorated his campaigning and inspired him to persevere until the end. He confided in her. He took comfort in her. He sought her advice. At this moment, O'Riordan recognized that he would not have made it to this point without her. This embrace was his way to say thank you.

"Now . . . I am a Member of the United States House of Representatives," said O'Riordan confidently, as he pulled away from Gabriella. "The people need to hear from me. I need to get out there and reassure them that I am okay and everything will be okay."

O'Riordan took one step to leave the room. He stopped in his tracks as he heard someone turning the outside knob to the holding room's door. He waited for the door to open.

"Bob," said O'Riordan enthusiastically and with a big smile on his face. He went straight up to Bob Jaworski and gave him a light man hug. He whispered gleefully into Jaworski's ear.

"I did it."

"What's wrong?" asked O'Riordan, as he pulled away from a cold embrace with Jaworski.

O'Riordan stood in the middle of the DoubleTree's holding room, with Gabriella three feet behind him and Jaworski three feet in front of him.

Jaworski's hulking frame filled the doorframe. O'Riordan took several steps backward to size up Jaworski. He noticed that the grizzled union boss did not share his excitement.

"Don't tell me that you are about to get all emotional about this kid," said O'Riordan. "Look, I know that you and Jimmy had some kind of father-son relationship. But he's dead now and there's nothing you can do it about. So don't worry about it. It's over. We won."

Jaworski stood there silently, not taking his eyes off O'Riordan. His reaction did not change.

"C'mon, Bob, you can't worry about this. It's a tragedy, sure, but it's over. It's done with. There is nothing you can do to change it. Let's celebrate the good news, not dwell on the bad news."

O'Riordan's big smile, wild gesticulations and calls for celebration failed to sway his longtime political adviser. Jaworski continued staring at O'Riordan. He did not show any emotion.

"I won Bob. Don't you get it? The election is over and I won once again. You should be happy right now."

O'Riordan paused. Still no response from Jaworski.

"Sure, the people cast their ballots for me . . . Michael O'Riordan. But you should celebrate this victory as well. A win for Michael O'Riordan is a win for the people. Everyone should take part in the celebration. Even you, Bob. My victory is your victory."

O'Riordan extended an open palm to shake Jaworski's hand. Jaworski ignored O'Riordan's offer.

"What's the matter? Are you not one for celebrations? Does the big tough guy not show any emotions in general or is it that he does not like to get excited?" asked O'Riordan, starting to sound very sarcastic. "Is this all part of your tough guy routine? Is this what works with those lackey workers of yours? Well, if that's what suits you, then fine. You can stay in character. Don't worry, I won't tell anyone."

O'Riordan stood there for several seconds assessing whether Jaworski was playing a role or whether there might be some other explanation for Jaworski's steely glare.

"Or is it something else?" asked O'Riordan, suspiciously. "Is there another reason why you refuse to celebrate my victory? What are you hiding from me, Bob?"

O'Riordan now appeared skeptical. He couldn't understand why Jaworski wasn't sharing in his excitement. This should have been a celebratory moment for the Chairman of the St. Joseph County Democratic Party.

"Don't tell me you wanted that little kid to win?" asked O'Riordan. "Is that it? You wanted your son's little best friend to take me down?"

The tone in O'Riordan's voice gradually turned angry. The wide smile disappeared from his face. He narrowed his eyes.

"Is that why you weren't much help this time around? Oh, I noticed Bob, don't think that I didn't. Every time I needed you, you were nowhere to be found. I had to run this entire campaign myself. I did it myself . . . And I won by myself."

O'Riordan inched closer to Jaworski.

"That's right. I did this myself. I won this election. The people want me. I am not going to let you ruin my moment."

O'Riordan came within inches of Jaworski's face.

"Or is there another reason all together, Bob?" asked O'Riordan in a whisper.

O'Riordan took one step back from Jaworski.

"Is that it? This is about something else?" asked O'Riordan, raising his voice. "That's it, isn't it?"

Jaworski did not respond nor change his steely glare. The lack of a response infuriated O'Riordan.

"It is something else. I knew it."

Still no response from Jaworski.

"You're jealous of me, Bob. You're jealous that it was *me* that the people of Northern Indiana elected. You're jealous that the people want *my* leadership. You're jealous that I am a Member of the United States House of Representatives," said O'Riordan.

O'Riordan's voice rose with each word. He jabbed his right index finger into Jaworski's chest to emphasize each statement. Jaworski remained undisturbed by O'Riordan's accusations. He had come here to do one thing only. He would not let O'Riordan distract him from that goal.

"I can't believe it's come to this. All of these years and I've been so good to you Bob. Are you going to turn your back on me now because you're jealous?" asked O'Riordan, within inches of Jaworski's face. "Fine. But don't try to ruin my moment. I don't need you anymore. I won this election without you and I'll do it again without you."

O'Riordan face was flushed red. Jaworski continued to stand there without reacting to any of the politician's threats.

"GET OUT!" shouted O'Riordan, thrusting his

hand in the air and pointing at the door. He stood there for several seconds staring Jaworski in the eyes. He steamed with anger.

When Jaworski did not move, O'Riordan backed down from his face. He turned toward Gabriella standing at the back of the room. His face was flushed. He put his hands on his hips. His heavy breathing was the only noise in the room until Jaworski spoke up.

"Why'd you do it?"

O'Riordan heard Jaworski, but he did not respond. He continued to stand with his hands on his hips, breathing deeply. As he caught his breath, he turned around to face Jaworski.

The union boss asked again.

"Why'd you do it?"

O'Riordan hesitated before responding.

"I don't know what you're talking about," said O'Riordan.

Jaworski lunged forward, catching O'Riordan by the throat. The thick, swollen fingers on his left hand slowly tightened around O'Riordan's neck. As Jaworski squeezed, O'Riordan began to suffocate and his arms flailed. His face turned from a beet red to a blueish-purple hue, and he dropped to his knees.

"I didn't do it," coughed O'Riordan.

Jaworski squeezed again. With his right hand, he punched O'Riordan in the face. O'Riordan's eyes bulged out from his head, and he gasped for air.

Jaworski struck him again.

O'Riordan had never experienced getting punched in the face. The first blow startled him. The second punch scared him. The fact that these punches came from his friend of over thirty years frightened him even more. He was in shock.

"Okay . . . okay," sputtered O'Riordan.

As he struggled to breath, the old politician also broke down into tears. He had avoided this moment for fifteen-years. But overcome by guilt and sensing that his demons had finally caught up with him, he decided to unload his heavy heart.

"I'll tell you everything."

Jaworski eased his grip, but continued to hold O'Riordan on his knees. O'Riordan struggled to suck in a deep breath of air. For only the second time in his life, he began to talk about that tragic event. He started slowly.

"She was the first one . . . Anna Passos, a Portuguese Brazilian, who had come over here on a Fulbright Scholarship. I gave a talk at the Kellogg Institute on the evolution of democracy in Latin American when she approached me with a question afterward. I saw her at several Kellogg events later, and she always impressed me with the depth of her questions."

"Get to the point," growled Jaworski, clamping down on O'Riordan's throat.

O'Riordan grasped and cried even more.

"Okay, okay, I'm getting there!" labored O'Riordan.

He struggled to breath, but he felt that he needed to tell the whole story. It was time to give the full confession and finally seek forgiveness.

"One day she asks to see a copy of my PhD thesis. I offered to drop one off at her house. She rents a garage apartment over in the River Bend historic district. I go in, she offers me a glass of wine. We sit and chat about Latin American politics. She keeps filling my glass. I keep drinking. She starts flirting with me. And I don't know what got into me . . ."

Tears were streaming down O'Riordan's face at this point. He struggled to compose himself and continue with the story.

"It had never happened before. But one thing leads

to another and I start kissing her neck and caressing her back. I don't know . . . it was just the combination of the alcohol and the discussion and her interest in my thesis. Oh my God . . . if only I had been a stronger man, none of this ever would have happened."

O'Riordan paused to catch his breath. The tears did not stop pouring from his eyes.

"Keep it going," grunted Jaworski, not offering any sympathy.

"I lost track of time and before I know it, it's nearly 6:00 p.m. I was supposed to give some introductory remarks at the Notre Dame Democrats Election Watch Party at 6:00 p.m. . . . I went rushing out of the apartment. By that point, I had had one too many drinks. I shouldn't even have been driving. But I jumped into my car and raced off.

As I'm rushing down Riverside Drive, I'm coming down a hill when a snowball smashes into the windshield. I didn't even see it until the last second. I swung the car to the left, trying to avoid the flying snow. With the ice on the ground and my impaired reflexes, I careened off the road. And I just hear this loud thud."

"What'd you do about it?" asked Jaworski, tightening his fingers around O'Riordan's throat one more time.

"I got out of the car to see what I hit . . . Oh God, Bob, I'm so sorry. I didn't know it was Tommy. I swear. I was drunk. And I didn't want to be caught. And I just panicked. I'm so sorry. I'm so . . ."

By this point, O'Riordan couldn't see through his tears. He made noise, but none of it was comprehensible. He simply babbled and cried. The politician dropped his head to avoid making eye contact with Jaworski, even as Jaworski kept his left hand clutching O'Riordan's throat.

"So you dragged him into the water and weighed him down with stones?" asked Jaworski.

"Bob, you've got to believe me. It was an accident.

I didn't mean to do it. I panicked. I'm so sorry. Please, please, you must forgive me," pleaded O'Riordan through his sobbing.

Jaworski began yelling at O'Riordan, as O'Riordan pleaded desperately for Jaworski's forgiveness.

"That was my son. I carried his cold, dead body out of the water in my own arms. I vowed that I would find the person who did this to him."

"Please, Bob, I'm begging you for your forgiveness!"

"For years I've been searching for that person."

"You've got to believe me, it was an accident."

"You buried him in that water."

"I panicked."

"He died there."

"I'm sorry."

"THAT WAS MY SON!"

"PLEASE!"

Jaworski released O'Riordan's throat from his grip. O'Riordan collapsed on the ground. His chest heaved up and down as he battled for oxygen. O'Riordan felt light-headed and strained to lift his head. He saw Jaworski towering over him from three feet away. He watched as Jaworski pulled a .357 Magnum revolver from the waist of his jeans. Jaworski took dead aim at O'Riordan.

"God is the only one who can deliver the forgiveness we both need."

BANG! BANG!

George DeMarco heard the two gunshots as he stepped inside the DoubleTree's lobby. He recognized the sound immediately. And he feared that he had arrived just a few seconds too late.

He scanned the lobby. Directly in front of him, two hotel staffers stood behind a front desk, exchanging nervous glances. To his right, a woman in a business suit with a suitcase at her side waited for the elevators and looked anxiously across the hotel lobby. He turned his head to the left side of the lobby just in time to see a set of double doors burst open.

A horde of volunteers rushed out of the Double-Tree's main ballroom. Middle aged women shrieked and screamed in fear. George knew this is where he had to start.

He raced against the crowd, pushing his way through the volunteers.

As he emerged from the flock of people and entered into the ballroom, he found a quiet, empty, wide open space. At the front of the room stood a podium, on top of a makeshift stage, decorated with an "O'Riordan for Congress" placard. Red, white and blue balloons hung in one corner, next to a helium tank. Several tables with wooden ballroom chairs sat in the back corner. The only noise came from a large flat screen television sitting on a pushcart to the left of the stage. The television's volume had been turned up to its loudest level. From across the ballroom, George could hear a CNN reporter providing Election Day updates.

George walked cautiously into the ballroom. He did not see anything suspicious nor did he hear anything other than the television noise. Despite the emptiness of the room, George sensed something was not right.

Where did those gunshots come from?

He surveyed the room again. This time it caught his eyes. On the left, behind the television, was a set of double doors that appeared to lead to the kitchen. On the right, George noticed a single door that opened to a hallway.

George made his way across the ballroom to that hallway. He looked around for anything that he could use as a weapon. He grabbed one of the wooden chairs and flipped it over. He kicked one of the legs until it broke off.

He snatched the severed piece of wood and slowly crept up to the single door. He nervously peered down the hallway to see three doors on the right side. With a firm grip on the chair leg, George silently moved forward.

Coming to the first door, he placed his ear against the outer frame to listen inside. He thought he heard movement from within the room, so he slowly turned the doorknob and pushed the door open. He raised the chair leg in anticipation for what he might encounter.

Nothing.

A tiny desk with a desk calendar, telephone, and a computer on top, sat in the middle of the room. No lights were on. It did not appear as if anyone had been in this office for a while. Yet George still heard human movement.

He moved slowly back into the hallway. He approached the second door. This door remained open, and George saw light radiating from the room. He put his back against the wall and listened carefully.

There it is.

He heard someone inside the room. He did not hear anyone speaking or any voices at all. He just heard some kind of movement. He raised the chair leg and took a quick glance inside the room.

Oh my God.

He pulled back from the doorframe and gripped the chair leg with both hands. Inside the room he saw a body lying on the floor, face down. A puddle of thick, red blood swirled around the head. George noticed that the dead man was not alone in the room, but the body startled him so much that he could not identify who else was inside. Leaning against the wall and gripping the wooden chair leg, George knew he could not allow whoever was in that room to get away. He had to take action.

George swiftly turned the corner into the room. He planted his feet, right next to the dead body. His left foot was a step in front of his right, allowing him to spring at any moment. He held the wooden chair leg like a baseball bat, ready to swing at whoever approached.

"Don't move," insisted Gabriella Silva, pointing a Beretta M9 at George's head.

She held the gun over the shoulder of a man who was hugging her. George stared at the back of the man's head. He did not who this couple was or why they were embracing. George kept his eyes focused as the man stopped hugging the woman, pulled away and turned toward George.

O'Riordan!

George identified him right away from all of the recent press coverage. He dressed like the stereotype of a university professor, sporting a bowtie and a houndstooth sports jacket with elbows pads. It was exactly how every news article had portrayed him.

George did not recognize the woman whom O'Riordan had been embracing. But based on his wife's descriptions and the fact that she stood here pointing a Beretta M9 at his face, he knew it could only be one person.

The Fox.

George tried to keep his eyes on the Fox, in case she made any quick moves. But he glanced down quickly enough to recognize the characteristics of the man on the ground.

Jaworski.

From this scene, George quickly pieced together that the Venezuelan had killed Jaworski. She stood there, gun in hand, while Jaworski lay dead on the floor. O'Riordan's face was puffy and red as if he had just done a lot of crying. It did not appear as if O'Riordan had the mental or physical strength to take out Jaworski.

He could not believe it. Lauren was right about the Fox being a cold-blooded killer. The only thing that Lauren had been wrong about was who the Venezuelan was going to kill.

George was not quite sure why she wanted Jaworski dead. He assumed it had something to do with him and O'Riordan. But he could not worry now about that now.

"Who are you?" asked Gabriella.

George remained calm. His feet were firmly planted on the ground and his hands wrapped tight around the chair leg.

"WHO ARE YOU?" shouted Gabriella, thrusting the gun in George's direction.

George held his ground, not intimidated by the sight of the gun.

"I know all about Jaworski."

"What do you know about him?" asked Gabriella.

"I know that he came here to kill you," said George, looking at O'Riordan when he made this statement.

George watched O'Riordan step out from behind the Fox. O'Riordan put his hand on Gabriella's arm as a motion for her to lower the pistol. She did not respond, but kept the gun aimed at George.

"He was about to kill me. He came in here with a gun. Fortunately Gabriella saved my life," said O'Riordan.

"I'm not so sure it happened exactly like that," said George, calmly but firmly.

"She saved my life. That maniac nearly shot me to death . . ."

"I know about Tommy Jaworski," said George, cutting off O'Riordan in mid sentence. As he spoke, George watched O'Riordan's face tense up.

"What do you think you know about Tommy Jaworski?" asked O'Riordan, in an angry tone.

"I know you killed him and covered it up fifteen years ago."

"Enough of this, Michael. Let me take care of him," interjected Gabriella, raising her Beretta again.

"But more importantly, I know that she's not who she says she is," said George, not giving O'Riordan enough time to consider what the Fox had just said.

The room fell quiet as O'Riordan looked at Gabriella. George and the Venezuelan kept their eyes fixed on each other, neither trusting what the other might do.

"What do you mean?" asked O'Riordan.

"I know Jaworski was going to kill you for what you did to his son fifteen years ago. But he's dead. So right now, both you and I have something else to worry about."

"And what's that?"

"The fact that your girlfriend here is a Venezuelan spy."

O'Riordan laughed at George's comment.

George remained calm, not showing any signs of joking. He also kept staring at the Fox. Out of the corner of his eye, he saw O'Riordan recognize George was being serious and glance at Gabriella to see her reaction.

"Don't take my word for it," said George. "Ask

her what she really did in Beirut. Ask her why she had to leave. Ask her what she's doing with a gun. And ask her how she learned to shoot like that."

"Gabriella, is this true?" asked O'Riordan.

"I think this man needs to go," responded Gabriella, without answering O'Riordan's question. "He has no business disrespecting a Member of Congress in this manner."

"Congressman, she's been working for Venezuelan intelligence her entire adult life. There's no telling what might happen to you or your career if it gets out that she's a spy."

"Has he no respect for a woman's honor? Michael, you must do something about this man or I will," insisted Gabriella.

O'Riordan stood silently as George and the Fox made their countering points. George refused to take his eyes off the Venezuelan, not trusting her for one moment. As the seconds ticked by and O'Riordan remained quiet, George wondered what else he needed to do to convince O'Riordan.

"Gabriella, tell me the truth."

"The truth is that this man is lying . . . and if you are too weak to take care of him . . . then I will."

BANG!

George heard the single, deafening gunshot as he fell to his knees. It sounded as if his right eardrum had just exploded. He heard nothing other than a constant ringing.

He couldn't hear a thing, but George knew that the ringing meant something very important.

He was not dead.

Right before he heard the gunshot, George felt someone kick him in the back of his right knee. The kick caused him to drop to the holding room floor. Kneeling on the ground, with his head hung low, he slowly opened his eyes to see what had happened.

Immediately to his left he saw Bob Jaworski's dead face staring back at him. Jaworski had one bullet hole in his forehead and the other in his right cheek. The union boss's head lay in a puddle of thick, red blood. Jaworski's body, however, was not his main concern.

George cautiously raised his head to see what had happened to everyone else in the room. As he lifted his eyes, he saw the Fox. The attractive Venezuelan with the thick, flowing brunette hair lay on the ground as well, with a single bullet hole right between her eyes. A stream of blood flowed from her forehead onto the floor. She still gripped her Beretta M9 in her right hand, but otherwise did not move. She most certainly was dead too – whoever had killed her was an excellent shot.

George continued to raise his head. As he did, he caught site of O'Riordan, standing two feet behind the Fox's body. O'Riordan had his hands raised in the air. His face look worried.

With his eyes still fixed on the Fox and O'Riordan, George felt a person's hand grip his shoulder. He could not tell if he was about to join Jaworski and the Venezuelan. His heart started racing again, and he braced himself for whatever fate might fall upon him.

Lauren?

A wave of relief washed over George. He watched as his wife passed him by and stepped up to the Fox. She kept her Sig Sauer P239 pointed at O'Riordan, while she bent down to pry the gun from Gabriella's hands. Lauren tucked the Fox's gun into her back waist and helped George to his feet. O'Riordan remained standing against the wall of the holding room. His raised hands signaled that he was not about to make any sudden moves.

George saw Lauren's mouth moving.

"I CAN'T HEAR YOU!" shouted George, the ringing just starting to die down.

Lauren kept moving her mouth.

"I CAN'T . . . I CAN'T . . ."

George caught himself when he realized he was shouting. The ringing had quieted enough for him to hear everything around him.

"George, are you okay?" asked Lauren, still pointing her gun at O'Riordan.

"WHAT?"

"Are you okay?"

"YES, I'M FINE . . . Sorry, I couldn't hear you over the ringing in my ears. What are you doing here?" asked George.

"Remember I told you that I found polonium in her dorm room?"

"Yeah, what about it?"

"Well, I found it a bit suspicious that she visited the hospital yesterday right before his daughter's death," said

Lauren, motioning at O'Riordan. "So I went to investigate it myself."

"That's when I saw you running into the hospital?"

"That's right. Thinking about the polonium overnight, I realized I had an old Geiger Counter stashed away in some boxes of equipment in the basement."

"Where'd you get a Geiger Counter?"

"The Agency gave it to me for dealing with Iranian agents. It wasn't much but it was effective in detecting minor traces of radiation. I thought I might be able to use it to see whether any traces came up on the daughter."

"And you found traces of polonium on Mary O'Riordan?"

"No, the body had already been moved to the city morgue. But I was able to find traces of polonium on the bed in the room where they had kept her. That was enough for me to connect the Fox to the daughter's death."

"But if Jaworski was behind the initial attack on his daughter, why would she have killed Mary? What good would that have done?"

"That I don't know. It could have been a lover jealous that the daughter was getting in her way. But my guess is that it had something to do with the election. It would be huge for a spook to be intimate with a member of Congress, especially one who sat on the Intelligence Committee. I bet she picked up a few stories that the folks back in Caracas found pretty interesting."

George looked at O'Riordan as Lauren made this comment. O'Riordan's face turned red in embarrassment. The Congressman averted his eyes from George's stare.

"If O'Riordan's no longer a Congressman, she no longer has a source for American intelligence info," continued Lauren. "And if she no longer has a source for American intelligence info, then she isn't worth much to Caracas. Her handlers would not have been happy that a multi-term

Congressman lost his seat under her watch. I can imagine she was already on probation for what happened in Beirut. A loss in today's election might have been a death sentence."

"So you were right all along about her," said George.

"I told you I wasn't making it up. I knew she was in South Bend for a specific reason. I just wish that I had realized that reason earlier."

"So how'd you know to come here?"

"I remembered seeing one of the local TV reporters broadcasting from outside the O'Riordan headquarters for the day. And she was standing outside the DoubleTree. I also remembered you saying something about going to see O'Riordan so I figured I should get there as soon as possible. And I'm glad that I got here just in time."

"So you didn't come here to save me?"

"No," said Lauren, smiling sheepishly and yet still aiming her handgun at O'Riordan. "But I'm glad it worked out that way. So you're not angry at me?"

"No . . . why?"

"Because you were all worried about me killing the Fox."

A smile came across George's face.

"Don't worry about that."

"Why not?"

"*Goetz.*"

"What?"

"Bernie Goetz . . . you had a reasonable belief that it was necessary to use deadly force."

Lauren shook her head and smiled. The husband and wife hugged.

"So," asked Lauren, motioning in the direction of O'Riordan, as the sound of a police siren in the distance grew closer. "What do you want to do about him?"

THE END

THE THRILLS
CONTINUE IN

THE
SAINT FRANCIS
REVELATION

BOOK CLUBS: HOST JOHN!

Is your book club interested in hosting John?

Do you have questions about *The Saint Joseph Plot* or the writing and publishing process?

Do you want to ask John about working in the White House, living in Australia, or competing at the U.S. Olympic Swimming Team Trials?

Curious about why John missed his own wedding?

John is willing to appear in person, via Skype, or via telephone with your book club.

E-mail bookclubs@johnmpersinger.com or visit www.johnmpersinger.com for more information on your book club hosting John.

DISCUSSION QUESTIONS

1. What do you think was going through Father Finnegan's mind when he found himself next to Mary O'Riordan?

2. Father Finnegan awakes each morning at 5:00 a.m. to pray, regardless of how much he may have drunk the previous night. How do you think someone balances the discipline to rise each morning at 5:00 a.m. to pray against excessive drinking?

3. Did you think that George made the right decision to help Father Finnegan? Would you have made that same decision? Would you have done that for a friend? A relative? An immediate family member?

4. George and Lauren are often crossing paths throughout the book. Do you think that they too often put their own individual interests ahead of supporting each other?

5. Several of the characters have parent-child relationships – O'Riordan and Mary, Jaworski and Jimmy, Father Finnegan and George. How does the parent-child relationship affect these characters interactions with each other?

6. Both O'Riordan and Jaworski suffer from the death of a child, but handle the losses differently. Why do you think that they had different reactions?

7. Were you surprised that Father Finnegan revealed O'Riordan's identity to Jaworski? Do you think he held out longer or shorter than expected?

8. How would you react if someone trusted you with a grave secret, like the way that O'Riordan confided in Father Finnegan? Would you abide by the person's wishes to keep quiet? Would you attempt to counsel the person?

9. Did you figure out who killed Jaworki's son before it was revealed? At what point did you realize who it was?
10. Why do you think that O'Riordan and Jaworski remained close throughout the years, despite what had happened to each man?
11. Who do you think deserved to win the election? Did you sympathize more with O'Riordan or Jimmy King? Neither?
12. Did you think that Notre Dame's campus was portrayed accurately? Were there other Notre Dame locations that should have been in the book?
13. What about the scenes outside Notre Dame's campus? Did you think that it was an accurate portrayal of the South Bend area?
14. What do you think happens to Michael O'Riordan at the end of the book? What about Father Finnegan?

ACKNOWLEDGMENTS

The first and most important thanks go to my wife Sarah. This novel would not have been possible without her love, support, feedback, and hard work. This novel was truly the result of a Team Persinger effort.

My extended family played a significant role as well. I must thank my parents – Joseph and Julia Persinger – for all of their support. They have sacrificed and worked so hard for our family for years. There is so much that I am grateful for, so suffice to say, a son could not have asked for better parents.

I also need to thank my sisters Emily, Cynthia, and Valerie; my brothers-in-law Tim Proctor and Mike Lisa; and, my in-laws Scott and Julie Smiles.

I met my two best friends, Andrew McConnell and Dan Shevchik, in college. I have relied on their advice and counsel since our time together at Harvard. I thank them for their feedback on the novel.

There are a number of people at the University of Notre Dame to whom I will forever be indebted. The list is far too long for me to name here. However, I must thank Bill and Margaret Kelley. They have been instrumental in a number of big events in my life. I thank them for their past, present, and continued support of all of my endeavors.

There are several people whom I met in Washington, D.C. that provided me with fantastic opportunities. First, I must thank Ambassador Robert McCallum and his wife Mimi McCallum. I also need to thank Harriet Miers, Ken Mehlman, and James Waters for hiring me at various stages in my career.

Speaking of hiring, I need to thank Russ Warner, Jay Alberstadt, Dan Miller, Jim Walczak and all of the partners, attorneys, and staff at MacDonald, Illig, Jones &

Britton LLP in Erie, Pennsylvania. Thank you to Virginia Madden for all of her marketing and promotional advice. In particular, I need to thank my colleague and friend Aggie Gausman for reading an early draft and providing feedback.

Lastly, but certainly not least, I need to thank my old friend Greg Henning. Despite being on vacation, Greg stepped up and helped to get this novel ready for release. I thank him for all of his work.

John M. Persinger graduated from Notre Dame Law School and Harvard College. While at Harvard, John co-captained the varsity swimming and diving team and competed at the 2000 U.S. Olympic Team Trials. In between college and law school, John worked in the White House and at the U.S. Embassy in Canberra, Australia. He practices law and lives with his family in Erie, Pennsylvania.

E-mail John at John@johnmpersinger.com

Visit www.johnmpersinger.com for news and exciting updates on forthcoming books.

Follow John:
Facebook.com/JohnMPersinger
Twitter @JohnMPersinger